USA Today bestseller Annette Das... ...
dozen novels including the five-... ...
Chambers mystery series about a paramedic-turned-coroner in
rural Pennsylvania. Her standalone, *Death By Equine*, won the
2021 Dr. Tony Ryan Book Award for excellence in
thoroughbred racing literature. *Where the Guilty Hide* is the first
in her new mystery series set along the shores of Lake Erie.
Annette and her husband live in the United States on ten acres
of what was her grandfather's Pennsylvania dairy farm with
one very spoiled cat.

www.annettedashofy.com

twitter.com / Annette_Dashofy
facebook.com / AnnetteDashofy

Also by Annette Dashofy

Zoe Chambers Mystery Series

Circle of Influence

Lost Legacy

Bridges Burned

With a Vengeance

No Way Home

Uneasy Prey

Cry Wolf

Fair Game

Under the Radar

Til Death

Fatal Reunion

Crime in the Country

Standalone titles

Death by Equine

WHERE THE GUILTY HIDE

ANNETTE DASHOFY

One More Chapter
a division of HarperCollins*Publishers*
1 London Bridge Street
London SE1 9GF
www.harpercollins.co.uk
HarperCollins*Publishers*
Macken House, 39/40 Mayor Street Upper,
Dublin 1, D01 C9W8

This paperback edition 2023

2

First published in Great Britain in ebook format
by HarperCollins*Publishers* 2023
Copyright © Annette Dashofy 2023
Annette Dashofy asserts the moral right to be identified
as the author of this work

A catalogue record of this book is available from the British Library

ISBN: 978-0-00-855624-2

Printed and bound in the UK using 100% Renewable Electricity
by CPI Group (UK) Ltd

To Ray with love. Always.

Chapter One

A lthough Detective Matthias Honeywell had seen more egregious crimes in his years with the Major Crime Unit and as a patrolman, home invasions always ripped open an old wound that never quite healed.

And now they'd had two in one week.

Matthias and his partner, Detective Cassie Malone, stood shoulder to shoulder at the end of the driveway, studying the South Shore Drive residence. A quartet of Erie City Police units lined the road. Two uniformed officers stood on the street, directing what little traffic there was away from the crime scene. The absence of an EmergyCare truck indicated a lack of injuries. Or worse.

"The family has good taste," Cassie mused.

"Expensive taste." The white English Tudor with vivid red awnings was smaller by half than the mansion they'd responded to three days ago, but Matthias suspected it was worth nearly twice as much. Property like this, backing onto Lake Erie, came at a premium.

"If you're going to hit a place in the middle of the afternoon, I suppose you need to make it worth the risk." Her gaze shifted to him and grew concerned. "You okay?" With her short-cropped gray hair and dark skin, Cassie was part mother hen, part Amazon warrior queen. "You've got that look."

According to her, he always had *that look*. It kept people from asking him stupid questions. Cassie, however, had long been immune. "I'm peachy." He made no attempt to cover the sarcasm. "Let's do this."

"Fine by me." She started across the pristine lawn toward the open garage door where three officers spoke with a woman, mid-forties, who held both fists clenched, shaking. A pair of tearful teens stood at her side.

"He's not answering his phone," the woman said, her voice raw with panic.

One of the uniforms broke away and approached the detectives.

"What's going on?" Cassie asked.

"Looks like the same crew as the break-in earlier this week. Tied up the family. Except this time, the husband managed to work his hands free when the assailants weren't paying attention. According to the wife, as soon as they left, he got loose, untied her, and took off after them in the family car. A silver Audi Q5 SUV. He called her right before we arrived, saying he was following them east on West Sixth, trying to get a license number. But she hasn't heard from him since, and now he's not answering his phone." The officer wagged his notebook. "I put out a BOLO on the Audi."

"Good. Now we wait," Matthias said as much to himself as to his partner or the uniform. Patience was not one of his strong suits. "What about the suspect's vehicle?"

"Late model white transport van, same as before. I updated the BOLO on it as well."

Matthias thanked the uniform, who tipped his head in acknowledgment and strode off.

"I hope the husband doesn't try to be a hero," Cassie said softly as they approached the family.

Matthias flinched at the word "hero". Cassie either didn't notice or decided to give him a pass. "You talk to the first responders," he said. "I'll question the wife."

Cassie caught his arm, bringing him to a stop. "No way. I'll take the wife."

He faced his partner. She didn't usually play the seniority card with him. "Why?"

"Oh, I don't know. Maybe because she's terrified." Cassie's tenor turned acerbic. "And you're so warm and fuzzy."

He matched her tone. "And you are?"

She gave him an exaggerated smile and batted unmascaraed lashes. "When I put my mind to it." Without giving him a chance to argue, she stalked away. All six feet of her.

Pissed, he watched her go. Tall, slender, but rock-solid, Cassie Malone was several inches taller than he was. But that wasn't what annoyed the hell out of him. She was tough, smart, and a damned good cop. She had his back and knew he had hers. One could make a case she was the best partner he'd ever had. No, what bugged him was the fact she was right.

Cassie guided the woman and her kids away from the remaining two uniformed officers, who turned to Matthias.

He flipped open his notebook. "Who wants to fill me in on the details?"

Officers Lyle and Kollmann exchanged a look before Lyle gave his partner a nod.

Kollmann referred to his notes. "The call came in at sixteen fifteen." Four fifteen. "The wife reported the robbery."

Matthias glanced at the house. "What about security?"

"They have a system, but it was disarmed. Wife says they never have it armed once the kids get home from school. They're in and out too much. Just easier to shut the thing off."

Same as Tuesday's job. "What company?"

Kollmann checked his notes. "Safe At Home Security."

Not so *safe at home*, Matthias thought. "They didn't smash all the phones?" At Tuesday's heist, while the crew hadn't bothered with small-ticket items, they had destroyed the cell phones and cut the wiring for the landlines.

"The only one they could find was the wife's. Apparently, the husband left his in the car and the wife confiscated the kids' phones and stuck them in one of the kitchen drawers. Something about limiting their screen time after school. The assailants didn't make the effort to search for them."

Matthias jabbed his pen in the direction of his partner and the wife. "Whose phone does she have?"

"One of the kids' phones."

Convenient, Matthias thought. "Go on."

Kollmann reiterated what the first patrolman had already told them. Four-man crew. Family tied up. Same as Tuesday. Husband got free and took off after them. Not at all like Tuesday. Someone on the crew had gotten sloppy.

"I hope your partner has better luck than we did with the wife and kids. The only description they could give us was the intruders were dressed all in black, wore ski masks, and had *big* guns."

Matthias scanned the lawn. The houses on either side, while relatively close, were shielded by a green wall of trees, providing privacy. For both the family and the armed assholes who robbed and terrified them. However, more upscale homes faced them from across the normally quiet street. "What about neighbors?"

Lyle waved a finger at the surrounding tree line. "There's no clear view from either side. We haven't had a chance to talk to the residents over there." He pointed toward South Shore Drive.

"You said the security system was turned off. What about cameras?"

"Offline." Lyle removed his hat and ran his handkerchief over his polished dome before replacing it. "I hope the husband gets back to us with a license number. That would be a huge help."

Matthias grunted. It would. "Has anyone contacted the cell service provider?"

"As soon as the wife stated he wasn't responding to her calls, we put in for an exigent circumstance ping," Lyle said. "Still waiting to hear back."

"While you wait, start canvassing the neighbors, especially the ones across the road. Find out if anyone saw the van and who was in it. And check their security cam footage."

"On it."

Matthias thanked the uniforms and headed toward the massive pine in the Tudor's side yard where Cassie had gathered the wife and kids.

Cassie turned to him as he approached. "Mrs. Simmons, this is my partner, Detective Honeywell." She introduced the woman to him as Barbara and the kids as Belle and Jake.

Barbara Simmons still clung to the phone with one trembling hand, but she no longer appeared on the verge of a nuclear meltdown. Belle, a more petite version of her mother, clutched a tissue and chewed her lip. Matthias guessed the boy, the younger of the two, to be about fourteen and unsure whether to tough it out like a man or burst into childish tears.

"Why don't you take the kids around back," Cassie suggested, "while I finish up with their mom?"

Matthias caught his partner's knowing lift of one eyebrow. Although he tended to intimidate adults, he'd always had a way with kids. Plus, she probably wanted to ask some harder questions of the mother.

"Sure." He gestured for the teens to join him. "I bet you guys have a great view of the bay."

Jake hung his head and shrugged. "I guess."

But he and his sister obediently followed Matthias to the backyard.

Calling the view "great" was a vast understatement. The manicured lawn and landscaping bordered a paved walkway leading to the water's edge. In the distance, Presque Isle's peninsula separated the bay from the lake. A stiff breeze churned the water's surface, giving a pair of ducks a rollicking ride worthy of Waldameer Amusement Park.

Matthias settled the kids on a low cement bench beneath a tree and knelt in front of them. "Can you tell me what happened?"

Jake, still slumped, gazed at his knees. "We already told the other cops."

Matthias gave both teens a smile. "I know. It's a pain in the ass, but I have to hear it from you."

The gentle swearing raised Jake's face and brought a

fleeting grin from the girl. The pair exchanged a look. Belle's nod was nearly imperceptible.

Jake straightened. "I was in the family room, you know, gaming. Don't tell my folks."

Matthias held his pen away from the page and feigned innocence. "Tell them what?"

Jake relaxed. "Next thing I knew, some dude busted down the door, charged in, and yanked me out of my chair."

"Did you get a look at his face?"

"Nah." Jake waved a finger in front of his mouth. "He had on a ski mask sort of thing."

"Okay. He yanked you out of your chair. Then what?"

"He had a gun and told me if I yelled or anything, he'd blow my head off. Then he dragged me into the dining room, where another guy had Mom and Dad tied up. A third guy came in with Belle. They tied us up too."

"I thought there were four men. You've mentioned three."

"The fourth one stayed by the front door and kept looking outside."

"You said the one who came and got you was wearing a mask. Did you see the faces of any of the others?"

Jake shook his head. "They were all dressed alike."

"Did you notice what color their eyes were?"

"All I saw were the guns they were pointing at us."

"All four of them had guns?"

"Yeah. Big ones."

Matthias turned his attention to the girl, whom he pegged to be around sixteen. "What about you?"

She shot another look at her brother before bringing her gaze back to Matthias. "I was doing my homework."

Jake rolled his eyes. "Geek," he mumbled.

"Hey. If I finish my homework Friday night, I don't have to worry about it all weekend, like somebody else I know."

Matthias lowered his face to conceal a smile. When he lifted it again, he asked, "Where were you doing your homework?"

"My room. I had the door open, but I had my earbuds in, so I didn't hear anything. He was just … there. I think I screamed. He pointed a gun at me and told me to move."

"He didn't touch you?"

"No." Belle sounded relieved. "Just waved the gun around. He kinda grunted orders at me and took me to the dining room and tied me up."

"Did you see anything to help identify them? Eye color? Maybe a scar?" Matthias touched the long-healed one on his upper lip, a memento from his brief stint with cage fighting back in his twenties.

Belle was silent for a moment. Shook her head.

Something about the brief hesitation made Matthias wonder. "Anything at all? When they spoke, did they have any kind of accent?"

"Uh-uh," Jake replied.

Belle took a moment longer. "No. Not really."

The chirp from Matthias's phone interrupted before he could inquire what "not really" meant. The text from Cassie read, **Need you up front. Now.**

He withdrew a pair of business cards from his pocket and handed one to each teen. "If you think of anything, anything at all, call me. Okay?"

Jake studied the card. Belle pocketed hers without looking at it.

Matthias herded the siblings back to the front of the house. Cassie waited for him halfway between the porch, where she'd left Mrs. Simmons, and the road. At his encouragement, the kids veered off toward their mother.

He approached his partner and didn't like the look on her face. "What's going on?"

"They found the Audi."

Matthias risked a glance at the Simmons family watching from the porch.

"I didn't tell them yet," Cassie responded to his unasked question. "Wesley wasn't in it."

Matthias, Cassie, and a dozen assorted city and state police gathered around the silver Q5 parked in the middle of the Erie Sand and Gravel Company. Mountains of crushed rock and stone surrounded them. Not a security camera to be seen.

"The crime scene unit's been notified," one of the state troopers said. "But they're working a homicide down in Meadville. It'll be a while before they get here. We already searched the area and are bringing in a K-9 unit to see if they can pick up a scent."

Matthias gazed at the heavy machinery and mounds of rocky material and sand dredged from the lake. What the hell had happened here?

Cassie nudged him. "I'm not waiting for CSU. I'll get the camera."

While his partner retreated to their car, Matthias studied the ground around the Q5. The sandy ground was anything but smooth. Signs of a struggle? Maybe. Or it could be signs of the business's work crews traipsing through the property.

Heavy equipment tracks crisscrossed with those of other, smaller vehicles.

Cassie returned with the DSLR they kept in the trunk. She clicked several photos of the car's exterior and the ground before handing the camera to him and heading to the driver's side.

He fired off a few more photos of the passenger side before slinging the strap over one shoulder and swinging the chunky camera around behind him.

Cassie peered through the windows on her side as Matthias wiggled his fingers into a pair of black nitrile gloves.

She tried the door. "It's unlocked."

His side was too.

Cassie surveyed the seat and dashboard. "No blood." She slid into the seat and pressed the start button. The Audi roared to life. Leaning over, she slipped her hand into the center cubby and came out with the key fob.

Matthias remained outside the vehicle, scanning for anything out of the ordinary. "He left his fifty-thousand-dollar car out here, unlocked, with the fob inside."

"Fifty thousand is probably the stripped-down model."

"Out of my budget either way." Matthias bent down and opened the glove box. Owner's manual, insurance card, and registration. "What about his phone?"

She extracted hers from her pocket, along with her notebook. Skimming through it, she fingered a page and keyed in a number.

Symphony music filled the interior. They both looked around for the source. Cassie swept the center cubby again and reached for the console lid.

Matthias knelt and reached under the seat. His fingers

closed around the device. "Got it." He took one look at the shattered screen and showed it to Cassie. "Looks like a job for the tech nerds." He pulled a small paper evidence bag from his hip pocket and deposited the phone into it.

Cassie scanned the interior of the car again and shut off the ignition. Stepping outside, she gazed at the barren landscape. "There's no blood." She said it again, firmer this time.

"Why leave the car here?" Matthias asked, more to himself than to his partner. "If the home invasion crew grabbed him, where'd they take him?"

Cassie eyed him and, for the third time, said, "There's no blood."

"I'm not deaf."

"No, but you're being dense."

He bristled and glared back at her.

Her expression softened. "Look, you need to consider the possibility that Simmons might not be the hero here."

Her suggestion took Matthias aback. "I never said he was a hero."

"No, but you're thinking it."

His partner knew him entirely too well.

"He got loose," she said. "How? Did someone get careless? Or maybe it was intentional. He conveniently left his phone in the car rather than bring it into his house. The home security system was conveniently shut off."

Matthias wanted to point out the same had been true with the earlier robbery but kept quiet. Cassie raised some interesting questions.

"Now, he's *conveniently* disappeared. The whole thing is too freaking convenient if you ask me."

"You think he knew them?"

"I think I want to look into Simmons's financials and phone records. And I want to see a list of stolen items. It wouldn't be the first time some rich son of a bitch faked a robbery to collect the insurance payoff."

Matthias considered his partner's theory. He pictured the two kids and the wife. Frantic. Terrified. Vulnerable. If the husband had been involved in a risky get-rich-quick scheme, Matthias would bet his last dollar the rest of the family knew nothing about it. "Let's get the car impounded and the phone to the lab. Both have GPS. I want to know where Simmons went. If he—and they—stopped elsewhere, we'll have another crime scene to process."

Cassie nodded. "And we'll check for nearby security and traffic cam footage. Just because there aren't any cameras here doesn't mean we don't have this car recorded somewhere."

"With any luck, we'll get a glimpse of the van he was following."

She keyed another number into her phone and wandered away. Matthias slammed the car's passenger door, picturing the man he'd never met behind the wheel, his laughing wife next to him, the kids in the back seat. A happy family.

Until a few hours ago.

He tried to shake the feeling of dread. Tried to gaze beyond the stark brown hills of gravel and sand to Presque Isle Bay.

Their home invasion case was now a missing person's investigation. Possibly insurance fraud.

He hoped like hell it didn't turn into a homicide.

Chapter Two

M ost folks avoided cemeteries at dusk. It was one of the reasons Emma Anderson favored wandering through the crowded rows of graves as the shadows lengthened. She preferred the privacy. And she didn't want to intrude on others who might be visiting their loved ones, especially since she lugged a Nikon and a backpack laden with lenses, filters, and a spare camera body. Alone, she didn't feel so much like a ghoul, a vulture, profiting from others' pain.

Not that it was much of a profit. Freelance work took on many faces. None of them paid well.

She paused to read the names carved into the granite markers. In her jeans pocket, she carried a folded scrap of paper, a short list of dead strangers, but she didn't need to refer to it. She'd memorized them. An old friend from her former home in the southwestern corner of Pennsylvania had hired her to help trace his family history. He had ancestors from Erie. He'd done the research, made the phone calls, and learned several were buried in this section of Trinity Cemetery. He wanted her to provide photographic evidence of their final resting spots.

Emma moved on. The cemetery was huge, the graves crammed together. Even knowing the general vicinity of the burial plots wasn't speeding the process. She might not mind strolling the grounds at dusk, but she'd watched too many spooky movies as a kid to want to stick around after dark.

The next row of stones didn't contain any of the names she searched for either, although another name, farthest from where she stood, stirred a shiver of dread. Anderson. Her surname. She tamped down the anxiety. The cemetery was Catholic, most of the graves old. Emma and her younger sister, Nell, had been raised Presbyterian. Emma started doing the math. Nell had been missing a little over two years. Emma's last contact with her had been about six months ago—shortly before Christmas—when she'd confessed she was living here in Erie, waitressing at a local restaurant. Nothing since then. Surely if Emma's little sister had died, someone would've notified her.

Emma picked her way down the row, careful to avoid stepping on a grave. Her father had pounded that into her brain when she'd been a child and they'd placed flowers on her grandparents' plots.

The Anderson marker stood watch over a couple who'd passed in the early 1900s. Relatives? Probably not. Anderson was a common name. She lifted her camera, focused, and tripped the shutter. Zoomed in and snapped a few more pictures. One never knew. Someday she might sign up for one of those ancestry websites and research whether she had family up here in Erie.

Besides Nell.

A nearby sound jarred her from her thoughts. A short, rattling crackle she couldn't quite identify. She moved toward a large shade tree and the direction from which the sound had come. Easing around the trunk, she realized she was wrong about being alone. Less than twenty feet away, a man sat on the ground in front of one of the granite markers, his back to her. His dark hair renewed the chill and stirred a tsunami-force wave of panic.

Clay had found her. Dear God, he'd found her.

Before she could bolt, her phone rang. The man at the grave turned towards the sound and her, his expression fierce. Even in the fading light, she could tell, other than the hair, he bore no resemblance to Clay.

Relieved, she lifted a hand toward the man and called, "Sorry," before ducking behind the tree. Caller ID displayed Robert DelGrosso, editor of *PA Living Magazine*. "Bob. Hi."

"You busy?"

"Always," she lied. "But never too busy for you." Not a lie. He paid well.

"You're in Erie, right?"

"Yes."

"Good. Judy Post just turned in an article about the beaches at Presque Isle. Nice piece, but her pictures suck. I want to get this in the next issue, so I need you to get me some photos by Monday. Can you do that?"

Judy Post was Bob's pet contributor. Emma had tried writing articles for the magazine, only to have Bob pay her for the photos and ask Judy to rewrite the copy. Other times, like this, he turned to Emma to provide the visuals for Judy's words. "Sure." Emma searched the ominous gray skies. The forecast called for storms tonight with gradual clearing Saturday. If the weathermen told the truth, Sunday would be glorious.

"Great. I'll email you the article. That way you'll know what kind of pictures I need. You're the best, Anderson." He ended the call.

Emma looked at the phone's screen. "Yeah. Thanks."

Bob was notoriously full of BS, layering on the praise, provided she told him what he wanted to hear.

Pocketing the device, she peered around the tree. The man at the grave was gone. Curious, she approached the stone where he'd been sitting.

The tombstone was a newer one surrounded by older monuments bearing the same last name. Glossy granite with an inset of a badge. An eagle topped a circle bearing the words Bureau of Police, City of Erie, PA. The carving identified the fallen officer as Nicholas Tucci and his date of death five years ago. Emma did the math. He'd been forty-nine. According to the other engravings, he'd been a beloved husband, father, and grandfather.

The ground in front of the stone had been dug up, red and white geraniums planted and recently dead-headed. Less decorative, two crumpled beer cans rested among the flowers.

That was the sound Emma had heard. Aluminum being crushed.

She searched the grounds for the man who'd left them behind, but only the dead and the long shadows cast by the trees remained. She knelt, lifted her camera, and captured several photos of the grave and the beer cans. There was a story here. But she remembered the ferocity of the man's expression when he realized he wasn't alone. Somehow, she didn't think it was a story he wanted to share.

The next morning, Emma climbed to the top of the sandy rise between the parking lot and Beach Ten at Pennsylvania's Presque Isle State Park. The wind that kept her up most of the night had diminished, but the clouds remained threatening, the lake choppy. Whitecaps punctuated the gray water, reflecting the dark sky. Waves rolled in, crashing on the sand. She closed her eyes, allowed the breeze to toss her hair, and, for a moment, imagined she was by the ocean. The fantasy was her favorite part of living here. Lake Erie was big enough to conceal the Canadian shore beyond the horizon. On a more settled day, boats—fishing, sailing, yachts, even the USS *Brig Niagara* when it was in port—dotted the vista. She opened her eyes again. Only one vessel risked the rough water this Saturday morning, a mere speck where the lake met the sky.

She sloughed down the slope toward the lake's edge, sand filling the old canvas sneakers she kept for this very purpose. Before reaching the waterline, she veered left.

The article Bob had sent her dealt with the kite flyers who met almost daily on the beach, taking advantage of the lake's constant breeze. Emma knew the spot where they gathered, just west of Beach Ten. They weren't likely to be there right now, but if the weather cleared as forecast, they'd be around later. Tomorrow for sure. This trip was a scouting mission. At least that was her excuse for taking a morning walk along the shore. She'd driven her twelve-year-old Subaru instead of riding her bike, and carried her phone instead of her heavy camera equipment.

She loved when the lake was like this. Angry. Roiling. Morose. Not the kind of pictures Bob wanted for his touristy magazine. No, he only wanted vivid blue skies and vibrant colors. Not the muted, moody stuff she captured on days such as today.

The overnight storm had washed debris onto the beach. Having long heard the stories and listened to the songs about shipwrecks in the Great Lakes, Emma dreamed of finding pieces of such a wreck among the other chunks of wood, water weeds, and trash. Squawking seagulls looped overhead. Some skittered along the sand, foraging for dead fish or bits of food left by yesterday's picnickers. Emma knelt with her phone set on camera, clicking a few pictures of the fearless scavengers before continuing down the beach.

She'd been partially right. There were a couple of kite flyers setting up, but she kept walking, the sand in her shoes rough on her feet. In the distance, she could make out a group of people but not what they were doing. Curiosity drove her on, stopping to grab shots of an interesting piece of driftwood or an especially brazen gull. Halfway to the group, she determined they were practicing yoga using beach towels instead of mats.

She debated sneaking some pictures and decided against it. If she'd had her Nikon with one of her long lenses, maybe. And she'd have to get permission to do anything with the photos. Maybe not legally. Out here on a public beach, there was no assumption of privacy, but common courtesy held her to her own rules, stricter than those of the legal system. She even hesitated to get any closer and risk disturbing their focus.

But she could see a massive pile of debris on the beach beyond them. Her shipwreck fantasies drove her onwards.

She slipped off her shoes and stepped into the water, the cold snatching her breath. Standing still, she let her lower extremities acclimate to the temperature as the waves lapped at her shins, burying her toes and feet deeper in the sand. It didn't take long for the water to feel almost tepid. Barefoot, she skirted the yoga class, which was being led by a shapely young woman with a purple-streaked ponytail and wearing violet yoga pants and tank top.

The woman spotted Emma. "Hey, come join us."

Emma lifted her hand, clutching her phone. "Maybe next time." She meant it. Sort of. It had been years since she'd taken one of Nell's yoga classes, although the memory of the inner calm it produced made her repeat, "Maybe next time," softer to herself.

The jumbled mass of lake trash bore no resemblance to any shipwreck Emma had imagined. A half dozen or more gulls were perched on it. Sodden plastic shopping bags, weeds, and what appeared to be a fair-sized length of old wood-slatted snow fence bound by rusty wire made up the bulk of the mess. From her photographer's eye, the birds were the most interesting part of the scene. Rather than risk scaring them off, she kept her distance. She clicked a few pictures, experimented with the rule of thirds composition, and toyed with zooming and exposure as much as she could on the phone.

"Hey."

Emma spun to see the yoga teacher approaching. Beyond, her students were stretched out, face up on their beach towels. *Savasana*. Corpse pose.

The teacher kept her voice soft, as if not wanting to disturb the class, although, from this distance, Emma doubted they'd hear her over the rush of the breaking waves. "I'm Kira Petersen." She extended a hand holding a business card. "I have a studio in town and teach classes here on the beach a few times a week, weather permitting."

Emma studied the card, printed in restful pastels. She felt the woman watching her expectantly and looked up. "Sorry. I'm Emma Anderson." She really needed to get new business cards made. "Freelance photographer."

Kira seemed surprised. "Oh. I thought maybe you were waiting to talk to me after class." She waved a hand at the mound. "And were just killing time by taking pictures of … garbage."

Emma choked a laugh. "No, I really am taking pictures of garbage."

"I guess it could be considered pop art." Kira sounded doubtful.

"I was hoping for wreckage from a long-lost ship."

Kira's eyes brightened. "The wreck of the Edmund Fitzgerald?"

"Wrong lake. But that's the idea." Emma automatically looked out over the water. "To be honest, I'm scouting." She gestured in the direction from which she'd come. "I have an assignment to shoot the guys who fly the kites, but I'll have to come back when the weather clears."

"Sounds like fun." Kira glanced toward her students before returning her gaze to Emma. "Seriously, though. You really a photographer?"

Realizing she looked like any other selfie-shooting tourist, she grinned sheepishly. "I am. I have actual cameras and lenses and flashes and everything."

"I've been thinking I should get some photos of me and my classes for my website and social media. You interested?"

"Sure." Emma hoped she didn't sound too eager.

"Great." Kira struck a dramatic and fashion-model-worthy pose. "How's this?"

Emma laughed and snapped a quick shot. "Perfect. Maybe not for promoting your yoga classes, though."

"What can I say? I'm a frustrated model." Kira wagged a finger at her. "You have my card. Call me. I'll see which of my students want to participate, and we'll set up a date."

"I will." As if on cue, Emma's phone rang and sounded ridiculously loud, although none of the resting yogis appeared to notice.

Kira turned to go. "Thanks. I better get back to my students."

Emma checked the screen. Caller ID only identified the incoming call as "Unknown", and the number wasn't familiar. Probably a scammer or telemarketer. She hit the red button, declining the call. Guilt, doubt, and regret slammed her. What if it had been Nell? True, Emma hadn't heard from her in months, but finding her sister was one of the reasons she now lived in Erie. As far as she knew, Nell was still here. Somewhere. Emma did her best to leave breadcrumbs, hoping Nell would reach out to her. What if that declined call was the one Emma had been waiting for?

Or it could've been Clay, the other reason Emma was in Erie, a hundred and fifty miles from the home she once loved.

Clay couldn't possibly have her number. Could he? She'd ditched her old cell—same as she'd hacked off her long red hair and dyed it a nondescript shade—before she'd moved. Since then, she'd battled with every decision regarding her contact information. Her clients in and around Erie had her number, as did Eric Baker, her best friend from back home ... the only person she trusted to keep her secrets ... and who'd sent her on the search for his ancestors' graves.

But she'd also trusted waitresses at seedy bars around the city with photos of Nell, Emma's number scrawled across the back. She prayed one of those photos never found its way into Clay's hands.

Between her sister and her ex, Emma teetered on a fine and very sharp blade, desperately wanting to be accessible to the first while remaining concealed from the other.

As if sensing her quandary, the phone rang again. This time, Emma answered. "Hello?"

Only silence responded.

She plugged her other ear, drowning out the surf and the seagulls. "Hello?" she said louder, hating the tremor in her voice.

The line went dead. Emma stared at the phone as if it might give up the caller's true identity. Family or foe?

Or someone trying to sell her an extended insurance policy on her car?

Hoping for the latter, she shook her head, took one last look at the pile of lake trash, and decided she'd had enough for one morning.

When Emma first moved to Erie, she'd made every attempt to wash or wipe all the sand from her feet and beat it off her shoes, before getting in her car. She soon learned it was an impossible task. Her Forester was now officially a beach vehicle with grit coating the all-weather floor mats.

She settled behind the wheel. The skies were already starting to lighten. Beach Ten's parking lot was filling. Families lugged coolers and towels towards the beach, anticipating the emergence of the sun. A lifeguard planted a flag indicating the beach was open and climbed to his perch on a high white chair.

Emma retrieved her laptop from under the passenger seat and pulled a cord from the center console. She plugged her phone into the computer to get a clearer look at the photos she'd taken.

Clicking through, she deleted some blurry seagull photos. Several of the angry lake pictures looked potentially good enough to print, frame, and offer for sale at one of the summer's arts and crafts shows. Or at one of the local eateries that displayed her work.

The pictures of driftwood lacked contrast and definition due to the flat lighting. Maybe when she came back to photograph the kites, she'd take another walk and try again.

The last photo was the purple-haired yoga instructor. For a quick shot, it wasn't bad. The flat lighting that didn't work for landscape shots was exquisite for portraiture.

As for the pictures of the mound of trash and the seagulls flocking over it, the yoga teacher had been right about the closeups of the tangled snow fence. They could almost be considered pop art. Almost. But not quite. Emma skimmed through, went back, and was about to hit delete when something caught her eye. Something that didn't fit with the rest of the plastic and wood and wire.

Emma touched the screen, enlarging the image. She squinted. Enlarged it again.

Realization took her breath away. That wasn't some random piece of plastic or a dead fish.

That was an arm protruding from the lake junk.

Chapter Three

The beach northeast of the Presque Isle lighthouse had already been cordoned off with yellow caution tape by the time Matthias and Cassie approached on foot. Park rangers from the PA Department of Natural Resources and officers from Pennsylvania State Police and Erie Police joined the Erie County Coroner at the scene.

"The gang's all here," Matthias said.

A homicide in the state park ordinarily wouldn't have landed in their laps but would've fallen under the PSP's jurisdiction. When Matthias's attempts at sleeping in on a Saturday morning were interrupted by his lieutenant, ordering him to the scene, he knew better than to ask why. He did, however, wisely choose an old pair of hiking boots as footwear.

Matthias lifted the tape for Cassie before ducking under it.

One of the state troopers spotted them and approached, nodding a greeting. "Detectives. Trooper Alex Gooding."

"Matthias Honeywell." He pointed at his partner. "Cassie Malone. What have we got?"

Gooding thumbed toward a jumble of rubbish at the water's edge. "The body's tangled up in that mess. Must've washed up overnight." He re-directed the thumb towards a young woman standing alone just outside the taped perimeter, hugging herself as if she were cold despite the rising temperature. "That's the reporting party. She was taking pictures with her phone and says she didn't notice him until she looked at the photos on her computer."

Matthias eyed the soggy pile of debris. "Taking pictures of trash?"

Gooding shrugged. "That's her story. She came back to make sure she'd seen what she thought she saw and then called it in." Gooding checked his notes. "Name's Emma Anderson. Gives her home address as Sara's Campground."

Cassie fixed the trooper with one of her withering glares. "Not that we don't love spending a Saturday morning at the beach, but isn't this a case for you guys and the rangers? Do you mind telling us why we're here?"

"Because of the decedent's ID. He came up in the system as a missing person in one of your investigations. Wesley Simmons of South Shore Drive."

Matthias sensed Cassie stiffen. "Has the family been notified?" he asked.

Gooding gave them a pained smile. "It's your case now. Looks like that task falls to you." He turned and walked away.

"Dammit," Matthias muttered. He glared at his partner. "I guess this rules out your insurance fraud idea."

"Not necessarily. No honor among thieves, as they say. Maybe he and his buddies had a falling out. Or he became a liability. Or they decided they didn't want to share." Cassie pointed towards the body. "If anything, this adds credence to my theory. Let's go talk to the coroner and then question the woman who found the body."

Matthias trailed his partner towards the water's edge, but his gaze drifted to the woman standing outside the yellow tape. Short dirty-blonde hair. A Pittsburgh Pirates T-shirt. Jeans rolled up to mid-calf. Something about her felt familiar, yet he was certain he'd never met her before.

Looking like a surfer dude with unruly sun-bleached hair, Felix Hamilton, Erie County Coroner, knelt beside the body. He directed two of his deputies, who struggled to disentangle the decedent from the water weeds and some wood pickets bound by wire.

"Hey, Ham," Cassie said. "Know anything yet?"

Hamilton lifted his pale blue gaze to the detectives before pointing at the body. "Our decedent suffered a deep penetrating wound, left side, just below the rib cage."

That brought Matthias's full attention to the victim. "He was stabbed?"

"Maybe. The wound could have been created by a knife or from some of this debris. I won't know anything for certain until I get him into autopsy." The coroner stood and stretched. "I understand he's someone you were looking for?"

"So we've been told," Cassie said.

"Mind if I take a look?" Matthias asked.

"Be my guest." Hamilton stepped back.

Matthias squatted and tipped his head sideways to view the man straight on. The victim must've washed up face down. The sand appeared disturbed, where someone had repositioned his head for a better look. The open, unseeing eyes were opaque. The skin was pale and waxy. Matthias thumbed through his phone's photo gallery to pull up the picture of Wesley Simmons the man's wife had given them yesterday. "It's him." Mental images of the two kids swam through Matthias's mind.

He stood and met his partner's gaze, betting from her expression she was thinking of them too.

"Let us know what you find out, Ham," Cassie said.

The coroner gave a nod before returning to his spot beside the body.

Without a word, Matthias trudged through the soft sand toward the crime scene tape and the blonde.

As they approached, Cassie whispered, "She's cute. You gonna ask her out?"

"Jesus," he muttered. "You're sick, you know that?"

She shrugged. "You've never been one to pass up an opportunity. Just sayin'."

The blonde looked up, her face tense. Her wide eyes reminded him of pictures he'd seen of the Caribbean Ocean, equal parts green and blue. Almost teal. He still sensed he knew her from somewhere.

Matthias introduced himself and his partner. "And you are?"

"Emma Anderson."

"You live around here?"

"At Sara's Campground. Site five eighteen."

Matthias studied her. "But where do you live?"

She met his gaze without wavering. "At Sara's Campground," she repeated, enunciating her words more clearly as if speaking to a child. "Site five eighteen."

"That's your mailing address?"

"It's the only address I have."

Matthias jotted a note. Was this woman a transient? The campground wasn't open year-round. She had to have another address.

While he puzzled over Emma's residence, Cassie stepped in to continue the questions. "I understand you found the body?"

"I guess so." Emma told them about walking along the beach taking pictures and about how she'd seen an arm sticking out of the debris once she'd blown up the photo on her computer. "I came back for a better look. That's when I saw it really was a person in there and called 911."

"You didn't see him before? When you were taking the pictures?"

"No. I wasn't paying attention to details. I was mostly trying to get shots of the gulls. I was using my phone."

"Do you always take pictures of garbage on the beach?" Matthias asked.

Those teal eyes came back to him. "I'm a freelance photographer. I take pictures of anything and everything."

That was why she looked familiar. Last night. At the cemetery. The woman lurking by the tree with the camera. He watched a flicker of some veiled emotion dance across her face before she blinked and masked her expression.

"I'd like copies of those photos, if you don't mind," Cassie said.

The "if you don't mind" part was Cassie's way of finding out how cooperative their witness was. Matthias expected an argument. Expected the blonde to say she did indeed mind.

"No problem." She tapped, swiped, and tapped again on her phone. "Give me your email address and I'll send them now."

Cassie moved to Emma's side and watched over her shoulder while spelling out the address. Emma didn't protest, didn't try to shield the screen. To the contrary, she held the phone so Cassie could see what must have been her photo gallery.

"These are the shots of the..."—Emma glanced toward the trash heap—"of where the body washed up. Do you want all of them?"

As the two women conferred, heads bent over the phone, Matthias turned his attention to the coroner and his deputies working over the decedent and to the lake beyond.

Presque Isle was a peninsula, jutting north into Lake Erie, narrow at the base, widening as it swept east. On the southern edge, Presque Isle Bay separated the peninsula from the city.

They'd found Simmons's car at the Sand and Gravel Company, on Erie's northern shore, across the bay from Presque Isle. If he'd been killed and dumped in the water there, his body would've had to make the unlikely journey through the channel, east into the Lake Erie Harbor, north around the far tip of the peninsula, and west through the lake to wash up on this sandy beach. A long trip for a dead man in a very short span of time.

"Who's that?"

His partner's question brought his focus back to the photographer. Cassie pointed at Emma's phone.

"Her name's Kira something. She was teaching a yoga class over there." Emma gestured. "We spoke briefly about doing some promotional photos." She dug in her pocket and came up with a business card. "Kira Petersen."

Matthias held out a hand for the card. "May I?" Like

Cassie's "if you don't mind" comment, his question was more of a test of Emma's cooperation than a polite request.

Again, she passed, handing him the card.

From his experience in the martial arts and eastern philosophy, Matthias recognized the circular design on the front as a *sri yantra*. Namaste Erie Yoga was printed in a font resembling Sanskrit. In smaller block letters, Kira Petersen, Proprietor, plus an address downtown and a phone number. "Mind if I keep this?"

This time, Emma hesitated. "Could I take a picture of it first?" When he gave her a look, she pointed at the card. "She was interested in hiring me for some work. Provided you don't arrest her for murder, I'd like to follow up."

He met her gaze, searching for any indication she was holding back. There was definitely something there, lurking in the depths of her eyes. But instinct told him it was less about the case or the yoga chick and more about him.

He scared her.

He'd been told he had that effect on people.

Matthias softened his expression and held the card toward her on the flat of his palm. "Don't wanna get in the way of a small business owner trying to make a living."

She snapped her photo, thanked him, and turned back to Cassie. "Any other shots you want me to send you?"

"The one of the yoga teacher. And any of her class."

Emma worked her thumbs over the screen. "I only took that one. It didn't feel right to intrude on the others in the middle of their practice."

"Then the one of Ms. Petersen will have to do."

Emma tapped the phone one more time. "Done."

After determining the photographer hadn't seen anything else useful, Matthias and Cassie gave her their cards.

He watched her go, climbing the sandy beach all the way to the grass line, giving the crime scene a wide berth. Cassie'd been right about her being cute. But what had she been doing taking his picture at the cemetery last night? She said she didn't feel right intruding on the yoga class but apparently didn't mind intruding on his privacy. Now wasn't the time to ask. Later, however, he intended to track her down at the campground.

If that was really where she lived.

"How the hell did Wesley Simmons wind up here?" Cassie mused.

Matthias turned his back on the departing blonde. Cassie was gazing out at the choppy water, much as he'd done a few minutes earlier.

"There's no way his body traveled all the way from where his car was abandoned in a matter of eighteen hours or so."

Cassie held up one finger. "Either he was killed there and his body moved, probably by boat, out to the lake and dumped—"

"No blood in or around his car."

She nodded and held up a second finger. "Or he was killed at a different location, dumped in the lake, and then his car was left where it was to distract us." A third finger. "Or he followed his killers to the sand company where they left his car and took him somewhere else where they killed him and dumped the body in the lake."

"My money's on door number two."

She closed her fist and lowered her hand. "Basically, we

have nothing. No primary crime scene, no murder weapon, no suspect."

"Some days I hate this job."

"What we do have," Cassie faced him, with her mouth drawn into a tight scowl, "is a family waiting for us to ruin their world." She pivoted and headed back towards their car.

Matthias gazed out at the lake for a moment longer. "Yeah. Today, I definitely hate this job."

Chapter Four

E mma wasn't sure which disturbed her more: finding a dead body washed up on the beach or the intensity of that police detective's eyes.

She hadn't recognized him at first. Last night, she'd averted her gaze the moment she realized she was mistaken. He'd been wearing a dark jacket over a hoodie. Today, he wore a polo shirt and dress trousers.

He made the connection before she did. Of that she was certain. His already clenched jaw tightened. His eyes sparked with the same thinly veiled hostility she'd seen at the cemetery. That was when she placed him. He tried to cover. But she'd known men with anger issues—especially the one she'd mistaken him for—and knew well enough to avoid them.

Emma knew she was projecting her fear onto this cop because of the flash of terror when she'd thought he was Clay. The detective's hair—dark and straight—triggered her reaction. Beyond that, the two men had little in common. The cop had a blockier build. Not tall, but broad-shouldered with a muscular frame born of hours spent pumping iron. And his eyes were what her mother would've called baby blue. The man she'd mistaken him for? Also broad-shouldered and strong, but refined. More of a long-distance runner's physique than that of a gym rat. Clay's dark eyes were almost black.

By the time she reached the state park's exit, the slow pace of cars traveling at the 25mph speed limit and the natural serenity of the green foliage to her left and the sandy dunes to her right had mollified her. Sara's Campground and the fifties-style restaurant owned by the same family bordered the park. Emma slowed even more to negotiate a pair of speed bumps in front of the diner before making the left turn. She cruised through the open gates and the private property sign and into the campground. A trio of youngsters played in a large water puddle, paying no heed to Emma's car. She steered around them and maneuvered along the blacktopped camp roads to her "neighborhood" of shaded seasonal sites. She parked on the concrete slab in front of her home, a seventeen-foot camper, and turned off the ignition. The other trailers dwarfed hers. Heck, some of them dwarfed the house she used to live in. But she'd been grateful to find this little one available, especially with an attached covered wooden deck, which almost doubled her living space.

Gathering her laptop, keys and phone, Emma climbed out of the Subaru and started toward the porch. A flutter of white cottonwood seeds drifted down and settled against the bases of the surrounding trees, like snow in May.

"Morning, neighbor."

She looked toward the voice. "Hey, Joe."

Joe Platt, one of the weekend regulars, occupied the shiny forty-foot Jayco next to hers. She guessed him to be in his mid to late fifties with a full head of white hair and a tanned and creased face hinting at years spent outdoors. As she watched, he dragged a vinyl cover from a massive grill.

Emma might have resented Joe's monster-sized trailer blocking her view, but she'd learned within her first week that it also shielded her from the guy on the other side of Joe's lot. Mick Harper liked to drink—a lot. He also liked to blast his radio and sing. Loudly. And not well. Not only did Joe's Jayco provide a physical buffer, but Joe had put Mick in his place more than once.

Joe shook out the grill cover, sending a spray of rainwater toward the road. "Did you get any good pictures?"

Telling him she'd found a dead body didn't seem appropriate. "Not really. I'll have to go back when the sun comes out."

He looked skyward. "Maybe later."

"Maybe." She took another step toward her deck.

"Hey, my daughter and grandkids are coming over for supper. We're cooking out if you care to join us." He patted the stainless-steel lid. "I know you're a vegetarian, but I'll be glad to slap one of those bean burgers on ol' Wanda Weber if you want."

The invitation was tempting. Joe often talked about his grandchildren and he'd shown Emma dozens of photos of them, but she'd never met them or his daughter. While curious, being social didn't appeal to her today. Still, she forced a smile. "I might just take you up on that. Thanks." She waved and stepped onto her porch, putting her camper between her and Joe.

She set her laptop on the cheap painted cabinet she'd claimed from someone's garbage and kept on the deck next to the door. A good catch-all and storage for the little odds and ends necessary to camping life. Citronella candles, mosquito repellent, a lighter, a coil of collapsible garden hose. As she inserted her key into the lock, her phone rang. The screen identified the incoming call as Unknown again. Emma froze. She should let it go to voicemail. But if it was Nell, she couldn't trust her baby sister to leave a message.

Emma swiped the green button. "Hello?"

She was greeted with silence. No. Not total silence. The faint scraping sound in the background told her someone was on the other end.

The line went dead.

Shedding her unease, Emma pocketed the phone, unlocked the camper's outer door, and secured it open with a bungee. Her new home needed work, but until she landed a real job as a staff photographer somewhere, she kept it held together with duct tape and bungees.

She stepped out of her canvas sneakers and slapped the soles together, knocking off any residual sand before depositing them on the deck. Collecting her laptop, she popped open the screen door and stepped inside.

Home sweet home. A seventeen-foot camper didn't provide a lot of elbow room, but for one woman who'd left most of what she owned and loved behind, this was all she needed.

Although a better space for her computer and photo editing equipment would be nice.

Emma set the laptop on the table that doubled as her desk before preparing the Mr. Coffee for her second pot of the day. She clicked the power button and listened to the gurgle and hiss of the unit coming to life. While it brewed, she cranked open the small window over the sink and the wider ones over the futon. Sliding onto the bench that served as both her office and kitchen seating, she raised the blinds and the window above the table, flooding the space with light. A deliciously warm spring breeze wafted through the camper carrying a hint of wood smoke.

Yes, she'd definitely worked in worse settings.

Emma wanted another look at the photos she'd taken on the beach a few hours ago. Not the ones with the trash-encrusted body. If anything looked print-worthy, she'd run them through Lightroom, her photo editing program, and email the files to the print shop in town.

One thing her small living space did not have room for was a quality color printer.

She plugged her phone into the laptop and the laptop into one of two large monitors. While the photos loaded, she turned to her second laptop, clicked on the email icon, and waded through the usual array of advertising and spam messages. Two legit emails caught her attention.

The first one was from Eric, inquiring about the gravestone photos. **How goes the quest? I've come up with a couple of additional names. Thanks for your help**.

He included the cemetery—a different one this time—and the plot locations. Looked like she'd be spending another evening searching tombstones. Hopefully, she wouldn't encounter the beer-drinking detective near any of them.

She pushed aside thoughts of the cop and fired off a reply to Eric, updated him on what she'd accomplished so far, and promised to get photos to him early in the week.

The second email was from her *PA Living Magazine* editor. Emma hesitated before clicking on it. Did he have another assignment for her? Or was he canceling the beach kites job?

Neither was the case. Instead, the message was a nudge. **Have you gotten my pictures yet? When can I expect them? Would like to get this edition put to bed**.

So much for having until Monday. And so much for waiting until tomorrow for better weather. She looked out the window at clouds that were starting to reveal peeks of blue.

Emma typed a reply. **Not yet. Bad weather. Hoping for later today or early tomorrow**. She considered mentioning his original deadline but decided against annoying her best source of income.

Fifteen minutes later, coffee mug half drained, she'd weeded out most of the morning's beach photos. Deleting more of the seagull pictures, she saved only a couple landscapes showing the whitecaps and monotone gray of water and sky. She also kept the quirky photo of the yoga instructor. She intended to send it to the purple-haired young woman as a gift.

Except Emma had turned over the business card to the police. She scrolled to find the photo she'd taken of it and came across the pictures of the debris. And the arm sticking from it.

Her coffee turned acidic in her stomach.

She contemplated deleting the pictures. Would she get in trouble with the cops if she did? They were crime scene photos, after all. Evidence. She'd emailed them to the woman detective. But still, these were the original source files. Not that they showed anything. An arm. Hardly something that would prove or disprove anything about the crime.

As she debated, the sound of factory-set ringtones drifted through the window over her sink. Joe's phone. She heard him answer with a cheery hello.

Emma decided to copy the disturbing photos to her

external hard drive in their own file before deleting them from her phone. That way, she wouldn't keep stumbling across them.

Outside, Joe's voice rose. "Oh, my God. Honey, are you sure there isn't some mistake?" He sounded anguished. Disbelieving.

Emma's curiosity battled with her determination to mind her own business.

"Oh, my God," he said again. "I'll come right over." Then after a pause, "Are you sure? Well, okay."

He continued to talk but softer. Emma tried to focus on her work. She found the picture of the yoga studio business card and made a note of the email address. Before she could finish typing it into a message, Joe's grief-stricken sobs drew her to the window. Outside, the older man sat on his deck, his head in his hands.

She charged outside barefoot and padded around her camper to his. "Joe? What's wrong?"

He lifted his face, tears streaming down his weathered cheeks. "I just got a call from my daughter. The police found her husband's body washed up on the beach this morning."

"This is it." Joe pointed at a driveway on the right side of South Side Drive.

Emma slowed and pulled in.

At first, he'd refused her offer to drive him to his daughter's house but reconsidered. "Barbie told me there wasn't anything I could do here," he said as they approached the Tudor. "But I'm her dad. I can't just sit around while my little girl's in pain."

"My dad was the same way." Emma shifted into park.

"You don't talk much about your folks."

Her throat closed. What could she say? They're dead, and it's my fault? Instead, she said, "Call me when you want me to pick you up."

"Let me introduce you first. Besides, she may tell me to leave." Joe didn't wait for a reply and climbed out.

"Wait. What?"

But he'd turned his back and was striding toward the house.

Emma turned off the ignition and watched him go. The last thing she wanted was to meet Joe's family under these circumstances. Grief was something she was all too familiar with and, in her opinion, was better dealt with in private.

She stepped from her car and hesitantly trailed her campground neighbor. The second half of his parting words stirred the bigger question. Why would his daughter ask him to leave?

Joe was already inside by the time Emma reached the front door. Distressed voices drifted through the glass panel. She stood on the small porch, her fists clenched. Should she ring the bell? Just let herself in? Or wait until Joe came looking for her? The doorbell wasn't one of those high-tech ones with a built-in camera. How long before someone noticed her standing there?

What felt like five minutes ticked by, and she decided on another option. What she should've done in the first place: wait in the car. She stepped off the porch and had taken two steps when the door opened behind her. She spun to find not Joe but the dark-haired cop from the cemetery and the beach. Guilt gripped her, as firmly as if she'd been trespassing and peeping into the house.

"What are you doing?" he asked.

Emma couldn't remember his name. "I drove Joe here to be with his daughter."

The cop's face exhibited none of the anger it had earlier but appeared carved in stone. "How do you know Joe Platt?"

"He's my neighbor."

"At the campground?"

She nodded.

"Why didn't you come inside with him?"

She was wondering the same thing. "Good question." She offered him a sheepish grin, hoping to soften the cop's granite-like features.

The attempt failed. He waited.

In her mind, Emma ran through the same options she had minutes earlier while standing at the door. If she tried to explain it all to him, he'd think she was a babbling idiot. "It didn't feel right, intruding at a time like this."

The answer seemed to appease him. He stepped back into the house and held the door. "Come in."

It sounded like a congenial offer, but she sensed it was a police order. "Thanks."

Inside, they followed the same distressed voices through a beautiful, lofty entryway to the biggest kitchen Emma had ever seen. She recognized the two teens perched at a massive island from Joe's photos. The girl's face was tear streaked. The boy's chin quivered, but his eyes were dry. The same female cop who'd been at the beach stood over a round table where a woman sat, tissues pressed to her mouth. Joe jumped from his seat across from her.

"Emma," he said. "I'm so sorry. I invited you in and then just left you out there."

"It's okay. You were focused on your daughter."

Joe rested a hand on the woman's shoulder. "Barbie, this is my new neighbor at the campground. Emma. I told you about her. The photographer."

"I'm so sorry for your loss, Barbie," Emma said softly.

"It's Barbara, not Barbie." The woman lifted her gaze for a fleeting moment, acknowledging Emma's presence before returning her focus to her tissue. "Thanks for driving Dad here. I'll make sure someone takes him home." She looked up again. "Or better yet, take him back with you."

Joe sputtered a protest.

"Dad, I told you on the phone not to come."

"You're my daughter."

Barbara's face turned cold. "You haven't been to my home in almost two years."

"That's not my fault," Joe said, his voice as cold as his daughter's expression. He shot a glance at the two cops. His next words were softer, imploring. "I thought we were working on it. You and the kids agreed to come to the campground this evening."

"Well, we won't be now." She met Emma's gaze. "Get him out of here. Please."

Emma looked from Barbara to Joe. How had she ended up in the middle of a family dispute?

"Barbie, honey," Joe said. "Please don't keep shutting me out."

Barbara's face flushed. She appeared on the verge of

spitting an angry retort, but her gaze shifted to the cops before coming back to her father. "We'll talk later." Her tone left no room for debate.

"If that's what you want." He looked at Emma. "Can you give me a ride?"

"Sure." She watched as he paused to give each of the kids a hug.

He stood over Barbara, but when she turned her face away, he settled on squeezing her shoulder. Facing Emma, he said, "Let's go."

She offered a weak smile and a nod to the cops, who hadn't budged or said a word, and headed back the way she'd come. Joe's soft footsteps told her he was right behind. Outside, she breathed a sigh of relief, grateful to be free of whatever family drama had been boiling between father and daughter. She slowed to allow Joe to catch up.

"I apologize for all that," he said. "Barbie and I haven't seen eye to eye for a long while."

Behind them, the door slammed. "Excuse me." The dark-haired cop's voice froze Emma mid stride.

They turned.

"Mr. Platt, I'd like to have a word with you." The cop's gaze settled on Emma. "You too, Ms. Anderson. If you don't mind."

Chapter Five

Death notifications sucked. Matthias would rather spend an afternoon in a drug house, breathing the stench of human excrement, than cope with the tortured faces of a family as their worlds were crushed. Cassie, despite her normal mother hen mentality, pulled rank for the second time in as many days and ordered him to take the lead.

He'd made no effort to ease into the news. Next of kin always saw through the small talk. Better to get it over with. "I'm sorry to have to tell you, we've found your husband's body."

"He's ... dead?" Barbara Simmons had squeaked out the question.

"Yes, ma'am."

At which point, he had to catch her before her weakened knees dropped her to the floor. Cassie offered to make tea. Mrs. Simmons gathered her children and told them the news. The daughter—Belle—broke into silent tears. The son—Jake—was

47

visibly shaken but held tough. He was now the proverbial man of the family and appeared to be contemplating the role.

There was nothing silent about the widow's grief. She sobbed into a tissue. Cassie located a fresh box for her in the entryway.

Matthias began to understand why his partner had made him the bearer of bad news. It allowed her to maintain the caregiver position. He was the bad guy who ruined their lives. She was the one who offered comfort.

"Is there anyone we can call for you?" Cassie asked.

Mrs. Simmons thanked her but said she'd make the call herself.

Which, in hindsight, was the moment things started going to hell.

She'd wept into her phone, telling her father what had happened but asking him to *not* come to the house. Matthias hadn't understood.

Until Joe Platt showed up about fifteen minutes later.

As Platt and Mrs. Simmons bickered, Matthias and Cassie remained silent observers. Mrs. Simmons didn't want her father there. Platt appeared all too eager to play protector while showing absolutely no sorrow over his son-in-law's demise.

The argument had started to subside when Matthias caught sight of someone at the front door. The silhouette retreated as he strode to the entryway, opened the door, and discovered the young woman who'd found Simmons's body. Bringing Emma Anderson into the house revealed one important fact. She and Barbara Simmons were strangers prior to this meeting. But Emma and Platt were well acquainted. Matthias had no idea what the connection meant. Yet.

Back outside with the pair, he considered separating them. Interviewing them individually was usually his preference but watching their reactions to each other might prove more enlightening. He guided them into the shade. The same spot where Cassie had spoken with Mrs. Simmons one day earlier.

Standing so he could still see Emma's expression, he focused his first question to Platt. "When was the last time you saw your son-in-law?"

Platt blew a noisy breath from his lips. "Hell, I couldn't even tell you. It's been years."

This drew a look of surprise from Emma. Matthias pretended not to notice. "What kind of relationship did you have with him?"

"A piss poor one." Platt shot an apologetic glance Emma's way. "I'm sorry. Wesley always brings out the worst in me."

"How so?" Matthias kept his tone curious and conversational.

"We were like oil and water from the first time Barbie brought him around. He wanted to be the only man she relied on. If I tried to help them, Wesley would tell me to butt out. He didn't need or want anything from me. He didn't want me at family gatherings. Said I was a bad influence on the kids."

Matthias noticed an uncomfortable reaction from Emma as Platt spoke and made a mental note.

Platt snorted again and continued. "Bad influence. I'm their grandpa, for crying out loud. I finally gave up even trying. Oh, I kept in touch with Barbie as much as I could. She'd sneak out with the kids to meet me at the park or for lunch, but never with Wesley's knowledge. And never here." He gestured at the house.

"You can't remember when you last saw your son-in-law?"

"Like I said. It's been years."

"Did you know about the break-in yesterday?"

Platt scowled. "What break-in?"

Matthias took that as a no. Mrs. Simmons hadn't looked to her father for solace following the home invasion. "Did you know Wesley Simmons was missing?"

Platt's face reddened. "All I know," he said stiffly, "is what Barbie told me on the phone. He's dead, and his body washed up on the shore."

Matthias shifted his gaze to Emma while still directing his questions to Platt. "Did you know Ms. Anderson's the one who found the body?"

If looks could kill, Emma's teal eyes would've ripped Matthias to shreds.

Platt turned to her, his face the picture of shock. "What? No. Emma?"

She held Matthias in her deadly stare for another beat before meeting Platt's gaze. "I'm so sorry. I didn't know he was your son-in-law."

Platt brought a hand to the top of his head, burying his fingers in his silver hair. "How many dead bodies wash up at Presque Isle?" he asked incredulously.

She stuttered. "As soon as you told me, I figured it had to be him. I should've said something, but I didn't know how."

"You should've figured out a way. I'd rather have heard it from you than from the police."

She shot another angry glance at Matthias. He could read her face clearer than any book. *See what you've done?*

To Platt, she said, "You're right. I've never found a dead body before and was—am—still trying to wrap my head around it. I'm truly sorry."

He considered her words and gave her a nod. *Apology accepted.* Or perhaps, *we'll continue this discussion in private.*

With the conflict momentarily settled, Matthias moved to the important question. "Mr. Platt, where were you between three o'clock yesterday afternoon and six this morning?"

"At the campground."

Emma must've become wise to Matthias's methods. She didn't blink, didn't flinch, didn't react at all.

Nor did she jump in and agree with Platt's alibi.

He amended his statement. "Most of that time, anyway. I pulled in around five yesterday." He looked at Emma. "Right?"

"A little after." She met Matthias's gaze. "I was working on my computer and noticed the time. It was a quarter past."

"And you didn't leave to go anywhere?" he asked Platt.

"Nope."

Matthias didn't confirm the answer with Emma. She wouldn't know. She'd been at the cemetery later that evening. "What about the time between three o'clock and five fifteen?"

Platt's eyes shifted but came back. "I left work at three and ran some errands. Stopped at the grocery store to stock up on food for the weekend. Got gas. Went to the bait shop."

"Where do you work?"

"Fort Niagara Investments."

Matthias flipped a page in his notebook and handed it over along with his pen. "Write down all your stops."

"You think I did this? You think I could cause my daughter and grandkids this kind of pain? I may not have gotten along with Wesley, but I'd never—"

Matthias stopped the rant with a raised palm. "I need to clear you. Confirming your story will help me do that and allow us to spend our time finding the real killer."

Platt stared at the notebook. His expression softened. "Fine."

"And if there's anyone who saw you at any of those places, write their names down as well." Matthias turned to Emma.

"I was in my camper working on my computer," she said before he could ask, "until seven thirty or so when I got an email from a client with the location of several of his ancestors' graves. I went to Trinity Cemetery to get the photos he requested."

That explained her presence there with the camera.

She raised one eyebrow. "I have a witness if you need him," she added with the slightest hint of snark.

For the first time in two days, Matthias fought a smile. "I don't think that'll be necessary."

Platt had his head tipped toward the notebook, but his puzzled gaze darted between Matthias and Emma. When he noticed Matthias looking at him, he returned to scribbling.

Once Platt completed his task, Matthias thanked both and watched them stroll away.

"Did you get her number?" Cassie asked.

He flinched and turned. "Dammit. You need to stop sneaking up on people."

"I wasn't sneaking. You were distracted." She gestured at the pair who were climbing into a white Forester. "Did you?"

"Did I what?"

"Get her number."

"You already got it yesterday."

"I can text it to you."

He glared at her. "I don't date women who are involved in an active case."

"Then we need to put this one to bed so you can take *her* to—"

He stopped her with a look. "Don't."

Cassie chuckled, then grew serious. "What do you think of the old man?"

Matthias waved his notebook before pocketing it. "He gave me a list of places he claims to have visited yesterday afternoon."

"Good. Because I learned a few interesting facts from Mrs. Simmons."

"Such as?"

"Mr. Platt and our victim had a tempestuous relationship at best."

"Platt never denied that."

"Did he mention he's been pressing his daughter hot and heavy to leave her husband?"

"No, he neglected to share that part." Matthias kept his gaze on the Forester as it backed onto South Shore Drive.

"I thought so."

"Did Mrs. Simmons mention why?"

"All she would say is her father and husband had butted heads from the first time she brought Wesley home. I tried to get more out of her, but she refused."

"Interesting." As the Forester disappeared around the bend in the road, Matthias brought his focus back to Cassie. "But what possible connection could Platt have with the home invasions?"

"If we knew that, we could close this case. And you could ask Ms. Anderson out on a date."

Chapter Six

The weather didn't clear until late Saturday afternoon at which point Emma returned to Presque Isle and captured dozens of kite photos. When she got back to her camper, she tried to concentrate on editing them, but the events of the day swirled through her mind, ruining her focus. Mentally and emotionally exhausted, she gave up.

Sunday morning, a bass beat and guitar rock'n'roll riffs blasted from Mick's radio two camps away as Emma picked up where she left off, both working on the photos and thinking about the body on the beach. Poor Joe. He'd been badly shaken when his daughter called him. Then that detective had the gall to insinuate he'd been involved.

Joe had never mentioned the tension between him and his son-in-law. The more Emma thought about it, she realized despite constantly bragging about his daughter and grandkids, he'd never once mentioned his son-in-law. Emma had assumed Barbara—Barbie as he always called her—was a single mom.

And now she was.

Emma took off her computer glasses and covered her eyes, blocking the glare from the screen but not the mental image of the debris on the beach.

Her phone rang. Caller ID showed *ErieNOW*, a digital news service to which she'd sold a couple of photos when she first arrived in town.

"Emma, this is Rudy Springstein." His words tumbled out. "We need to talk business."

"What kind of business?"

"Those photos you took yesterday."

She brought her focus back to the kite picture on her computer. Bob must've mentioned her assignment to Rudy.

"The crime scene photos at Presque Isle."

Her mouth went dry. "What about them?"

"I want them. How many did you take?"

Responses logjammed from her brain to her throat. How had he found out about the photos? Only one of them showed anything of the body, and it only revealed an arm. She needed money, but selling that image left a bitter taste on her tongue. She stuttered. "I don't think the police want me releasing that picture."

"Only one, huh? That's okay. One's enough. Two hundred and fifty dollars."

"Didn't you hear me? The police—"

"Don't own the rights to your photographs. You didn't sign anything, did you?"

"No, but—"

"Just as I thought. Okay, three hundred. And if the cops complain, I'll take care of it."

Sure he would.

Emma pictured Joe discovering the photo splashed across the digital news world. He'd know it was hers.

"Four hundred, but that's as high as I go," Rudy said, misinterpreting her silence.

"I'm sorry. It's not for sale." She almost added *until the police say so* to justify her refusal but knew Rudy. He'd be on the phone to the Erie PD for their okay and would be back to her within minutes. Her father had always told her not to make excuses. *It's hard to argue with no*, he'd say.

"Everything's for sale, honey," Rudy said. "Five hundred."

Even if she'd been inclined to cave, the condescending "honey" comment sealed the deal. "No, thanks, *sweetheart*." And she hung up.

She tamped down her irritation, returning to the vivid reds, blues, and yellows of the kite on her screen. The phone rang again. *ErieNOW*. Again. With a swipe of her thumb, she sent the call to voicemail.

How had Rudy learned about the photo? Had to be the police. That detective. She wouldn't put it past him. He'd pointed out to Joe that she'd discovered the body. The look on Joe's face, accusing her of … what? Withholding information? Deception? Neither had been her intention, and she'd planned on confessing to everything on the drive back to the campground. She'd been furious with—what was his name? Honeywell. Detective Honeywell. But then he'd slipped up when she mentioned the cemetery. He'd grinned. He tried to cover, but he'd definitely grinned.

Maybe there was a human behind those fierce blue eyes after all.

A half an hour later, she attached the final edited kite photos to an email and tapped the key that sent it off to Bob DelGrosso.

Next, she found her note with the yoga instructor's number, and keyed it into her phone.

A lilting and perky voice answered. "Namaste Erie Yoga. This is Kira. How may I help you?"

Emma introduced herself but didn't get beyond her name.

"The photographer taking pictures of trash. Hey, thanks for the photo you sent me. Is it okay if I use it as my social media profile?"

"It's yours to do with as you please."

"Super. Thanks. Hey, I'm glad to hear from you. I want to talk some more about you doing promotional photos for the studio."

"That's why I called."

"Oh, good. Have you ever taken a yoga class before?"

Emma smiled at the memory. "My sister used to be an instructor. I was her guinea pig when she was going through training. It's been a while, but yeah."

"Super. I'm teaching a beginners' class tomorrow at noon. Why don't you come? As my guest, of course. Afterwards, I'll take you out to lunch and we can discuss what all would be involved. You have the studio's address on my card." The words poured out without Kira taking a breath.

From Emma's experience, breath was important in yoga. She wondered what kind of teacher this bubbly personality would be. "You don't need to buy me lunch—"

"Nonsense. It'll be a business expense. Besides, I'm always ravenous after I teach." A melodic peal of laughter filtered through the phone. "Who am I kidding? I'm always ravenous. What d'ya say? See you in class?"

"I'll be there."

"Super. See you then."

With the call ended, Emma found herself grinning. Photographing purple-haired Super Kira should be fun.

The phone rang again as soon as Emma set it down. Had Kira forgotten to tell her something? No. The caller ID registered four letters. One of the Erie television stations. On the heels of the call from Rudy, she answered with a professional but cautious "This is Emma Anderson."

"Ms. Anderson, this is Wade Davison of WERI-TV. We're interested in purchasing the photo you took yesterday of the homicide scene at Presque Isle."

She closed her eyes. She needed to come up with a pat response if this was going to continue. "I'm sorry but—"

"Seven hundred dollars for national rights for one year."

Her reply stuck in her throat. The business side of her brain did the math. Finally, she stuttered, "National rights for a year?"

"You're right. Make it eight fifty."

Emma sat back. Her inner accountant calculated how far that would go toward replenishing the dwindling stash of cash she kept hidden within the camper. Her gaze drifted to the window over her sink. The one that looked out on Joe's campsite. "I'm sorry. No."

She ended the call as Wade Davison from WERI-TV was in the midst of upping the offer. Part of her wondered how high he'd have gone. Part of her didn't want to know. Nell's voice tickled her memory. *I'm not cheap but I can be bought*, she'd joke.

Eight hundred and fifty dollars. Not only would it be a start at bolstering Emma's life savings, it could help pay for a private investigator to find her kid sister.

Emma shook her head. No. She'd track Nell down. But not that way.

Raised voices mingled with Mick's loud music drew Emma to the window over her petite kitchen sink. Joe's camper blocked her view, but as the argument amplified, she could tell the voices belonged to Joe and Mick. The music made it impossible to make out exact words. The tone, however, was undoubtedly heated, headed toward boiling.

Emma slipped into her battered sneakers and hurried across her porch and onto the camp road. Clear of Joe's camper, she spotted the two men. Mick stood on the deck like a lord and master of his kingdom, fists planted against hips, chest puffed. Emma wasn't sure if his crimson face was a result of sun, rage, or booze. Or a combination.

Joe stood at the edge of Mick's campsite, hands clenched as if wanting to either choke or pummel the man. "It's Sunday morning, for crying out loud. Some people would appreciate a little peace and quiet. Why can't you get that through your thick skull?"

Emma edged closer. She had no idea what she could do to help but wanted Mick to realize there was a witness to whatever was about to transpire.

Mick gave no indication of noticing her. "You want peace and quiet on a Sunday? Go to your goddamn church. I paid good money for this rig and for this site. I can do what I damn well please." Despite the hour and day of the week, his slurred speech was evidence he'd already been hitting the bottle.

Joe advanced to the base of Mick's stairs. "Not when it infringes on everyone around you." Joe swept a hand at the other campers who'd either come outside or stopped what they were doing to watch the argument. Emma wasn't the sole witness. "You're the only one who blasts your music at all hours, every single day."

"You don't like it? Go to management. They'll tell you the same thing I did. Quiet hours are eleven at night to eight in the morning. I'm not violating any of your precious rules."

Joe's entire body trembled. Emma edged up behind him, afraid he was on the verge of a stroke. She noticed his shoulders rise on a deep in breath and slowly lower as he exhaled. While it appeared to take a herculean effort, he brought his arms down to his sides, opening his fingers.

When he again spoke, his voice was quieter. "All I'm asking is for you to turn it down for the next hour. Is that too much? I have a pounding headache and would like to be able to hear myself think."

"You got a headache?" Mick's gaze settled on Emma. He brought his focus back to Joe but jutted his chin in her direction. "You and your little girlfriend there party too much last night?" He picked up a mostly empty bottle of Jack Daniels and held it toward Joe. "I'm such a nice guy, I'll share my medicine with both of you."

"Go to hell." Joe took the steps to Mick's deck faster than Emma had ever seen him move. He reached not for the bottle but for Mick's neck.

The loudmouth backpedaled, slamming into his screen door. The Jack Daniels crashed to the deck. Glass shattered, splattering the whiskey remnants across the wood planks.

Joe's fingers closed around Mick's throat. "Let go of me, you son of a bitch," Mick squeaked.

Emma bounded up the steps and put a hand on Joe's arm. "Don't do this," she said, keeping her voice low.

For a painfully long moment, she feared he hadn't heard her over Mick's music. Or was ignoring her. But then he stepped back and released Mick. The words Joe uttered next were so quiet, Emma almost couldn't hear them.

"One of these days, Harper, you're going to push me too far." Joe turned away from Mick and from Emma.

"I guess I should be happy your girlfriend is here to keep you in line," Mick said, rubbing his neck with one hand.

Joe wheeled back toward him.

But Mick had the other hand on his doorlatch and staggered backward into his camper. The radio continued to blare.

Instead of following him, Joe stopped, pivoted, and came face to face with Emma. "What are you doing here? Did you come to take pictures of the neighborhood brawl?"

The sharpness of his words stung. "I wanted to make sure you're okay."

He stormed past her, thudding down the steps. "Well, I'm not."

She followed him to his porch. "Can we talk?"

He crossed the wooden decking and reached for the door. "No."

She stopped shy of putting a foot on the deck. "About yesterday. I'm so sorry."

Joe froze, hand on the knob. His head lowered. Slowly, he faced her. "You've got nothing to be sorry for. I'm the one who owes you an apology."

"You don't—"

"Yes, I do. I shouldn't have dragged you into my family

mess yesterday. And I shouldn't have gotten so angry when I found out you'd been the one to find the body."

"You had every right—"

"No, I didn't. You had no idea it was Wesley. How could you? I never mentioned him to you before."

Emma decided agreeing might not be the way to go.

With the gait of an old man, as if he'd used up his day's supply of vigor during his encounter with Mick, Joe shuffled to one of his deck chairs and dropped into it.

She didn't wait on an invitation and took a seat on another one. "What happened? Between you and Wesley, I mean?"

Joe's gaze turned icy. "Nothing happened. I hadn't seen the bastard in years."

"Before that. Why didn't the two of you get along?"

"You heard what I told those detectives."

"Yes," she said, dragging out the word. "I just have the feeling there's more. If you want to talk about it, I mean."

Joe's cold expression didn't thaw but his eyes shifted, gazing beyond her. "My son-in-law was a controlling bastard. He charmed his way into Barbie's good graces, acting like everything he did was to protect her. But I saw what he was doing. Driving a wedge between her and her mother and me. Even when my wife passed, Wesley didn't want Barbie attending the funeral."

"Did she?" Emma asked.

Joe's gaze met hers. "Yes. But I suspect she paid dearly for disobeying his wishes."

Emma felt a chill rise from the pit of her stomach. Joe could've been talking about Clay.

"You know I work in finance. I'm good at my job. Wesley thought he was good with investments too. Better than me."

Joe looked over Emma's shoulder. "He wasn't. I offered to help. To teach him what I knew. He acted like I was insulting his manhood. Told me—told Barbie—I hated him and wanted to break them up. And you know what? He was right about that. I'd be willing to bet he'd been abusive. If not to my grandkids, then at least to my daughter." Joe's voice lowered, as if speaking to himself rather than Emma. "If I'd ever caught him laying a hand on any of them..." He let the words evaporate, blinked, and met Emma's eyes, appearing as if he'd forgotten she was there.

But she was. And she was thinking of her own past with abuse. Feeling the impact of Clay's fist as if it was happening all over again.

"You've never talked about your past," Joe said, his voice still barely above a whisper. "I've always had a feeling you're hiding here. From something ... someone. Am I wrong?"

Her mouth went dry. "No."

He gave a nod of understanding. "Thought so. I see in you the same thing I see in Barbie. Only you got away on your own."

That last phrase settled on Emma's stomach like a lead weight. *On your own.* "Did you help her?"

Joe looked puzzled.

Emma knew she shouldn't ask but the question escaped unbidden. "Did you help your daughter get away from her abusive marriage?"

"You think I'm guilty of killing my daughter's no-good husband?"

His amused tone stiffened Emma's spine. "Are you?"

The question took him aback. "No. I did not kill Wesley Simmons. Though God knows, I'm not at all sorry he's gone."

Joe lowered his gaze to his hands, folded in his lap. "I would never do that to my daughter. Or my grandkids." A hint of a smile crossed his lips and quickly faded.

Emma watched as Joe's face flushed and the ice returned to his eyes.

"Best thing that's ever happened to my daughter happened Friday night when Wesley Simmons was killed."

Chapter Seven

"Looking for Love in All the Wrong Places" was Matthias's mother's favorite song. God rest her soul. She'd sure been in the wrong place when she'd met his father. As Matthias walked the two blocks from his loft apartment to the station, he mused on his own lackluster history with women. His head throbbed from last night's time spent at the Tap House. He hadn't been looking for love, which was good because he didn't find it. He almost picked up a cute blonde with a killer smile and a low-cut, very tightly stretched tank top. At the last minute, though, he thought of his mother, his father, and that song. He'd left alone.

He didn't blame the country classic or his father, who was still in the Oklahoma State Penitentiary, for his lack of a committed relationship. For that, he let the blame fall squarely on the very sexy shoulders of the only woman he'd ever proposed to. Melissa was the reason he'd made the move to Erie. But when he popped the question, she told him she could never be married to a cop. Two months later, she got engaged to a lawyer and moved away.

That was over twenty years ago, and at forty-three, he still felt the old wound whenever an attraction threatened to become more than physical. His mother would've told him to get over it.

If she'd still been alive. Which she wasn't. Thanks to dear old Dad.

The newly renovated gym at the station was empty on this late Sunday morning, for which Matthias was grateful. He pulled on his workout gloves, snugging the Velcro strap around his wrists, and spent the next hour focused on sweating and grunting his way through the machines until his muscles burned and memories of his distant past were stuffed back into the recesses of his mind, where they belonged.

He showered, changed into his polo shirt and dress slacks, and climbed the stairs to the Major Crimes Unit, a long, narrow room with seven cubicles along one wall. The set up reminded him of his grandfather's horse farm back in Oklahoma. A row of stalls housed Quarter Horses there. Housed detectives here.

Matthias expected to find Cassie already at her desk in the cubby next to his. She wasn't.

The entire detectives' floor was quiet. Most of the unit had weekends off unless they were on call or working a time-sensitive case. Like the Simmons homicide. Which is what made Cassie's absence concerning.

He dumped the day-old coffee dregs and grounds from one of the two industrial-grade urns on the break room table and refilled the basket. By the time he poured fresh brew into his mug, he heard footsteps on the stairs. A moment later, Cassie bustled through the break room and into Major Crimes without stopping or acknowledging him.

He tailed after her and watched as she dropped into her chair and faced her computer, her expression a study in poorly concealed rage.

"What's going on?" he asked.

Cassie didn't look up. Nor did she answer his question. Instead she asked, "How was your date?"

"What makes you think I had a date?"

Cassie's annoyed gaze lifted to meet his. "Last night was Saturday. You always have a date on Saturday." Her eyes lowered once again to her computer monitor. "Just never twice with the same woman."

He gave her a look.

"Am I wrong?"

Not entirely, although he had no intention of agreeing with her. His near miss with marriage—if having his proposal thrown back in his face could be considered a near miss—had taught him that a wife, family, and his chosen career were not compatible. The rejection scarred him deeper than he wanted to admit. Never again would he open himself up, be that vulnerable. But while he may have been burned big time where personal relationships were concerned, he didn't intend on becoming a monk. Women, he liked. Commitment? That ship had sailed.

And sunk like the *Titanic*.

He sipped his coffee. "I did not have a date last night. And you're avoiding my question. You're upset about something."

She huffed a loud sigh and pivoted her chair to face him squarely. "It's Alissa."

He glanced at the half dozen photos thumbtacked to the

wall of Cassie's cubicle. All featured her eight-year-old granddaughter, whom Cassie recently had taken in when the girl's mother deployed overseas. Cassie didn't talk much about her Army Sergeant daughter—only enough that Matthias knew his partner was equal parts proud and terrified. Alissa's father had died when she was two, so her mom and grandparents were all the family she had left. "Is she okay?"

"Define 'okay'." Cassie breathed another sigh, softer this time. "There's a kid in school who's bullying her. Calling her names. Pushing her around. All because she's the new kid in class. You've seen that child. She's a bitty thing. It's not like she can fight back. That isn't a solution anyway." Cassie rubbed her eyes. "I've been trying for days to reach the school counselor and set up a meeting. He keeps putting me off. This morning, Alissa told me she didn't want to go to school tomorrow. Started crying when I told her she had to. That did it. I got on the phone and tracked the man down. Told him I didn't care it was Sunday. He and I were going to meet, or I was going to show up at his family dinner and wasn't going to be quiet about my grievances."

Matthias clamped his jaw shut to keep from smiling at the mental picture of Cassie Malone calling out some unsuspecting grade school guidance counselor. "I gather you got your message across."

"Damn straight. We have a meeting for seven o'clock tomorrow morning."

"Wesley Simmons's autopsy is tomorrow morning."

"I know. I don't expect it'll take me long to make my concerns clear." She lifted her chin and fixed Matthias with a hard glare. "If I'm late, I'm sure you'll be on time for the postmortem."

He hated autopsies, and she knew it. "I'll be there."

"And another thing," Cassie went on. "*I'm* going to attend Alissa's career day next week instead of Shawn."

Matthias feigned shock. "You really think those kids would rather hear from a city cop instead of your veterinarian husband with his show-and-tell foster kittens?"

She gave Matthias a scowl. "Doesn't matter anymore who they'd rather hear from. I want to see this bully for myself and put the fear of God into the boy."

Matthias almost felt sorry for the kid.

Cassie swiveled back to her computer. "Enough about my problems. Let's get to work. I want to find out what Patrol learned from canvassing the Simmonses' neighborhood. You can start on Wesley's financials."

Matthias considered suggesting a swap. Wading through numbers ranked low on his list of favored activities. But Cassie still appeared ready to march into battle. He'd rather tackle the financial records than Cassie when she was in attack mode.

He took a seat in his cubicle, set the coffee on the desk, and logged into his computer. A check of his emails offered nothing from the banks. "No financials yet. Still waiting on the bank to send them over."

"Naturally," she replied. "It's the weekend."

His inbox didn't contain anything from the tech nerds processing the collected evidence, either. He clicked open the file with all the reports posted by the uniforms at Friday's crime scene. He skimmed through the stuff he already knew, looking for what he didn't. In the third report, he found it. The preliminary list of what had been stolen. Electronics. Some silver that had been a family heirloom. But the biggest-ticket items were four paintings. Matthias had never been an art aficionado and didn't recognize the first three artists. But even he had heard of Jackson Pollock. If Wesley Simmons really had been part of an insurance fraud scheme, that one painting might make it worth his while.

"Have you seen the list of stolen merchandise from the Simmons robbery?" he asked.

"Yes, I have," came Cassie's response. "Nice haul, huh?"

"That's one way of putting it." Matthias closed out the reports and decided to look into another part of the case that was bugging him.

He'd drained his coffee mug by the time Cassie rolled her chair into the aisle.

"Patrol finished canvassing the Simmonses' neighborhood," she said. "Only about half answered their doors. Of those who did, only two stated they saw anything on Friday. White van. They assumed Wesley and Barbara were having some work done. No one reported noticing the van's occupants." Cassie paused before continuing. "It's probably nothing, but the neighbors directly across the street mentioned hearing Wesley and Barbara arguing. Said it wasn't unusual though. That's just how some couples communicate."

Matthias had witnessed that style of communication between his parents. He didn't want to tell Cassie how that turned out.

"Uniforms will be back out today, knocking on the doors of those who weren't home yesterday," Cassie said.

"What about security cams?"

"We were able to gain access to two so far. That's what I've been watching."

Matthias stood, stretched, and moved next to her so he could see the footage.

"In this one, the family had their RV parked so it blocked any view of the Simmons house." She clicked her mouse. "The other catches a glimpse of the van driving by. Bad angle though. Can't make out the occupants or the license number."

"That's it?"

"So far."

He tipped his head toward his cubby. "Come check this out."

She pushed up from her chair and followed him.

"The theory of Wesley's body being dumped into the bay at the Sand and Gravel Company and then carried around to the lake side of Presque Isle has been bugging the hell out of me," Matthias said, reclaiming his seat.

"Same here. Total impossibility."

"Agreed. I pulled up the lake current charts for this time of year."

The map on his computer showed Erie's shoreline with lines marking the flow of the currents. He clicked twice, enlarging the map until the northern edge of Presque Isle filled the screen. "Look at this." He pinned a finger at the spot between beaches nine and ten, where the body had washed up.

Cassie leaned over his shoulder and nudged his hand away. She traced the line for herself. "The current is moving northeast."

"Parallel to the shore," Matthias said. "Wesley wasn't in the water all that long. No way was his body tossed into the lake from the Sand and Gravel Company. Or from the shore anywhere around here." The map confirmed what Matthias had thought all along. "Someone took him out in a boat and tossed him overboard."

Cassie continued to study the monitor, the hint of a smile

crossing her lips. "All we have to do is find someone with a boat."

"Narrows it down to about three quarters of the population of Erie."

"You're forgetting all the tourists and fishermen who bring their boats to our fair city. I can look up the numbers for you."

"That won't be necessary." He tapped the computer screen again. "On its own this may not narrow our search. But we find someone who has motive and opportunity, and if they also have access to a boat? We might just have our killer."

Monday morning, Matthias timed his morgue arrival almost perfectly. One of the young autopsy technicians was closing up the body as Coroner Felix Hamilton and Dr. Alexandra Browning, the forensic pathologist, conferred over a computer. Visually, the pair were polar opposites. Thirtyish Hamilton looked like he'd just carried his surfboard across a California beach. Dr. Browning had at least twenty years and thirty pounds on him. She wore her storm-cloud gray hair in a perennial bun that Matthias was convinced could survive a typhoon unscathed. Her dark eyes were razor sharp and never missed a thing, a stark contrast to skin so pale it could rarely have seen the sun.

Matthias had not arrived before Cassie, which was the less-than-perfect part of his timing. Arms crossed, she glowered at him from her position next to a wheeled cart, which held several evidence bags. Despite her ominous expression, he crossed to her side. "How'd the meeting with the school counselor go?"

She grunted. "Let's just say he is well aware of the situation and of whom he's dealing with. He promised to have a talk with the child in question."

"Do you think it'll help?"

She raised an eyebrow in Matthias's direction. "If it doesn't, there's always Career Day."

Hamilton straightened and looked in their direction. "Detective Honeywell. I thought you'd be here earlier."

"Running late," Matthias said. He wasn't. At least not accidentally. Cassie always insisted on being there for the whole thing. He'd rather face a sword-wielding ninja than watch a human body being carved up. "What'd you find out about our drowning victim?"

"He didn't drown."

Matthias assumed as much.

"Wesley Simmons had no water in his lungs. He was dead before he hit the lake. Cause of death was exsanguination from a penetrating wound to the anterior upper left quadrant of the abdomen. He probably bled out in a matter of fifteen to twenty minutes."

The longest fifteen to twenty minutes in Wesley Simmons's too-short life.

Matthias looked toward the stainless-steel table and the body stretched out on it. In addition to the various incisions made during the postmortem, the injury evident yesterday morning on the beach stood out against the pale flesh. "He was stabbed." If Simmons died before going into the lake, the theory about debris causing the wound was null and void.

"He was definitely stabbed," Dr. Browning said. "The blade was roughly three and a half inches long and just under an inch wide. The handle of the knife made marks on the skin around the wound."

"If we find the murder weapon…" Matthias left the question hanging.

Browning responded with a nod. "We might be able to match it."

Matthias thought of the car and the sign of a struggle at the Sand and Gravel Company. "There should've been blood."

"Not necessarily." Hamilton leaned forward to tap the computer keys. "There might've been some cast-off from the knife, but these kinds of injuries hemorrhage internally. When we opened him up, the peritoneum was filled with blood."

Dr. Browning cleared her throat. "There would be more blood from his nose than from the stab wound."

Matthias looked at the pathologist. "His nose?"

"It had been broken recently. No signs of healing, so in my opinion, the break likely happened during the same struggle as when he got knifed. Like Ham said, the victim would've been alive and conscious for quite a while as he bled out. During that time, he sustained the injury to his nose and a compressed skull fracture consistent with being struck with a rock. Or he might've fallen and hit his head. Also perimortem and very recent."

Matthias ran the murder scene through his mind. The debate he and Cassie'd had remained unanswered. Was Simmons an accomplice to the home invasion or attempting to be a hero?

"What are you thinking, Detective?" Hamilton asked.

"There was no blood where we found his vehicle. Not even a drop from a bloody nose."

Hamilton gave a knowing nod. "I'm not surprised. We found residue on the decedent's wrists and face."

"Residue?"

"Consistent with duct tape."

"He was bound."

"And gagged and blindfolded," Hamilton said. "We found fibers in his airway. I can't say for sure until the trace lab confirms, but I'd venture a guess the killer or killers stuffed something in the victim's mouth and taped over it. They taped over his eyes as well."

The last part raised another question. Why blindfold him if they planned to kill him? A dead man can't identify his assailants. And if he'd been part of the team, he'd already know what they looked like.

Matthias could only conclude the home invaders hadn't intended to kill Simmons. Something had gone wrong.

"Or you have it backwards," Cassie said in response to Matthias when they returned to their desks after logging Wesley's clothes into evidence. "Maybe the homicide was always the endgame, and the home invasion was a cover."

"That makes no sense either. Binding his wrists, gagging him, I get. Why the blindfold if they planned to kill him all along?"

Cassie leaned back, her mouth drawn to one side—her usual *I'm thinking* expression. "We don't have enough evidence yet for conclusive answers," she finally said, her voice flat.

"You're the one who always tells me to keep an open mind." Matthias knew quoting her "teaching moments" back to her never failed to get on her last nerve. "Fixating on one theory only blinds us to evidence pointing in a different direction."

She gave him the side-eye before recovering her senior-detective façade. "Exactly. You can't assume your scenario is the only possibility."

Wasn't that what he'd just said?

His phone rang. "Detective Honeywell."

"This is Jeff in the lab. I have the GPS results from Wesley Simmons's car."

Finally. Something that might prove useful. "Can you email them to me?"

"Already did. Check your inbox."

Matthias thanked him, hung up, and faced his computer screen.

"What've you got?" Cassie asked.

Before responding, he clicked on the new message and opened the attached image. "See for yourself."

She joined him in his cubicle and peered over his shoulder.

The image was timestamped Friday afternoon. Point A identified the Simmons residence on South Shore Drive as the start of the trip. The path Wesley's Audi took to West Lake Road was direct. Once he approached downtown, however, the line veered north, then west, then south, then east. Right and left turns every block or so until the map pinned Erie Sand and Gravel as the end of the trip.

"Looks like that cartoon where little Billy travels all over the neighborhood between the school bus and his house," Cassie said.

Matthias couldn't argue with the comparison. "According

to the wife, he was trailing the van. If that's true, they were doing their best to lose him."

"Through Friday night rush-hour traffic." Cassie straightened. "Why not just get the license number, report it to the police, and give it up?"

"Beats the hell out of me." Matthias enlarged the map. "At least this gives us his exact path, and presumably the van's as well. Let's find out which businesses and homes on these streets have security cameras and get their footage. Someone has to have an angle that'll give us a view of the license number."

"Or a shot of the driver or passenger."

"One can hope."

Chapter Eight

In spite of Kira's perky voice and runway-model pose for the photo on the beach, Emma found the young woman's in-class persona and tone comforting. She was gentle with her students, guiding them into the best version of the pose for their body. And her soothing, lyrical voice eased Emma into a deep state of relaxation during *savasana*.

The same way Nell used to.

Kira brought the class back out of "corpse pose" with an equally calming tone. Emma joined the other students in exchanging a round of *namastes*, feeling more relaxed than she had in months.

"I really needed that," Emma told Kira after replacing her rolled yoga mat in the woven basket.

Kira grinned. "You know what I need? Food. You still on for lunch? We can talk photography."

Fifteen minutes later, Emma sat across from the yoga teacher in a vegetarian restaurant a block from the studio. "This is great." Emma looked around at the brick walls and exposed pipes and ductwork strung with Buddhist prayer flags. "I didn't know I could get real vegetarian food around here."

"It's only been open since February. I'm trying to direct business their way." Kira shot a glance at a bulletin board next to the door. "And they've been kind enough to let me put up flyers and posters about the yoga studio."

A waitress with a piercing in her nose, a wisp of purple in her bangs, and the initials JJ on a name badge approached, pen and pad in hand.

Emma had been too busy gawking at the décor to study the menu in depth. She made a snap decision. "I'll take the Peanuty Thai Tofu Wrap." The beverage list caught her eye. "And a chai."

Kira handed her menu to the waitress. "Sounds good. I'll have the same."

When the waitress walked away, Emma eyed Kira. "Copycat."

She shrugged one shoulder. "It's so hard to choose. There aren't many restaurants where I have that problem."

Emma nodded in agreement. "Our waitress is a copycat too. She stole your shade of hair color."

Kira beamed. "She did, but she likes her natural color too much to tint any more of it."

While they waited for their meals, they discussed the business at hand. Kira had lined up several students willing to strike some yoga poses for Emma's camera. She'd even compiled a list of when everyone could be available.

Emma's schedule was wide open, making it easy to settle on the following evening. She laughed softly. "I wish all my clients were this organized."

"I run a business." Kira turned serious. "It's not a side gig. It's how I put food on the table."

As if on cue, the waitress appeared, balancing a large tray on one hand. She deposited plates and steaming mugs in front of them, asked if they needed anything else—they didn't—and bustled away.

Kira inspected her wrap. "Anyhow, everyone thinks I'm a flake because I have purple hair and chant. But I'm a businesswoman under it all. Being organized is essential to survival."

"Good to know."

They fell into a comfortable silence for several minutes as they put dents in their lunch. After devouring the first half of her wrap, Kira's hunger was apparently sated enough for further conversation. She wiped the peanut sauce from her fingers and studied Emma. "What about you? Is photography your sole gig or a sideline?"

Emma chewed and swallowed. "It's all I have." The word "literally" didn't pass her lips but leapt to the front of her brain.

"So you know what I mean. You do whatever you have to in order to stay afloat." Kira paused before adding, "Like taking pictures of trash."

Emma winced and wondered if she knew what had been in that trash. She didn't have to wonder long.

"Horrible about that poor man."

"I didn't see him at first." The words tumbled out unbidden. "Not until I got back to my car and viewed them on my computer."

"It's okay. I know you didn't."

Emma looked down at her hands resting beside her plate,

surprised to see them trembling. She quickly slid them onto her lap, hidden from view by the table. But the move did nothing to quell the internal quaking. What was going on? It had been three days since she'd discovered the body tangled in the debris. Beyond the initial shock, she'd been fine.

"Have you ever seen a dead body before?" Kira asked in her calming yoga voice.

"No." It was a lie, and somehow, Emma had a feeling Kira knew that.

"It's unnerving."

"No kidding." Emma drew a breath to subdue the sudden rush of anxiety. "How did you find out about my photo?"

Kira laughed. "I saw you taking it, remember?"

"You saw me taking a photo of trash and seagulls."

The laughter and smile faded. "I saw it on the news."

"The photo?" Emma asked, shocked. She'd turned down the media requests. Who had gotten their hands on it?

"No. The news story. They said where it happened. I put two and two together."

Emma exhaled a sigh. Of course. The whole incident had clearly rattled her more than she realized.

Kira rested an elbow on the table. "You want to talk about it?"

"There's nothing to say. I didn't know the victim." Not directly.

"That's not what I mean."

Emma met Kira's gaze and had an uneasy sense that the woman's talents went beyond yoga and chanting, venturing into clairvoyance.

"You weren't exactly truthful when you said you'd never

seen a dead body before," Kira said, then slowly repeated, "Do you want to talk about it?"

Images, long ago memories washed over Emma. Mental photos she tried to delete. The car crash. She'd not been in it. But she should've been. Only ten miles from home. They'd almost made it all the way from Ocean City. A trip her parents had begged her to go on with them. Her and Nell. Neither had wanted to. To their mother's disappointment, the sisters insisted on staying behind.

No. *Emma* had insisted on staying behind. Nell simply followed her sister's lead.

A half hour later, Emma took a wavering breath, having poured out the story. A story she hadn't shared with anyone.

Except Clay.

"Dad fell asleep at the wheel," she said. "If Nell and I had gone with them, we could've helped with the driving. I never understood why Dad wouldn't let Mom drive, but he was fine with either of us."

Kira hadn't moved from her elbow-on-table, chin-cupped-in-palm position, but her expression reflected Emma's grief. "I am so sorry. I had no idea."

And yet, she'd sensed something under the surface. A wound Emma kept covered and private.

"How old were you when it happened?"

"It was four years ago. I was twenty-six. Nell was twenty."

The pierced waitress returned. "Can I get you ladies anything? More chai?"

Emma looked down at the uneaten half of her wrap and the cold dregs of her tea, her appetite gone.

Kira hadn't touched the remainder of her meal either.

"Nothing, thanks. Just a couple of boxes please. And the check."

"Sure thing." With a pirouette worthy of a ballerina, the waitress departed.

"What about Nell?"

The question jarred Emma again. She didn't know how to answer.

"I can tell from your voice that you're carrying some unsettled energy where your sister's concerned." Kira's brow furrowed. "Oh, no. Is she … dead?"

Emma wanted to say, *No, she's fine.* Instead, the truth forced its way from her throat. "I don't know." She'd already spilled her guts about the loss of her parents to a virtual stranger. She wasn't going to share Nell's demons.

Kira nodded as if she understood.

But how could she when Emma didn't?

"You'll find her," Kira said.

Emma met her gaze, stunned. "I didn't say she was missing."

Kira gave her a sad, knowing smile. "You didn't have to." She came forward, resting her elbows on the table. "What will you do when you find her?"

The optimism brought a short laugh. It also made Emma realize she hadn't considered what was next. Rehab. For as long as it took. Not that she would tell Kira that. Instead, Emma thought further back to the sisters' dream before life went sideways. "I still own our grandparents' farmhouse down in Washington County. Nell and I always talked about converting it into a bed and breakfast." Maybe someday.

"That sounds amazing. You must do it. Don't let go of your dreams."

If only it was that easy.

The waitress cruised past, depositing two cardboard take-out boxes and a black vinyl folder containing the check on the table without slowing. Emma reached for the folder only to have Kira snatch it from her.

"I told you I was buying."

"That was before you realized you were going to get stuck in a therapy session."

Kira dismissed her with a flip of her hand. "What are friends for?"

Emma rolled the word over in her mind. When was the last time she'd had a friend? Clay had driven all of hers away. She hadn't realized it at first. Not until he'd tried—and succeeded—in cutting her off from Nell too.

With the bill paid and their take-out boxes sealed, they strolled through a spring drizzle back to the yoga studio. The conversation lightened with Kira expressing her fascination with life in a campground. As they stopped at the front door, she asked, "Are you planning to stay in Erie?"

Plan? "Yeah. I guess so."

"You know Sara's Campground is closed in the winter, don't you? What will you do?"

Emma pondered the question. "Honestly? I don't know. I haven't thought that far ahead."

Kira gave her a puzzled look. Maybe she wasn't clairvoyant after all. She didn't know *why* Emma was hiding out in a seventeen-foot camper. She didn't know Emma was being stalked. "Okay. Well, I need to go inside and do some paperwork before I head home. Thanks for joining me for lunch."

"Sorry I dumped on you."

Kira waved away the apology. "I'll see you tomorrow evening for our photo shoot." Then she grabbed Emma in a quick hug before spinning away and breezing through the door.

Alone, Emma flipped up the hood on her jacket against the steady drizzle. She'd parked one block over on State Street but turned to look north towards the marina. She'd spent most of her time around Presque Isle since she'd moved, with only a few excursions to various locations around the city for photo assignments. Even with the rain, the temperature was mild. She considered walking to the marina to look at the gorgeous sailboats moored there. Possibly check out the Maritime Museum.

Mother Nature immediately squelched any such plans. The drizzle intensified into a driving spring shower. So much for taking a stroll.

Emma started south toward her car at a jog. A chill brought her to a stop, but the goosebumps on her arms weren't a result of the rain. She sensed she was being watched. A quick look around failed to support the sensation. No one was spying on her. No one was paying her any attention at all. She shook her head against the paranoia and continued toward her Subaru.

She'd almost reached it when she heard her name being called. Stopping, she searched for the source and spotted a tall gray-haired man lumbering her way, waving. It took a few moments before she recognized the face. Bob DelGrosso, her editor at *PA Living*. She'd only met him in person once, years ago. Back then, and on the website, he had dark hair.

"Emma Anderson." Bob smiled through his labored breathing. "I thought that was you."

She shook the hand he offered. "What are you doing in Erie? I thought you lived in Scranton."

He dug a handkerchief from his pocket and mopped his head. "You haven't read the magazine in a while, have you?"

"Yes, I have."

Bob glanced around before gesturing toward an awning on the next storefront. "Let's get out of the rain." Once they'd taken shelter, he pocketed the handkerchief. "After my wife and I divorced a couple years ago, I moved back here. I grew up in Erie, and while most of my family has passed on, I still have a brother nearby. It felt like a good place to start over. I'm renting space over on French Street to run the business."

Emma realized her mouth was hanging open. "I'm so sorry about your divorce. I confess, I skim through the magazine but don't usually look at the information in the front."

"Now you know. But, hey, it's good having you in town too. I loved the kite beach photos."

"Good."

He took a furtive glance around, and his expression tensed. "I hear the kites weren't the only things you photographed over there."

Emma's shoulders tightened. She hoped he was talking about seagulls or driftwood.

Bob lowered his face and his voice. "The body that washed up. You're the one who found it." Not a question. "You have pictures." Also not a question.

"One," she said. "*One* picture." Before she could add *of an arm*, he interrupted her.

"I understand the news outlets have been hounding you to sell it."

She wanted to ask him where he'd heard, but the words

stuck in her throat, blocked by a bigger question. Where was he headed with this? She couldn't bring herself to ask that one either.

She didn't have to.

"Let me buy the rights to it."

Not what she'd expected. "Why? Pictures of debris with an arm sticking out aren't exactly suitable for your magazine."

He looked around again. Did he expect a band of roving news media zombies to descend upon them? "*PA Living*? No. You're right." He chuffed a dry laugh. "The fact is I have plans to start a new publication. Edgier. It'll focus on some of the notorious incidents that have happened around Erie and the vicinity. You know. The Pizza Bomber. Now this."

Emma wondered how many notorious incidents Bob had in mind. It would take more than two to fill a magazine or a book.

"Besides all that though, I'm thinking of you."

"Me?"

"I know you could use the money. Plus, if you sell me lifetime exclusive rights, it'll keep the other outlets away. You'll have nothing to offer them. They can hound me if they want, but I'll put them off."

She studied Bob's face and had a feeling he wasn't being completely straight with her. If he owned the rights to that picture, he could then sell it over and over, making more than whatever he paid her. Which brought up another question. "How much are we talking about for lifetime exclusive rights?"

His Adam's apple bobbed. "Twenty-five hundred?"

Emma battled to keep her face neutral. She dared not say anything for fear of choking.

"Not enough? Name your price."

She slowed her breathing, thinking of Kira softly luring her into a state of deep relaxation not long ago. Finally, Emma managed to force words from her dry mouth. "I'll have to think about it."

The creases in Bob's forehead deepened but he nodded. "I understand. Just, please, don't sell that photo elsewhere without giving me a shot at it." His smile returned but it was forced. "After all, I've been buying your stuff for a long time. That should earn me some loyalty. Right?"

"Right." She gave him a tight grin, as forced as his. "You have my word. I won't sell it out from under you."

He stepped back and raised both hands. "That's all I ask." He lifted his gaze to the leaden gray sky still dumping rain on them. "Looks like it's not gonna let up so I better run. Call me. I'll make it worth your time." Without waiting for a response, he jogged away.

Emma didn't move. Externally. Internally, her mind raced. *Name your price.* For a single photo. Bob was right about one thing. She'd be grateful to have that image off her computer, no longer her responsibility. But Bob DelGrosso offering top dollar? For anything? Then again, maybe he really was serious about this new publication he mentioned.

And then there was Joe. He'd granted her an uneasy reprieve for not being the one to tell him about that blasted picture. What would he say if she blatantly made a profit from it? Even if Joe wasn't in the equation, the thought of making money off the heartache of another never sat well with her. It's why she'd never pursued a career in real photojournalism.

At least Bob hadn't pressured her for an answer. For that, she was grateful. She needed time to think.

She stepped into the rain and headed for her car. At the

crosswalk, she checked the traffic before looking over at the opposite curb.

A man stood next to her Subaru, his head lowered as his thumbs tapped his phone screen. A hoodie and his dark hair shielded his face for the most part. But his stance and his physique screamed at her.

Clay.

She thought about turning and running. She could make it back to the yoga studio, but he'd obviously spotted her and was waiting. He would follow her. Ultimately, Emma would be putting Kira in danger if she lured him there.

A large delivery truck sloshed by, blocking her view. Emma inhaled, praying once it passed, he'd be gone. Another figment of her overactive imagination. No such luck. The truck moved on. Clay was still there, texting.

The police department was only a couple of blocks away. Not that it mattered. She couldn't outrun him if he tried anything. They'd never hear her scream from that distance. Emma steeled herself. They were on a public street. There were pedestrians everywhere. Safety in numbers. The walk sign lit, and she started towards her car and the man who terrified her like no other.

He didn't look up. She circled to approach from behind him.

"Clay." She managed to keep her voice firm.

He lifted his head and turned.

The man standing by Emma's car wasn't Clay.

This guy was younger, his face rounder, his eyes a lighter shade of brown. He looked at her puzzled. "Can I help you?"

Heat seared her cheeks. She stuttered. "I'm sorry. I thought you were someone else." In truth, she wasn't sorry at all.

"No problem." The man gave her a tight smile, pocketed his device, and strode away.

Emma rounded the front of the Subaru, so rattled she almost stepped out in front of a truck. He blared his horn, and she staggered back. Closing her eyes, she took a deep breath to compose herself. Checking for traffic, she moved to her driver's door and fumbled for her keys. It took two tries to hit the unlock button on the fob. She slid behind the wheel, relocked the door, and exhaled, letting her head drop back against the rest.

She really was losing it. Thinking every man she saw was her stalker. Fear was exhausting. And senseless. Clay Bauer was probably still in the Pittsburgh area. He'd probably found another woman to charm and then possess. He'd probably put Emma completely out of his mind.

Please, God, she breathed. Let him have put her far out of his mind.

So she could put him out of hers.

Emma withdrew her phone from her pocket, reached for the charger cord, and spotted a notification for a missed call. She'd set the phone on silent for the yoga class and forgot to turn the volume back on afterward. She punched in her PIN and tapped the icon for recent calls. Another private number. No name. But this time, there was a voice message.

Probably another car warranty call.

She hit play.

"Emma, it's me, Nell…"

Emma's breath caught.

"I'm sorry I missed you. I wanted you to know I'm okay."

She didn't sound okay. Not by a long shot.

"You don't need to call back. This isn't my phone. I'll try to call you another time. Love you. Bye."

The message ended.

Emma hit the green re-call button. It didn't ring but went straight to a recorded voice. "The number you are trying to reach is out of service."

The screen blurred as tears flooded her eyes. How could the number be out of service? Nell had just called from it. How long ago? Emma swiped an arm across her face, clearing her vision. She checked the time on the incoming call. Fifteen minutes ago. If she'd remembered to turn the sound back on, she'd have answered. She'd have been able to talk to her sister for the first time in five months.

Emma hadn't been face to face with Nell for more than two years. The last encounter was ugly—Nell pleading for money, claiming she needed it for rent. Emma knew the real reason. Drugs. Emma supporting her sister infuriated Clay, whom Emma had been dating for a while by then. "You're enabling her," he would rant. And he was right. But that evening when Emma heeded his advice and told Nell no, she'd gone into a rage. She shoved Emma. Told her she hated her. Insisted Emma cared more for Clay than for her own sibling. Nell said Emma would never see her again and stormed off.

She'd made good on the threat. Emma hadn't seen her since. Nell would call sporadically, apologizing, alleging she was getting help, cleaning up. But she was still unwilling to forgive Emma for cutting her off. For choosing Clay over her. No matter how strongly Emma asserted that was miles from the truth.

The call five months ago had been subtly different. Nell gave up her location. She was in Erie. Desperate to make amends, Emma begged her to come home, promising things would be different. Nell still refused. "Not as long as Clay's around," she'd stated. But she'd admitted Emma hadn't been entirely wrong. "I need to get clean. For real this time. I need to learn to fend for myself."

As sincere as Nell had sounded, Emma sensed she wasn't doing either.

She hit play on the message and listened to it a second time. And a third. Tried to read between the proverbial lines.

Don't need to call back. Isn't my phone. I'm okay.

The desperation in Nell's voice said more than the words did. Nell was crying out for help. And Emma didn't know how to reach her.

Chapter Nine

By mid-afternoon, Matthias and Cassie returned to the office having walked the streets of downtown, following the erratic path Wesley had taken on Friday. An annoyingly small percentage of the businesses with CCTV willingly agreed to turn over their recordings without a warrant. In most cases, the employees were uncomfortable releasing videos without the owner's or manager's consent. Matthias and Cassie left business cards with those and would have to follow up.

Cassie's phone chirped as she stuffed her purse in her desk's bottom drawer. She squinted at the screen. "Wesley's financial records are in. Do you want them, or do you want to start watching the security footage?"

"Doesn't matter." Matthias dug a quarter from his pocket. "Flip you for it."

She shook her head. "Rock, paper, scissors."

"No way. You cheat."

"How can you cheat at rock, paper, scissors?" she asked innocently.

He didn't know, but she won every time. He thought about it and realized she usually won the coin tosses as well. "I'll take the videos." Hours of watching traffic passing by in the hopes of spotting one white van versus crunching numbers? Traffic won by a slim margin.

A couple of hours later, as other detectives filed out of the office, heading home, Matthias reached the conclusion he'd chosen wrong. He rubbed his eyes against the strain of watching grainy CCTV footage. For his effort, he'd found the van and Wesley's Audi exactly once. Matthias noted and time-stamped the location, hoping to eventually piece it with more sightings. One thing was evident. Wesley had been following the van. Not the other way around. And he'd kept several car lengths between them.

What Matthias saw matched the wife's story of her husband trying to get a license number.

Cassie rolled her chair from the confines of her cubby. "You want a break?"

Hell yes. "Why? You find anything?"

She gave him an evil grin, crooked her finger, and rolled back into the cubicle.

Matthias stood, stretched, and moved to her side. Her desk was stacked with papers and her computer screen revealed a spreadsheet filled with numbers and calculations. "Whatcha got?" he asked.

"Wesley Simmons was a financial train wreck."

Not what Matthias had expected. "Really?"

"The man has made and lost several fortunes in investments. Lately, he's been solidly in the loss column." Cassie rearranged some of the papers. "He's bleeding money. Behind on all his payments. That Audi? I'm willing to bet the loan company is already in the process of repossessing it. He's on the verge of losing that beautiful South Shore house too."

"Wow." Matthias held up a wait-a-minute finger and backtracked to grab his chair, dragging it next to Cassie's.

She folded her arms. "Supports my theory. Wesley desperately needed cash. What better way to get a nice check than to file an insurance claim?"

"Except he ended up dead."

"Clearly not part of his plan."

Matthias stared at the spreadsheet without truly seeing it. Instead, he held a mental picture of Wesley's wife and kids Friday afternoon, distraught at not knowing where he was. Then on Saturday morning, gathered in their upscale kitchen as Matthias and Cassie shattered their world. Or had they? "What about Barbara Simmons?"

"She's another good possibility." Cassie thumbed through the paperwork to settle on a copy of the mortgage. "She co-signed for the loan on the house."

"I'd love to find out how much she knew about Wesley's financial troubles."

Cassie grunted. "If I found out my husband had lost a small fortune and we were about to be out on the street, I'd be sorely tempted to bury his ass. Maybe I'm right about half of it. The heist was staged, but Barbara's the one who set it up. Wesley getting loose and chasing the van would screw up a perfectly good plan."

Matthias brought his mental image of the beautiful grief-stricken blonde into closer focus. Distraught? Or a good actress? "What about her father? Joe Platt."

"She'd been vocal about not wanting him there."

"Maybe afraid he'd let something slip?"

"Where did he say he worked?" Cassie paged through her notebook. "Fort Niagara Investments. Interesting. None of Wesley's investments are with them. In fact, looks like he didn't use an advisor from any of the big firms. He made all his trades online, on his own."

Matthias huffed a laugh. "Must be like lawyers. A person who represents himself in court has a fool for a client."

"Apparently so." Cassie leaned back. "Platt said he'd offered to help Wesley, but he refused. What if the wife got tired of her husband turning down her father's helping hand?"

"Or Platt could've arranged it without Barbara knowing." The idea of those two kids losing both parents—one in jail, one in the ground—hit too close to home for him.

"Arranged 'it'?" Cassie echoed. "The robbery or the murder?"

He pondered the question. "I don't see any reason for Platt to set up a home invasion at his daughter's house. If he wanted to help her financially, he could just write a check."

"Except it sounds like Wesley would never accept Platt's money." Cassie swiveled toward a second computer keyboard and monitor on her desk, pulled up the NCIC database, entered the home invasion's case number, and typed in Joseph Platt. It didn't take long for Platt's history to load on the screen. "Well, look at that. Mr. Platt has a criminal record. Simple assault. Aggravated assault. Multiple DUIs."

Matthias stood and looked over Cassie's shoulder. "All back in the nineties. Nothing, not even a parking ticket, since then."

"So he cleaned up his act. Doesn't mean he isn't still capable of opening a can of whoop ass."

Matthias snorted. "If he hired the crew to take care of the

problem, he wouldn't need a can opener."

Cassie looked up at him. "You told me you weren't convinced his alibi would hold up. Maybe you should have another talk with the photographer babe."

He refused to let his partner know he'd already planned to do just that. "I'll add it to my list. Right after we finish canvassing the Simmonses' neighbors on South Shore Drive, going over all the surveillance videos, checking the pawn shops for the stolen merchandise—"

"Don't forget we need to interview the yoga instructor too."

He hadn't. "Lower priority."

"She was at the crime scene."

"After the fact. And with a good reason. Besides, she owns a local business. I don't see her as at flight risk."

"As opposed to Joe Platt and Emma Anderson who both own campers and could pull up stakes at any moment."

Good point. Platt was less of at flight risk. He was employed and had family—family he might have been willing to kill to protect—in Erie. But Emma Anderson? No permanent address and only a camera as a career.

Cassie stretched with a groan. "It's been a long ass day. I don't know about you, but I'm going home and get some rest. I just hope and pray I don't have to deal with a crying granddaughter tonight."

Matthias glanced at his watch. Six o'clock. "I'll be right behind you."

"Uh-huh," she said, her words and expression thick with sarcasm. "You better be. Tomorrow's another day." She logged out of her computer and retrieved her purse from its drawer. Scooping up a stack of paper files piled on her desk, she strode out of the office.

He watched her go and briefly considered heeding her suggestion. Instead, he reclaimed his seat and pulled up the next video.

The long evening proved productive on the CCTV front. It was midnight before Matthias tumbled into bed.

As usual, Cassie was already at her computer when Matthias entered Major Crimes the next morning, a cup of dark roast from the nearby coffee shop in one hand. Both urns were full, and a large box of doughnuts claimed the space next to them on the break room table, but he preferred to start the day with a higher quality brew. In addition, the pastries would put him in a sugar coma, which he did not need after last night.

She shot a glance his way. "I half expected to find you sleeping on your desk."

"You told me to go home. I went home."

"When?"

He set his coffee shop brew on his desk and didn't reply.

She grunted. "Right." With a nod toward his cup she asked, "Why do you waste your money on that fancy schmancy organic crap when we have plenty of coffee here?"

"Maybe I care about what I put in my body. Maybe I care about the Earth."

"Bull. I've seen you guzzle two gallons of our grocery store grind on a single shift."

"Only because I can't keep running out for the good stuff. But at least I can start my day with it."

Cassie sniffed. "What did you find? Before you 'went home', I mean."

"I spotted the van and the Audi four more times along Wesley's route. From what I could tell, he never gained ground on the suspects. What I don't know is whether the van driver was that good at evasion or if Wesley was intentionally lagging back." Matthias took a sip of coffee. He nodded toward the stack of paperwork Cassie had lugged home and which was now back on her desk. "How about you?"

She gave him her innocent grin. "I just got here. It's not like I've had time to do much."

He held her gaze, unblinking. After a few seconds, she let the act drop, as he knew she would.

"A deeper dive into Wesley's financials only revealed more of the same. Progressively bigger and riskier investments followed by huge losses. He was nearly six months in arrears on the house. About the same on his car payments. I can't believe the repo guys weren't already knocking on his door."

"Maybe they were."

"Maybe," she echoed. "What do you say we get outta here and go get some answers?"

Their first stop was South Shore Drive with a list of residents who had failed to answer their doors on Saturday. Matthias and Cassie split the list and headed in opposite directions. When he received no answer at the first four houses, he scribbled notes on his business cards and left one in each door.

At the fifth house, Matthias rang a fancy security doorbell and didn't have to wait long for a female voice to respond from thin air. "Yes? May I help you?"

Matthias stepped back and looked at the doorbell.

"Detective Matthias Honeywell, Erie Police." He checked his list for a name. "Ms. Riley?"

"Yes?" Her tone was cautious.

"Are you home by any chance?" He'd rather see her face and eyes, especially since she could see him.

A brief pause was followed by, "Yes, but I'm quite busy. What's this about?"

Apparently, she hadn't seen the news or spoken with her neighbors. "I'd like to ask you a few questions about Friday's home invasion."

"Home invasion?" she asked, shocked. "Someone broke into my house? Why wasn't I notified?"

"It wasn't your house. Where exactly are you?"

Another pause. "I'd rather not say."

Matthias pinched the bridge of his nose. "I'm with the police, ma'am. I'm not one of the burglars."

"How can I know that?"

He unclipped his badge from his belt and held it up to the camera followed by his ID.

"I don't know that that's real."

He jammed his badge back on his belt. "Tell you what. Why don't you call the Erie Bureau of Police and give them my name? Ask them if I'm legit. Have them describe me to you. Would that convince you?"

Yet another pause. "Yes, that would. Could you spell your name, please?"

He obliged.

"Thanks. Stay there. I'll get right back to you."

Exasperated, he turned to gaze at the street, hoping like hell Ms. Riley wouldn't come back only to have absolutely nothing for him. He looked toward the Simmons house, across the street and two houses to the west. If the van had been facing east, there was a slim chance the license plate may have been visible from here.

"Hello? Detective Honeywell?"

He wheeled to face the doorbell. "Yes."

"They verified you're who you say you are." There was a smile in her voice, replacing the caution. "How can I help you?"

He told her about Friday's illicit activity in her neighborhood. "Wesley Simmons's body was discovered Saturday morning. If there's anything you might have seen during the time of the break-in, even if it seems inconsequential, it might help us with our investigation."

"Wesley's dead? That's horrible. I'm sorry but I'm in Cancun on vacation. Have been for the last two weeks, so I'm afraid I'm of no help."

Matthias took note of the placard indicating the name of her security company. Not the same one the Simmons family used. "Would it be all right if we accessed your security camera footage? It might have caught something useful."

Once again, she hesitated. "You can see my company's name, right?"

"Yes, ma'am."

"Good. Then you get a court order and serve it on them. I'm sure they'll be happy to give you what you need. Good day, Detective."

Matthias sensed he'd had the virtual door slammed in his face. He jotted a note, shot a curled lip snarl at the camera just in case Ms. Riley was still watching, and headed to the next house.

An hour later, after exhausting any hopes of gaining a good

lead on South Shore Drive, Matthias and Cassie headed to their next stop. Fort Niagara Investments.

A dark-haired woman with large designer glasses and the posture of a castle sentry took their names and asked them to have a seat. The atrium soared three stories. Light from the front wall of glass flooded the space, which was filled with greenery. Matthias suspected the company spent more on décor in this one lobby than he spent on a year's rent for his apartment.

"Remind me not to give these guys any of my money," Cassie said, clearly having made the same observation he had. "I can't imagine the percentage they keep in order to pay for this place."

"They're making a statement. They're successful. Would you trust an investment firm that operated out of a shack?"

She considered it. "Guess not."

High heels clacked across the marble floor bringing the raven-haired sentry with them. Matthias rose, Cassie a split second behind him.

"Follow me, please," the receptionist said and continued past them towards an open doorway to a small conference room at the edge of the atrium. She stopped at the entry and gestured them into the room. "I'm afraid Mr. Platt is out of the office today. Mr. Castillo will be out to speak with you shortly. Can I bring you anything? Coffee? Tea? Water?"

"No, thank you," Cassie replied.

The sentry clacked back to her desk.

Matthias circled the oval table, which held one telephone and was surrounded by eight leather chairs. "Maybe Joe's at the campground."

"That would be convenient. We'll make it our next stop. If

he's there, I'll talk to him. You can talk to the cute photographer."

Matthias gave Cassie his best evil eye knowing she was immune.

"You know you want to ask her out."

"She's part of the investigation."

"I'm well aware. As I've said before, all the more reason we need to clear this case."

A man in an expensive-looking suit strode into the room, interrupting Cassie's matchmaking efforts. He closed the door behind him, plastered a well-practiced smile on his face, and extended a hand to Cassie. "Detectives. I'm Eugene Castillo."

After Castillo and Cassie shook, he offered the hand to Matthias.

"Detectives Malone and Honeywell," Cassie said. "We were hoping to speak with Joseph Platt."

"Yes." Castillo gestured to the chairs. Once they were seated, he said, "Joe's off this week, I'm afraid. Is there something I can help you with?"

"We're trying to determine Mr. Platt's whereabouts on Friday afternoon," Matthias said. "Can you tell us what time he left?"

"This past Friday?" Castillo scowled.

"Yes, sir." Matthias could see the man thinking and had a feeling his thought process involved more than simply trying to remember.

Castillo pulled the phone closer, picked up the receiver, and punched a button. "Maria? Can you check to see when Joe Platt checked in and out on Friday?"

A moment later, the receptionist entered the room and

clacked her way to Castillo, handing him a sheet of paper. He thanked her and she sashayed out the way she came.

Castillo's scowl deepened as he studied the sheet. "It appears Joe Platt only worked half a day." He turned the printout and handed it to Matthias. "This is the record of his logging in and out for the last week. As you can see, he left before noon on Friday."

Matthias scanned the report, holding it so Cassie could read it as well. Their eyes met, and he knew she'd noticed the same thing he had.

"Is there a chance Mr. Platt could've come back to his office without it showing up here?" Cassie asked.

Castillo shook his head. "The only way anyone can access the upper floors where the offices are is to use one of the elevators or the stairwell. All require us to swipe our ID." He tapped his own security badge clipped to his jacket lapel. "Each swipe is recorded." He pointed at the paper in Matthias's hands and offered a weak grin. "Unless he scaled the side of the building and broke a window, his comings and goings are listed right there."

Cassie took the page and held it up. "May we keep this?"

"Please do."

After thanking Castillo and leaving their business cards with him, they left Fort Niagara Investments, silent until safely back in their sedan. Again, their eyes met.

"Joe Platt has no alibi for Friday afternoon," Cassie said.

Matthias held her knowing gaze. "He also left early last Tuesday."

The day of the previous home invasion.

Chapter Ten

Nell's voicemail haunted Emma. She'd spent the rest of Monday afternoon and evening calling the number. Each time, she got the recording about it being out of service. While spending the bulk of the night staring at the ceiling, she decided she couldn't simply wait around for another call. She was dressed, in her Forester, and headed downtown by the time the sun cleared the horizon.

Back in December, Nell had told Emma she was working at the Blue Goat Restaurant and Pub on French Street. Emma checked it out when she first arrived only to discover dark windows and a for-rent sign tacked to the door. She didn't know what she expected to find there today. As far as she knew, the business remained shuttered. Still, it was the only solid address she had.

She found a vacant parking spot a half block away and maneuvered her car into it. The usual pride she took in her parallel parking skills quickly faded as she climbed out and strode down the street. The sidewalk was void of pedestrians and yet she had that prickling sensation along her neck and shoulders … that feeling of being watched.

At one time, the old redbrick building which housed the Blue Goat had been a fire station. The restaurant owners converted the massive arched doorways into windows, which were now dark. Emma cupped her hands over her brow and alongside her face, pressing close to the glass, cutting the glare. The shadowy interior gave nothing away, all vestiges of the dining décor having been stripped.

What had she expected? To find Nell hanging out at her former place of employment?

"Can I help you with something?"

Emma spun to face a woman she guessed to be in her fifties with a long braid draped over her shoulder. "I doubt it," Emma said, feeling foolish. "My sister used to work here and…" What? I don't know where she is so I was hoping she might have left a note on the window?

"So did I," the woman said with a sad smile. "It was such a great place. Plus, I live right across the street, so the commute was perfect."

Emma pointed at the vacant building. "You worked here?"

"For close to twenty years. What's your sister's name?"

Emma's heart rate kicked into high. "Nell Anderson."

The woman's smile faded. Emma thought she noticed a small intake of breath. "I remember Nell," the woman said. "Sweet young woman. But … troubled."

Emma's pulse and hopes dropped. "That's her. I don't suppose you know where she lives."

The woman studied Emma through narrowed eyes. "No. We didn't socialize."

"Oh." Emma should've known this would get her nowhere.

"I do remember where she went to work after she left though, if that would help."

"It would."

"A place called Fortune's Bar on Sassafras, down near Thirteenth, I think. It's … not as nice as this was."

Emma caught the innuendo in her tone and thanked her before jogging back to the Forester. She had to look Fortune's Bar up on her phone's GPS. According to the posting, it didn't open for a few more hours. Nevertheless, she was only blocks away. Too close to not give it a shot.

Fortune's small gravel lot saved Emma from testing her parallel parking skills this time. Two pickups, both in need of a trip through the car wash, flanked a dumpster and service door near the rear, giving her hope that someone might be inside. Emma parked close to the street, stepped out, and strode to the front of the building.

When the woman with the braid had said it wasn't as nice as the Blue Goat—even in its current condition—she hadn't been exaggerating. Fortune's Bar boasted one small filthy window set high in a graffitied brick façade. A discolored and cracked sign with the business's name hung from a pole protruding from the mortar. The plain steel door wore a faded warning that minors would not be served. Emma grasped the latch, expecting it to be locked. It clicked, and she heaved the door open.

It took a minute for her eyes to acclimate to the dark interior. As she stood there, the feeling of being watched returned. She shivered and shook it off.

Other than the muted sunshine filtering through the grimy window and puddling on the floor, the only lighting came from a row of bulbs over the bar. A tall, slim man wearing a white T-shirt and dark hair pulled into a ponytail looked up from wiping glasses.

"Can I help you?" he asked, his voice surprisingly gentle.

Emma moved toward him, startled to find the floor wasn't tacky beneath her shoes. "I hope so. I'm trying to locate my sister and was told she worked here. Her name's Nell Anderson."

He eyed her. "You're Nell's sister?"

"Yes. Emma." She extended a hand toward him.

He wiped his on the towel he was using before shaking hers. "Okay. Yeah. I recall her mentioning you."

"You know her then? She does work here?"

"Yes and no." He set one of the wiped glasses on a shelf next to dozens of liquor bottles before picking up the next. "I knew her. She *did* work here. Doesn't anymore."

Emma perched on one of the bar stools. "What happened?"

He shrugged. "She was a good waitress. Good bartender. For a while. Working in a place like this ... it's not advisable to sample the product. You get my meaning?"

"I do," Emma said. All too well. "Do you know where I can find her? Where she lives? Where she might work now?"

"I have no idea where she works." He jerked a thumb toward the ceiling. "She used to rent an apartment from me upstairs. But when I had to let her go, she got pissed and packed her stuff." His mouth dipped in a frown. "Now that I think about it, she never paid her last month's rent."

Emma tensed. She'd heard variations of this theme before Nell had taken off, usually followed by a request that Emma pay off her sister's debts.

The barkeeper's frown softened into not quite a grin. "Don't worry. I'm not expecting you to make good on it. I keep hoping she'll get clean and come back. To be honest, I'm glad to know someone cares about her. I wish I could help."

"So do I."

He paused in his glass wiping. "Why don't you leave me a number where I can reach you. If Nell shows up, I'll give you a call."

Emma opened her mouth, then closed it. Once again, she felt the agony of her conundrum. This man had seen Nell more recently than anyone else Emma had encountered. Nell very well might return to pay her debts. And yet Emma couldn't shake the feeling she was being watched. Did she risk leaving her number with a stranger? Risk having it fall into Clay's hands? She'd done it before with other bartenders and waitresses around town. But each time she upped the chance of Clay, not Nell, finding her.

Emma glanced around the darkened bar, her eyes now more accustomed to the low lighting. She and the bartender were alone. At least as far as she could tell. Still, her intuition—or her paranoia—screamed *no*.

She stood. "Just tell her to call me if she comes in. She has my number."

He continued wiping the glass in his hand. "Fair enough."

Emma started to turn away but faced him again. "How long has it been since you last saw her?"

"Four, no, five weeks ago."

She thanked him for his time and crossed to the door. Outside, the sunlight momentarily blinded her. Five weeks.

How far could Nell have gotten in five weeks?

Back at her camper, Emma brewed another pot of coffee. Mug in hand, she settled into one of her lawn chairs and breathed through her frustration.

The campground should've been quiet. Kids were still in school for a few more weeks. Weekenders were gone, including Joe. Not so for the next camp up the hill. Mick's radio blasted an old rock song that she might have enjoyed if it wasn't cranked to the decibel level of a jet engine.

As if on cue, Mick appeared, headed up the road toward his place. He waved and approached. "Yo, Emily."

She didn't bother to correct him. She'd already told him her name was Emma at least twenty times. He clearly didn't care. She raised a hand in acknowledgement, wishing he would keep walking.

No such luck.

His uneven gait suggested he'd already consumed a few alcoholic beverages despite the hour. He stopped at the edge of her deck and leaned on the railing, a smirk on his bloated face. "I'm having a big campfire tonight. Everyone's coming. You should come too."

Mick's version of a "big campfire" was a bunch of his loudmouth friends growing even louder because of an abundance of booze. He'd asked her to join them about as many times as he'd gotten her name wrong. She'd rather go swimming with alligators.

She faked a smile. "I'll do my best."

"Great! See you then." He waved, pivoted away, and continued toward his camp.

"Ain't happening," she muttered under her breath. "No way."

The sound of an approaching vehicle drew her attention

away from her annoying neighbor. She didn't recognize the black Impala, but it only took a moment to identify it as an unmarked police vehicle. It came to a stop in front of her camper and the same detective from the cemetery, the beach, and Joe's daughter's house stepped from behind the wheel. A tall woman with brown skin and short cropped white hair climbed from the passenger side. Emma remembered her from the beach too.

Now what?

"Ms. Anderson," the woman said and introduced herself as Detective Malone.

Emma already knew Detective Honeywell. She rose and crossed to the edge of her deck. "How can I help you?"

The Malone woman pointed at the next site. "Is that Joe Platt's camp?"

"It is, but he's not here. He works during the week."

Malone and Honeywell exchanged looks. Emma sensed they were having a silent conversation she wasn't privy to. Malone said something that Emma couldn't make out over the music and then strode up the road in Mick's direction.

Maybe she'd write him a ticket for noise pollution.

Instead of following his partner, Honeywell approached Emma. "Do you mind if I ask you a few questions?"

Uneasy, she said, "I suppose."

He tipped his head toward her lawn chairs. "May I?"

She stepped back. "Sure."

Once seated, he pulled out a notebook. "So this is where you call home?"

"It is."

"You don't have a permanent address?"

"This is as permanent as it gets for now."

The music from Mick's place fell silent. The woman detective had succeeded where everyone else had failed.

Honeywell took in the older-model small camper. Emma searched his face for signs of disapproval or judgment. If it was there, he masked it well. "Nice campground. I stayed here once when I first moved to Erie."

"When was that?" Emma winced. Why had she asked? She didn't really care.

He blew a breath. "Oh. Man, it's been close to twenty years now." He gave her a tight-lipped smile—one she sensed was standard issue, along with his badge. "I'm originally from Oklahoma."

"Really?" Again, she cringed. He was drawing her in, trying to put her at ease. And being an idiot, she was falling for it. "You don't sound like you're from Oklahoma."

"Well, thank ya, ma'am," he said with a drawl thick enough to choke a bull elephant. Or an armadillo.

Did they have armadillos in Oklahoma? She knew they didn't have elephants.

"I guess I've lost the drawl. Mostly. What about you? Where are you from?"

There it was. The real reason he was sharing with her. A backdoor into finding out about her. "Pennsylvania," she replied dryly. Not a lie.

The slant of his mouth told her he knew he'd been busted.

In spite of herself, Emma lowered her face and snickered.

It drew a more genuine grin. "You're not going to make this easy, are you?"

"No, I am not." She studied him, catching a glimpse of the man who'd smiled when she'd asked if he needed a witness to her being at the cemetery. For a fleeting moment, she considered spilling everything to him. Where she was from. Why she was hiding.

Could he help her find Nell?

Before she gave it more thought, he broke the spell. "I need you to tell me what time you saw Joe Platt on Friday."

"I already told you."

"No. He did. You agreed with him."

"Same thing."

"No. It's not. I need you to tell me in your words."

Emma studied Honeywell's face. The intense blue eyes. The strong jaw. But no sign of the rage she'd witnessed at the cemetery. *What's the story about the beer drinking at that gravesite?* She wanted to ask but didn't.

"What time did you see him arrive?"

"Like I said before, about a quarter after five."

"How did he seem?"

"What do you mean?"

"Was he relaxed? Happy to be here? Stressed? Upset?"

"I don't know. I didn't speak with him until Saturday morning, after..." She couldn't say it.

"After you found his son-in-law's body."

"I didn't know who it was at the time."

Honeywell held up one hand. "You don't have to convince me. I know you didn't."

Did he really? "Yeah. After that."

Honeywell glanced at his notes. "Did you happen to see Joe around here last Tuesday?"

The change in date threw her. "No. I told you. He works during the week."

"But you did see Joe arrive on Friday?"

"Yes."

"And you didn't notice if he was acting normal or not?"

"No, I didn't."

"How about when you talked to him Saturday? How did he seem then?"

Emma was tiring of this. "He seemed fine. He was planning a cookout and was excited that his daughter and grandkids were coming. He invited me to join them. Even offered to cook a veggie burger especially for me."

Honeywell paused in his notetaking to hike an eyebrow at her. "A veggie burger? You're a vegetarian?" He made an exaggerated show of disgust at the word.

"Pescatarian."

"You eat fish."

She was surprised. Most people didn't know what the term meant. "It's necessary to survival if I ever want to eat out around here."

The stoic cop façade slipped, and she again caught a glimpse of a genuine smile.

"I'll tell you something else. I overheard him on the phone when his daughter called and told him about her husband. I heard him crying. It wasn't for show. The news upset him. Bad."

Honeywell's head came up, a thoughtful scowl on his face. "He was upset by the phone call?"

"Yes. Very."

"But you don't know if he was upset because he learned his son-in-law, whom he admits he disliked, died. Or because his daughter told him she didn't want him to come to the house."

She opened her mouth to give the detective a sharp retort. Except she thought about what he was saying. And about her unsettling conversation with Joe. "No," she said reluctantly. "I don't."

"Has he ever talked to you about his daughter and grandkids?"

"On occasion."

Honeywell's gaze remained fixed on her. She knew he was waiting for more. She also knew Joe would not appreciate her blabbing about him and his family. "He's proud of his grandkids," she said. "What grandfather isn't? He showed me pictures on his phone. That sort of thing."

"What about his daughter?"

"She wasn't in any of the pictures. I guess she was the one taking them."

"Did Joe ever talk about her?"

"Not really."

"Had you ever met Joe's family before Saturday?"

"No, but I don't think that means anything. I haven't lived here long."

"Yet he knows you well enough to know you don't eat meat. And to invite you to a cookout."

"He was being nice. He's a *nice* guy." The music was back and even louder if that was possible. Emma winced. "Unlike Mick. Mick's a partier and a bully. If Joe was here, he'd put him in his place."

"Put him in his place? How?" Honeywell had to raise his voice.

"Joe keeps Mick from harassing me and some of the others." Emma swept an arm, indicating the surrounding campers. "Mick can't push Joe around. If Joe tells him to turn it down, he does. He'll grouch, but he'll do it. Usually."

"Did you ever see them get physical?"

She thought about earlier. Joe's grip on Mick's throat.

"I'm just wondering how Joe kept Mick in line," Honeywell said when she didn't answer. "Did they have a fight at some point?"

Emma knew what the detective was up to. He was insinuating Joe had a violent streak. Aside from the earlier confrontation, when Mick had pushed all of Joe's buttons, she'd never seen a hint of violence from her neighbor. But if she revealed that one incident, even if it was deserved, it proved Joe had the propensity for violence. She chose her words carefully. "Like I said. I'm new here. But I can't picture Joe ever punching anyone." Which was the truth. "He just doesn't tolerate Mick's bluster. Unlike most people, who are scared of him."

"Are you?"

She didn't have to think long. "Yeah. Kinda. I stay away from Mick as much as possible." She'd spent enough up-close-and-personal time with a bully.

"Has he ever tried anything with you?"

"Mick? Other than smarmy invitations to his beer parties, no."

Honeywell nodded as he scribbled in his notebook.

His partner appeared around the front of Emma's camper, a sour look on her face. "How has that man not been kicked out of this campground?"

"He abides by the rules just enough to avoid trouble with management." Emma felt a headache coming on. "He always points out that he adheres to the quiet hours. And his music isn't usually this loud. Did you ask him to turn it down?"

"I told him to turn it off so we could talk. Once we were finished, I asked him to keep the volume at a reasonable level.

If this is 'reasonable,' I hate to see what cranking it up means to the man."

"That's the problem. Anytime someone complains to him, he turns it up. Once you're gone, he'll lower it. I hope."

From somewhere nearby, a voice bellowed, "TURN OFF THAT DAMNED MUSIC."

Nothing changed. Emma suspected the volume was already set as high as it would go. "A couple weeks ago, someone snuck onto his deck in the middle of the night and cut the radio's power cord." She smiled at the memory of Mick's temper tantrum the following morning when he discovered the vandalism. "We thought we'd have a little peace and quiet at least until he bought a new one. Instead, he stuck batteries in it and kept on blasting it."

Honeywell studied her and one side of his mouth slanted upward. "That's good to know." He stood and stormed off Emma's deck, disappearing around the end of her camper.

Detective Malone smiled. "Oh, this should be good." She trailed after her partner. At least as far as the camp road.

Emma followed. She and Malone stood on the gravel lane to watch. Other nearby campers were observing the scene from their decks or in front of their sites.

Honeywell strode to Mick's camper and climbed the three wooden steps to the deck. Without waiting for an invitation, he crossed to the radio, a big old boom box-type thing.

"Hey!" Mick, who'd been sitting in one of his Adirondack chairs, came to his feet. "Who the hell are you and what the fuck are you doing?"

Honeywell picked up the player, and for one long moment, Emma thought he was going to smash it, something she'd dreamed of doing more than once. Instead, he flipped it over and thumbed open the battery compartment. The radio fell silent as he ripped out the D-cells. One hit the decking with a *thunk*. Honeywell palmed the rest. He set the player back down—maybe a little too hard—and tromped off the porch with Mick on his heels, spewing a string of profanity that was hardly appropriate for a family-friendly campground.

Once Honeywell was off the steps, he turned to face the wooded hillside behind Mick's camp. He wound up with the grace of a major-league ball player and sent the fistful of batteries sailing and scattering into the greenery.

Still swearing, Mick came up behind him, fists clenched. That's when Emma realized Mick towered over the cop. Although Mick's narrow shoulders and ballooning beer belly appeared no match for Honeywell and his gym-rat physique, she pictured her drunken neighbor flattening Honeywell and his partner hauling Mick off to jail for assaulting a law enforcement officer.

Instead, Honeywell spun to face him. Emma had seen that expression on the detective's face before. At the cemetery.

Despite his height advantage, Mick backed off.

"If I hear that you're playing that thing at that decibel level again, I'm coming back, and I'll confiscate the whole radio. And I'll write you up for violating noise pollution laws."

Mick regained some of his bravado. "Damn cop. You can't do that. I'll just buy a new one."

"And I'll confiscate that one too." Honeywell gave him a quick finger-jab to his chest. Just enough to drive home his message and make Mick flinch. Honeywell brushed past the taller man and strode down the hill. Not directly toward Emma and Malone but toward the unmarked car.

"Those batteries are expensive," Mick bellowed after him, the distance reinflating his swagger.

"Send me a bill," Honeywell growled back. "Mail it to Erie Police Headquarters, State Street."

As Malone and Emma watched, Honeywell yanked open the car door and got in behind the wheel.

Several of the neighbors who'd been observing the scene broke into applause.

Malone faced Emma with a tight grin. "Well then. I guess we're done here. If you think of anything that might help—"

"I have your cards."

Malone gave a nod before striding back to the car and climbing in beside her partner.

Emma watched the vehicle reverse down the hill and into the lower crossroad where it shifted into drive and headed toward the entrance. She didn't dare look in Mick's direction. Head down, she returned to her camper.

Chapter Eleven

"Nice bit of showing off for the photographer," Cassie said as Matthias dodged a steady stream of cars entering and exiting Presque Isle State Park to turn left on Peninsula Drive.

"I wasn't showing off. That guy is an ass."

Cassie hiccupped a laugh. "You didn't have the honor of interviewing him like I did."

Matthias had almost forgotten their purpose for the visit. "Did he have anything interesting to say?"

"Let's see." The fact that she didn't refer to her notes said a lot. "Emily is a stuck-up snob."

"Who's Emily?"

"As far as I can tell, Emma Anderson."

"Ah."

"And Joe Platt is a busybody and a pushy loudmouth who can't mind his own business."

"Coming from that asshole, Platt should be flattered." Matthias shot another look at his partner. "That's it?"

"Oh, no. He also says he thinks Joe and Emily are fooling around."

"*What?*"

Cassie waved a dismissive hand. "I get the impression he suspects everyone in the campground is fooling around with everyone else. Harper claims Joe treats Emily like a little princess, but admitted he's never seen either of them going into the other's camper. The only time he saw them even so much as get in a car together was Saturday afternoon."

"She drove him to his daughter's house."

"Exactly."

"Well, that was a waste of time."

"Not entirely."

"Oh?" Matthias glanced at his partner's profile and smug smile.

"Harper claims Joe tried to kill him a couple days ago. Said he marched onto his deck unprovoked and strangled him."

"You believe him?"

"The unprovoked part? Not really. Hell, I was on the verge of choking him back there myself. But Harper had bruises on his neck and wasn't shy about pointing them out to me. I asked if he wanted to press charges. He said he was thinking about it."

"Interesting."

"Harper also said it was Emily who convinced Joe to let him go."

"Also interesting. She never mentioned that to me."

"Maybe there really is something going on between those two."

Matthias considered the possibility. "I don't buy it."

"I don't either," Cassie admitted. "What I do buy is the part about Joe losing control and going after Harper. It fits with his criminal record and proves he may not have left his violent tendencies in the past." She held up a finger. "But wait. There's more." She used a damn good impersonation of one of those television ads offering a bonus if one merely paid additional shipping fees. "According to our Mick Harper, Joe Platt has a big-ass fishing boat."

Matthias thought about their supposition that Wesley had been taken out into the lake and dumped overboard. "I bet ninety-five percent of the people who have camps at Sara's own boats."

"Probably. Mick admitted he had one too." Cassie shifted in her seat to face Matthias. "The thing is Mick isn't a person of interest in Wesley Simmons's murder. Nor are ninety-five percent of Sara's campers."

While Matthias drove to the address listed as the Platt residence, Cassie tracked down information about Joe's boat. By the time they pulled into the driveway, she'd learned he had a fifteen-year-old, forty-one-foot Meridian 411 Sedan registered in his name.

"That's not a 'boat'," she said. "That's a yacht."

What she couldn't track down yet was at which marina the boat was docked.

Platt's single-story bungalow with a detached one-car garage sat on a small lot. If Matthias was to judge, he'd have to say the guy's Jayco had more square feet than this house. No one responded to the knock on the door. Cassie stood on her toes to peer through the garage door's window and reported it was empty. They wandered around to the back of the house, which appeared in dire need of a power washing. The lawn was neatly mown, but there was no landscaping beyond a solitary tree casting shade on a cracked square of concrete outside a pair of sliding glass doors.

Cassie circled to the front again. "I'm willing to bet good old Joe spends more time at his camp or on his boat than he does here at home."

"I think it's a safe bet he spends more money on them than on his house too." Matthias stuck another business card in the storm door.

As they pulled out, Cassie thumbed through her notebook. "Now what? He's not at home. He's not at work. He's not at his camp."

"He might be on his boat."

"Maybe. If he's our man, he might be destroying any evidence of his son-in-law's body ever being on it."

Matthias was thinking the same thing. "I guess we'll have to try again later."

Cassie looked over at him, a cheesy smile on her face. "In the meantime, there's someone else we haven't talked to yet. Head back downtown."

Namaste Erie Yoga occupied a small storefront on Peach Street, only a few blocks from police headquarters. A single window was decorated with the same *sri yantra* design Matthias

recalled from her business card. Lights from ins.
hope that Kira Petersen was in. He tried the doorkno
clicked open.

The interior smelled of incense. Hindu deities perched o.
shelf above a counter. Other shelves held items marked with
prices. Candles. Boxes of incense. Small silk bundles with a
sign labeling them as "eye pillows." A large woven basket in
the corner held cellophane-wrapped yoga mats for sale.

A doorway to one side of the counter opened to another
room from which soft eastern music wafted.

"Hello?" Cassie called. "Ms. Petersen?"

A voice from the back replied, "Just a minute. I'll be right
there."

A few seconds later, a woman breezed through the door.
Matthias recognized her from the photo Emma had taken.
Shapely and fit, Kira Petersen wore yoga tights and a form-
hugging tank top covered by a sheer, flowing drape of some
sort. The gauzy wrap did nothing to hide her figure.

"I'm Kira," she said with a bright smile. "How can I help
you?"

Matthias tapped the badge on his belt and introduced
himself and Cassie.

Kira slipped behind the counter and rested her elbows on
it. "This is about the body at Presque Isle Saturday morning,
right?"

"Yes, ma'am." Matthias stepped closer. "Can you tell us
what you were doing on the beach that morning?"

"Teaching yoga. But you already know that." She leaned
forward, her arms squeezing her breasts, creating some
amazing cleavage.

Matthias was well aware the move was intentional. He fought to maintain eye contact. "We do. But I was hoping you could take us through the morning in your own words. Tell us what you saw."

"I didn't really see anything. I teach a class there every Saturday morning during the spring, summer, and fall. Weather permitting, of course. There'd been storms overnight, so there was more stuff washed up on the beach than usual. I didn't think anything of it. Toward the end of class, a woman walked by, taking pictures."

"Emma Anderson," Matthias said.

"Yes. I talked to her a while." Kira flashed him a flirtatious smile. "I thought it was funny that she was taking pictures of trash. She assured me she was a real photographer and even took a picture of me, which she emailed me later. And that's pretty much it. I didn't notice a body in all that garbage. I wasn't looking for one. It wasn't until I saw the news later that I made the connection." Kira leaned farther forward, aiming her ample cleavage in Matthias's direction. "I figured eventually the police would come by. I'm sorry I can't be of any help though."

"Can you tell us where you were Friday between three and seven?"

"I taught a class from one until two in the afternoon. After that, I stuck around here to do some paperwork. Then I went straight home and fixed myself supper." She gave him a slow, sensual blink. "I'm very good in the kitchen."

He battled to rid his mind of a mental picture of her being "good" in the kitchen. "Was anyone with you during that time?"

"No. I was all alone," she said with a breathy sigh.

"Did you stop anywhere? Maybe to get gas or to pick up something at the store?"

"Afraid not. I'm sorry, but I have no alibi for whatever you're asking about." She gave him a devious grin. "Do you want to handcuff me?"

"That won't be necessary."

"Too bad. I think it'd be fun."

Matthias let his gaze dip for a moment. He blinked and met Kira's eyes again. Her smile widened.

"Has anyone ever told you that you have the sexiest blue eyes?" Her voice had deepened into a purr.

From behind Matthias, Cassie choked.

He fumbled for, and almost dropped, a business card, which he placed on the counter. "If you think of anything—"

Kira reached for the card, her fingers brushing his. "I'll definitely give you a call," she said.

He could almost hear Cassie's eyeroll. "You do that," he said, lowering his own voice.

Back in the car, Cassie started cackling.

"What?" he demanded.

"'*You do that*'," Cassie said in a throaty whisper, apparently imitating his voice. She snickered. "Why didn't you just ask her out right then and there? You didn't need to be shy on account of me."

"She's involved with the case."

"No, she's not. She didn't see anything."

"As far as we know. She didn't have an alibi for the time of the home invasion."

This time, Cassie rolled her eyes so hard her whole head

made the loop. "Then we need to find our killer so you can ask Miss Kira and the photographer out on dates."

He started the car. "The photographer isn't my type."

"Too girl-next-door? Okay, I'll grant you that. But Kira Petersen? She's definitely your type. Hell, she's ready to jump your bones right now. And I bet she's super flexible too."

"Stop," he growled, although he'd thought the same thing about Kira. Once this case was cleared, he wouldn't mind finding out just how flexible.

Cassie's expression grew serious. "Tell me something. Why are you so determined to avoid a long-term relationship? How old are you? Forty-five?"

"Forty-three," he said and instantly regretted answering her question. Cassie damned well knew his age. Throwing out a number two years older was a ploy. Like an idiot, he'd fallen for it.

"Exactly," she said. "You aren't getting any younger. What are you waiting for?"

"The right woman." He allowed the sarcasm to saturate his words. "But you're already taken."

"Smart ass."

At least the quip had derailed her mother hen routine. Matthias was completely aware of his age and his ongoing single status. Emma Anderson's face with those almost teal eyes drifted across his mind. He quickly blinked it away. She was the type of woman who scared the hell out of him. Not because she was the girl next door, as Cassie had claimed. Rather, Emma was someone he could have real feelings for.

Which was exactly the reason he wouldn't consider asking her out.

He'd opened his heart once. No way would he make that mistake again.

―――――

As soon as Matthias hit the top of the stairs at the station with Cassie on his heels, Brad Frazier, one of the other Major Crimes detectives, greeted them. "We got it."

"What have we got?" Matthias asked.

"And is it contagious?" Cassie added and snickered, pleased with herself.

Brad, while a damn good cop, was notorious for having been born without an ounce of humor and ignored her quip. "The van. A Ms. Riley, who lives across from the Simmons place, had her security company send us footage."

Matthias shot a look at his partner. The woman who was vacationing in Cancun had come through after all. "And?"

"I watched it while you were out. Sure enough, one angle caught a great shot of the license. I ran it and it came up as stolen."

"Big shocker," Cassie said.

"I've already put out a BOLO on it." Brad gave them a self-satisfied smile. "Now we just have to wait."

"Don't suppose you could see who was inside the van?" Cassie asked.

"Unfortunately, no."

Matthias brushed past the other detective. "Is the footage still up on your computer?"

"Yep. Feel free to take a look, but I'm telling you: the plate is all you can make out."

Matthias slipped into Brad's cubicle and wheeled his chair

over to the monitor still showing a freezeframe of the license enlarged. While pixelated, the numbers were unmistakable. He reversed the video to the point where the white van first appeared and checked the timestamp. Fifteen forty-nine. Eleven minutes before four. The van nosed into the driveway right up to the open garage door. From the angle, only the driver's side was visible. Shadows and blurred movement hinted at two or more people exiting the opposite side and entering through the garage. The driver stayed in the vehicle. A moment later, the van backed out, which was when the image of the license plate was captured. The driver pulled forward, and then backed into the driveway. From there, the crew was able to load their haul into the rear doors of the van and climb in afterward without being caught on camera.

"Son of a bitch," Cassie muttered from over Matthias's shoulder.

He glanced at her. "Pretty slick. They must have known about the camera."

"And as far as we've been able to discern, there weren't any cameras on the other side of the residence to catch them getting out."

"Wouldn't matter. They wore masks." Matthias fast-forwarded as nothing else was visible until nearly twenty minutes later when the van pulled out. Almost immediately, Wesley Simmons charged across the lawn to his car, jumped in, and screeched off after the thieves. "We need to go through all the footage from these cameras going back at least a week. See if we can spot any vehicles cruising the neighborhood, casing the residences." When Cassie didn't comment, Matthias turned to look at her. "What?"

"Oh, you're right, of course. But I keep thinking they

might've had help. Someone at the Simmons house would've known their neighbors' camera set-ups."

"You're still stuck on your theory that Wesley had something to do with it?"

She shrugged. "Wesley isn't the only one living there who was dealing with losing their home." Meeting Matthias's eyes, Cassie added, "But he is the only one who ended up dead."

Chapter Twelve

A pparently, Mick didn't have extra batteries. After the detectives left, the only music came from birdsongs and the only noise was the whir of a distant weed eater. At least until Mick slammed his Corvette's door, revved its throaty engine, and roared past on his way to the exit.

Off to buy new batteries, Emma guessed. Or a whole new radio.

Taking advantage of the tranquility, she sat at her laptop and opened her email account. Nell's call ate at her. For the umpteenth time, Emma picked up her phone, found the message her sister had left, and clicked on the green phone icon. For the umpteenth time, the recording about the number being out of service played. Muttering a few choice words, Emma set the phone down and rested her fingers on the keyboard.

When she'd left her home in Washington County to start a new life in hiding, one of the things she'd done was delete her social media accounts. She didn't want a cyber trail that Clay could follow. Unfortunately, it limited her ability to keep tabs on Nell.

Emma tapped a few keys and pulled up Facebook's log-in page. She typed in her old username. Had she been using her old laptop—something else she'd ditched to avoid being tracked—it would've auto filled her long-forgotten password. She backspaced, clearing the box. Not remembering her password might be a blessing—the Universe telling her Facebook was a bad idea.

But she needed to find out if Nell had added a post since the last time she checked.

Emma clicked on the button to set up a new account and stared at the required fields. First name. Last name. The simplest questions for most people. The hardest for her. She wanted Nell to recognize the name, but she needed to stay anonymous where Clay was concerned.

She pondered her options. What name could she use that Nell would recognize and Clay would not?

Her first inclination was using Nell's first name and their mother's maiden name. Nell Miller. But Clay was smart. He'd figure it out in a heartbeat. No, Emma needed something more obscure.

She and Nell had always shared a passion for reading along with their mother. Mom's favorite book was a tattered volume of *Rebecca* by Daphne Du Maurier. Every few years, Emma, her mother, and her sister would reread the novel and spend evenings drinking hot cocoa and discussing the rich characters and setting. *Last night I dreamt I went to Manderley again*. The opening line became a password of sorts between Emma and Nell. A signal that all was well.

The name jumped into Emma's brain. Rebecca Manderley. Obvious enough that Nell would make the connection. But not Clay.

Emma typed it in.

Other than creating a password, she didn't fill out the profile information. No picture. No location. No past.

She located Nell's profile and was grateful the majority of her posts were set as public. The most recent was a re-post of an old photo of Nell looking haggard. The same one had been there before Emma went off-grid. Nell's bio information was also outdated. She still listed the Blue Goat as her place of employment and Erie as her current residence. Emma could only hope that was still true.

She sent her sister a friend request, just in case she happened to log in.

Emma continued to stare at the screen wondering if Clay had kept his profile. She typed his name into the search bar. Sure enough, a link to his page popped up with a thumbnail of Clay the smiling charmer. Emma recoiled.

She battled to tamp down the anxiety, but paranoia overwhelmed logic. Would Clay be able to learn "Rebecca Manderley" had searched his page? Panic gripped Emma. Had she and Nell ever talked books in front of Clay? Emma remembered one time, but Clay had been engrossed in some online game with lots of gunfire and explosions. And she couldn't recall which book they'd been chatting about. Odds were good it was some other novel.

Emma recalled Kira leading her yoga class, imploring her students to breathe and let go. Emma tried. She didn't entirely succeed, but breath gave her courage. She clicked the link and was taken to Clay's page. She immediately regretted the decision.

Clay Bauer was a handsome devil. Emma had fallen for the handsome part only later to learn about the devil half. Her worst fears were that she'd find photos of him in Erie. Or photos on his page of *her* in Erie. She let out a relieved sigh when she saw there were none of those.

His photos, at least the public ones, were all set at various locations in Washington County. She recognized them with a jolt of homesickness. Selfies of Clay at the Wild Things baseball park. Of Clay on Washington's Main Street. Of Clay in front of the house they'd shared.

And a couple photos of Clay with his arm draped around the shoulders of a gorgeous redhead.

Not Emma. She had to scroll way back to find pictures with her in them. She returned to more recent posts of the couple. Apparently, he still had a thing for flaming red hair.

Good. As long as it wasn't *her* red hair, she was fine.

Emma returned to the most recent post and checked the date. Two weeks ago. She'd have been happier if it had shown him a hundred and fifty miles away yesterday. Still, those pictures of Clay and the redhead eased her mind. She'd been praying he'd find someone else to obsess over. Emma didn't recognize the woman or her name. When she clicked on it, the page that came up, unlike Nell's and Clay's, had stiffer privacy settings, blocking Emma from learning more. Not that she cared. But seeing the words "In a relationship with Clay Bauer" would've been worthy of a celebration. She'd have to settle for the sight of Clay and the redhead looking like they were in love.

And not in Erie.

Satisfied, Emma closed the tab. Part of her wanted to close the new account as well, but on the off-chance Nell might see and recognize the friend request, Emma left it.

Her phone rang, giving her a momentary jolt of adrenaline, but caller ID showed Eric Baker, her friend from back home. He probably wanted to know when she was going to send him more tombstone photos.

She hit the green button. "Hey, Eric."

"Hi." He sounded quiet, almost cautious. "How are you?" Not the casual, generic greeting. His voice carried a note of genuine concern.

"I'm good. How about you?"

After a long moment of hesitation, he said, "I gather you haven't heard the news."

A litany of horrible developments raced through her mind, most involving Nell or Clay. "What news?"

"There's been a fire. At your grandparents' old farmhouse. It's gone, Emma. Burnt to the ground."

She was glad she was already seated. She'd grown up in that house. Three generations. Her mom's parents. Her mom and dad. Nell and her. Plus, cattle, horses, and chickens inhabited the farm. It had been a fabulous childhood. Grandma left them first when a stroke took her unexpectedly on New Year's Day years ago. Grandpap developed cancer and died five years later. Her dad sold the cattle and chickens. And eventually, against Nell's and Emma's wishes, even the horses. Shortly after that, he'd decided the large and ancient farmhouse was too much work and he'd built a smaller bungalow on the property. That was when Emma and Nell started talking about someday converting the big house into a bed and breakfast. They'd even had discussions with a banker about a business loan.

Then came the tragedy that claimed her folks and Nell's subsequent spiral into drugs and alcohol.

Three years ago, Emma had met Clay and he moved into the bungalow with her. The farmhouse remained empty but was still in her name. Clay decided the smaller house was cramped. The farmhouse too decrepit. Without consulting her, he bought a new house. When she'd been at work, he packed her stuff and moved her into their home. She'd rebelled. Refused to unpack, determined to move back into the bungalow her dad built.

Then it mysteriously burned down.

Now here she was in Erie. The farmhouse, while vacant, remained Emma's anchor. It symbolized family, roots, and better times. She dreamed of being able to return eventually. Emma *and* Nell.

Emma finally found her voice. "Gone?"

"The chimneys and foundation are still standing. Sort of. Nothing else. Emma, I am so sorry."

"How?" She tried to block her first thought. The most obvious. The bungalow fire had been determined to be arson, but no one was ever arrested. Although Clay had a solid alibi, Emma never believed he was innocent. Before she'd left, she made sure the power was cut off to the old farmhouse to prevent an electrical fire like the one they'd squelched a decade ago. Most of the structure had been rewired, but some old knob and tube wiring remained.

"I don't know. I'll try to reach someone at the fire department and find out for you."

Another even more devastating thought crossed her mind. Nell. Had she gone home? "When did this happen?"

"Sunday night. Or early yesterday morning, I guess."

Emma exhaled. Nell's missed call had come in after noon on Monday. She wasn't in the house when it burned. Emma still had to ask, "You haven't seen or heard from my sister, have you?"

"No. I'm sorry."

She hadn't really expected he would.

"There's one other thing…"

She waited.

"The fire investigator might need to be in touch with you since you're the owner on record. I know you didn't leave any kind of contact information." Eric fell silent. When he spoke again, he asked, "How do you want me to handle it?"

The question brought a resurgence of the same paranoia she always suffered at the thought of someone needing to contact her. Would giving her location away bring Clay to her door?

She covered her face with her free hand and tried to think. "I'll get back to you. If anyone asks, tell them you'll see what you can find out. Or something to that effect." She lifted her head from her palm. "But don't give out this number or my email address."

"Got it. You'll need to get in touch with your insurance company too."

If Clay had something to do with the inferno, he would be anticipating that phone call. "I'll deal with that later," Emma said.

"Gotcha. I'll be in touch as soon as I know anything about the cause of the fire."

She thanked him and ended the call. Gazing beyond her computer and out the windows, she watched her campground neighbor across the road as he washed down his RV. What she visualized was her childhood on the farm. Her family. Her home.

And now it was all gone.

Home, even in her dreams, no longer existed.

Chapter Thirteen

After lunch, Matthias returned to his desk and checked his voicemail. Most of the messages needed a follow-up call although none were urgent. One piqued his curiosity. A state cop from Troop E station in Crawford County asked Matthias to contact him, stating he might have information on a missing van.

Matthias punched the trooper's name and number into his phone and identified himself when the trooper answered.

"I understand you have a BOLO out on a van involved in a homicide?"

"That's correct."

A heavy sigh filtered through the phone's speaker. "I'm afraid we have your van—or what's left of it. We discovered it on a backroad late Friday night."

"Do you have it in your impound? I can be there within an hour."

"It's in impound, but I doubt it will be much help in your case."

"Why not?"

"Our arson investigator has already gone over it."

"Arson investigator?"

"Your van was torched."

Torched was an understatement.

Matthias and Cassie stood in the Troop E evidence garage staring at the bones of a van laid bare of paint and with little more than springs and metal framing where the seats had been. The area around the blackened vehicle reeked of smoke and burnt chemicals.

"Why are we only now seeing this?" Matthias asked, as much to himself as to anyone else.

"The report of a vehicle fire out on a deserted stretch of Williamson Road came in late Friday night," the arson investigator, a trooper by the name of DeLuca, said. He looked at his notes. "Twenty-two thirty-nine to be exact."

Almost twenty minutes to eleven.

"By the time the fire department arrived, the vehicle was fully involved. The license plate had been removed. It wasn't until we received your BOLO and the VIN matched that we made the connection to your case."

Cassie had buried her nose in the crook of her elbow but lowered her arm to ask, "Anybody inside?"

"No, thank goodness. I found traces of an accelerant, probably gasoline, both inside and out. There were also traces of charred fabric—possibly clothing—in the cargo area, and I do mean *charred*."

Matthias pressed a handkerchief to his nose, trying to block the stench. "Don't suppose you found any artwork, electronics, or jewelry."

"No. Of that, I'm sure. We did find a knife though."

Matthias shot a look at his partner. "What kind of knife?"

DeLuca removed his phone from his pocket. After tapping on the screen, he turned it over to Matthias. "The blade measured three and a half inches long and seven eighths of an inch wide."

Matthias studied the photo of a blackened knife with its scorched handle, aware of Cassie thumbing through her notebook.

She stopped on the page she'd searched for. "Coroner's report states the murder weapon's blade was roughly three and a half inches long and just under an inch wide." She met Matthias's gaze. "Sounds like a match."

He turned the phone so she could see. "A lot of good it does us."

DeLuca reclaimed his cell. "I'll send you all the photos and my report. And as soon as the lab gets done processing the fabric, I'll send that report too."

Cassie thanked him, and he walked away. She elbowed Matthias. "Let's get outta here."

Clear of the building, he drank in the fresh air. Cassie went into a coughing fit.

"That was rank," she said once she caught her breath.

He couldn't argue the point but said, "You never so much as wrinkle your nose during an autopsy."

"I'm used to that. But the chemical smell of a fire chokes me."

Back in the car, Matthias sat behind the wheel without

reaching for the key. "Well, this throws a wrench in our timeline."

Cassie pondered his statement. "Maybe."

He looked over at her. "You're the one who's been convinced Joe Platt is behind this. He couldn't be in two places at one time. We know he arrived at his camp at quarter after five. If the report of the fire came in when it did, he's not the one who drove."

"Are we certain he never left the campground again later that evening?"

Matthias thought back to his interview with Emma and Joe. She'd confirmed his arrival time, but Matthias hadn't asked what she'd seen later because she'd been at the cemetery. "Certain? No." He needed to follow up with the photographer and check with their other neighbors.

"It doesn't matter. He may not have been behind the wheel, but that's not to say he wasn't in on it. Hell, he might've been the one calling the shots."

Matthias ran her scenario through his brain. Cassie's theory put the puzzle pieces together, but it felt like she was using a sledgehammer to make them fit. He started the car and aimed it north. "None of this feels right. We're missing something."

"No argument there," she replied.

A little over an hour later, they were back at the station, standing in front of a whiteboard, each with a marker in hand.

On the far right of the board, Matthias had scrawled the details of Saturday morning's discovery of Wesley Simmons's body. From there, they worked backward. Friday's break-in, Wesley giving chase, and his car found at Erie Sand and Gravel.

They went further into the past, jotting notes about the

victim's financial problems and listing Joe Platt and Barbara Simmons. Joe's alibi had holes big enough to sail the USS *Brig Niagara* through it. Barbara? Speaking with her again was at the top of the to-do list.

Matthias really hoped she wasn't involved. Those two kids had already lost one parent. But he was well aware the reason spouses always topped the suspect list was because they were often guilty.

He stepped back and studied the board. "You know why I'm not buying into this whole Wesley, Barbara, and Platt triangle?"

Cassie capped her marker. "Why?"

Matthias stepped up to the board again and wrote Tuesday at the top center, circling it twice. "Because we keep getting away from the fact the Simmons robbery wasn't the first."

"Okay." Cassie moved to her cubicle and, without taking a seat, pulled up another set of police reports. "The call for that one came in at seventeen twenty-one Tuesday afternoon."

Twenty-one minutes after five.

"The reporting party was Debra Ingram, the homeowner."

Matthias knew all that. He and Cassie had been there and done the interviews. The house on Pepperwood Circle was larger than the Simmons place on South Shore Drive and boasted more acreage but lacked a lakeside location. Despite remembering the house and family well, he let her continue with the recap to refresh his memory and perhaps catch something he'd overlooked.

Just like the Simmons robbery, three armed assailants entered while the security system was disarmed. The parents stated, like Barbara, the kids were running in and out. A fourth masked assailant stood guard at the door.

"Which security company?" Matthias asked.

"Beldon Security."

"No link there."

"A lot of people with burglar alarms leave them turned off. Go figure."

"What was taken?"

Cassie fired off a list of computers, gaming systems, several antique rifles, quite a few pieces of expensive jewelry, and four museum-quality paintings. She blew a low whistle.

"What?" Matthias asked.

"One of the pieces was a Van Gogh. Real. Not a reproduction." She kept reading. "The family's cell phones were all destroyed. The haul was loaded directly from the garage into the back of a white van. No descriptions of the assailants beyond they were masked and carrying big guns."

"What are the odds these are two different crews?" Matthias asked sarcastically.

"I think we're safe in assuming the two robberies were pulled off by the same assailants."

"What I'd like to know is if there are any ties between the Simmons family and the Ingrams."

Cassie straightened. "I'll do some preliminary digging on that. Then, let's pay visits to Barbara Simmons and Debra Ingram."

Linking the two families would've been a huge leap forward on the case, but Cassie found nothing obvious.

They debated who to visit first. Cassie pushed for the Ingrams. "They only lost personal property, not a family member. I'd like to know if they happen to have dealings with Fort Niagara Investments before we chat with Barbara."

Debra Ingram and her husband, Grant, invited Matthias and Cassie into a grand living room with vaulted ceilings and lots of polished wood.

"We heard on the news about that family up on the lake." Debra settled on the couch next to her husband and took his hand. "How horrible. Having those awful people come into our house, tie us up, and take our possessions was bad enough. The thought of losing my husband too?" Damp-eyed, she looked at Grant. "I can't even fathom what that would be like."

"How are your kids?" Cassie asked.

"Traumatized. Like us. But they seem to be bouncing back reasonably well. The boys are actually enjoying themselves, shopping for a new gaming system." She offered a weak smile. "I'm making them wait until the insurance check comes in. They already think dear old dad is made of money. It'll do them good to learn delayed gratification."

Matthias made a note and wondered about her words. Have your outdated electronics stolen. Get paid. Buy all new stuff. It sounded a lot like Cassie's insurance fraud suspicions regarding Wesley.

Cassie perched on the edge of an overstuffed chair. "I was hoping you'd be willing to answer some questions. Now that we have a second incident, we're trying to find out if there are any links between you and the Simmons family that might assist us in locating the culprits."

"Of course. We'll do anything to help. What do you want to know?"

Matthias kept notes while Cassie asked questions. None of

the answers offered much. The Ingram boys went to different schools than the Simmons kids. Debra promised to ask them specifically about Jake and Belle when they got home. Matthias had little hope. The Ingrams' children were several years younger and wouldn't likely cross paths at school functions. Nor did they share any sports or after-school activities.

Matthias had already taken notice of the Beldon Security placards out on the lawn, but Cassie mentioned the company anyway. "How long have you had your security system?"

The couple exchanged looks, clearly trying to count. "Gosh, I don't know. Ten, maybe fifteen, years?"

Matthias wondered, although Cassie didn't ask, how long they'd been leaving it turned off when they were home.

"Have you ever done business with Fort Niagara Investments?" Cassie asked.

"No," Grant Ingram said. "My sister's husband takes care of our stock portfolios. He works at Prominent Financial."

"Wait." Debra tapped him on the knee. "Before your sister met him, we were with another firm. Remember? When we were first married. Which one was that?"

"Great Lakes Trust."

"Oh, that's right."

Something sparked in the back of Matthias's memory. Before Cassie could ask her next question, he said, "Do either of you know anyone by the name of Joe or Joseph Platt?"

They looked at each other scowling before shaking their heads. "I don't believe so," Debra said.

Cassie continued down her list of questions. What church they attended. What fitness and country clubs they belonged to. Even what restaurants they frequented. She finished up by asking if they might have remembered anything about the men who had entered their home and tied them up.

"I'm afraid not," Grant said. "All I recall is the big black gun the one man aimed at my face."

Debra shivered. "And I only remember the big chrome one another guy was pointing at my boys."

Cassie thanked the couple for their time. As they returned to their vehicle, Matthias pulled out his phone, opened his search engine, and typed in Great Lakes Trust.

"What are you doing?" she asked when he continued to scroll, clicking a couple of dead-end links before finding the information he wanted.

"Ingram said they'd once had their investments with Great Lakes Trust."

"So?"

Matthias handed her his phone. "Great Lakes Trust hasn't been in business under that name in quite a while. I didn't want to say anything until I double-checked in case I was remembering wrong. Great Lakes Trust was part of a big merger sixteen years ago." He aimed a thumb at the phone in Cassie's hand before turning the key and starting the car. "After the merger, they were renamed—"

Cassie finished his sentence. "Fort Niagara Investments."

A pale and haggard Barbara Simmons greeted them at the door. "Have you caught the men who killed my husband?"

"Not yet," Cassie said. "Could we come in and ask you a few more questions?"

Barbara leaned on one side of the doorframe and placed a

hand on the opposite side, blocking their entrance. "What kind of questions? I've already told you all I know, which is nothing."

"There was another home invasion a few days before yours—"

"You mean you could've prevented all this from happening if you'd only done your jobs and caught those bastards after their first heist?"

Matthias tensed, partly because he couldn't argue with her.

"We've spoken with the other victims and hope to find a common denominator between their activities and yours that might lead us to the suspects."

"You're blaming my activities, my lifestyle, for what happened?"

Matthias leaned forward, wanting to calm Barbara down, but Cassie stopped him with a hand on his arm.

"We're not blaming you or anyone, Mrs. Simmons," Cassie said, her voice slipping deeper into her soothing mother-hen tone. "We're just trying to catch whoever killed your husband and stop these men before they strike again."

Barbara continued to barricade the doorway but appeared to consider Cassie's words.

"I know you don't want something like this to happen to anyone else and their family."

Barbara's shoulders sagged. She dropped her arm and stepped aside. "Come in. But I don't have much time. I have a funeral to plan."

They gathered in the kitchen where Matthias and Cassie had broken the news about Wesley three days earlier. Cassie asked about the children.

"How do you think they are?" Barbara snapped. "They've lost their dad. They're distraught. So am I."

Cassie went through the same questions she'd asked the Ingrams. The Simmons family attended a different church, didn't belong to a country club, did belong to a fitness club but a different one than Debra had named.

"How long have you used Safe At Home as your security company?" Cassie asked.

"About three years."

Matthias paused, his pen at the ready.

"What about before that?"

She named a well-known national company.

Matthias cleared his throat. "Have you ever used Beldon?"

"No." Barbara's frown deepened. "Why?"

"Like we told you. We're trying to find a common denominator."

"And have you?"

"Not yet."

Cassie leaned on the kitchen island, striking a casual pose. "Who took care of the family finances?"

Matthias caught the faintest twitch at the corner of Barbara's right eye. "Wesley did. That's one more thing that'll fall to me now."

"Did he ever use Prominent Financial?"

"No. Why?"

Cassie offered a tight smile. "As I said, we're looking for common denominators."

Barbara's expression relaxed.

"What about Fort Niagara?"

The eased tension was short lived. Barbara's jaw clenched. "Wesley would never go through my father's company."

"How about Great Lakes Trust?" Matthias asked.

Barbara turned her scowl on him. "I just told you. Wesley would've never dealt with a company my father worked at."

Matthias hadn't expected that response. "Your father worked for Great Lakes Trust?"

"Right up until the merger. That's when he moved to Fort Niagara."

As Matthias scribbled a note, Cassie asked, "Did your husband consult with you on money decisions?"

"Never," she said quickly. Too quickly.

"Were you aware that he'd lost considerable money in recent months?"

"He mentioned a few investments had fallen through."

"Did he mention he'd missed the last five payments on the house? And on his Audi?"

Barbara's expression darkened. "What are you implying?"

Cassie opened both palms upward. "I'm just trying to get to know the victim."

"The victim?" Barbara slammed her hands down on the counter. "The victim, as you call him, had a name. Wesley. And Wesley was a fine man. I won't have you suggesting that he's in any way at fault in this."

In the middle of the tirade, Matthias caught a glimpse of sixteen-year-old Belle and fourteen-year-old Jake peering into the kitchen from the next room but making no move to come closer.

"You cops are just like my father. Blaming my husband for everything bad that's ever happened. I won't have it. I simply won't allow it anymore. Not from him. And definitely not from you." Barbara stepped back and extended one arm, pointing toward the front of the house. "I've answered all the questions I intend to. Now leave."

Matthias closed his notebook and slid it back into his pocket.

As he and Cassie headed toward the door, Barbara shouted after them, "You can direct any future questions to my attorney."

Chapter Fourteen

E mma created a new email account, something she should've done months ago. While she'd closed down all her old accounts, she'd only opened a new one under Lake Erie Photography for business purposes. Now she opened one as Rebecca Manderley for everything else. She connected to her VPN before emailing Eric and directing him to give the new address to anyone who needed to reach her regarding the fire.

Late afternoon, she slung the duffel bag containing her camera and lighting equipment over one shoulder and lugged it to her Subaru. The stillness surprised her. Mick's car remained absent. How far did he have to go to buy new batteries? He could be adding to his stash of booze for his campfire as well. A real possibility.

Emma climbed into her Forester and nosed it down the hill.

Finding a parking spot near Namaste Erie Yoga was harder than it had been yesterday. She circled a two-block stretch three times before lucking out as an SUV relinquished its spot. She parallel-parked, a skill she was rather proud of, especially considering she'd spent the majority of her life on the farm, grabbed her gear, and hoofed it the block and a half to the studio.

Kira had rounded up four of her students for the photo shoot. Emma remembered seeing two of them in the class she'd taken. Then they'd been bare faced. Now, they and the others wore makeup and yoga gear that looked newly purchased. An ancient movie quote echoed in Emma's mind.

I'm ready for my close-up.

Kira looked especially stunning in a violet unitard that showed all of her curves, topped with a flowing translucent tunic that hung to her knees and floated around her as she crossed the yoga room, setting out blankets, blocks, and other props next to each mat.

Emma set up her portable studio lights and checked the lighting with her meter. It had been a while since she'd done a shoot like this, and she missed it.

The students were natural born models. And yoginis. Emma photographed all five of the women, simulating a real class. She staged scenes of Kira working with one of the students as if adjusting a pose. One of the women gracefully kicked up into a handstand with Kira nearby, acting as if ready to catch her if she wobbled.

Had Emma attempted such a pose, she'd never have gotten up. And if she had, she'd probably have gone all the way over and landed on her back.

Finally, each student posed in her favorite asana as Emma shot away. Kira was last, striking several arm balances before back bending all the way over until her hands reached the floor, arched into what Emma knew as wheel pose.

Nell had been able to do all of those asanas. Emma? Not so much.

When Kira was satisfied they'd captured enough images for her advertising purposes, the students grabbed bottles of water and left, their laughter lingering behind them.

Kira led the way to the reception area at the front of the studio. "That was fun." She handed another bottle to Emma. "I can't wait to see the finished result."

Emma set her Nikon on the counter and patted it. "I'll work on them tonight. I won't have to do a lot of Photoshopping, so I should be able to send you the files sometime tomorrow."

"Sounds good." Kira checked the clock on the wall. "I have dinner plans tonight, but you're welcome to join us."

Emma took a long swig from the water bottle and waved the idea away. "Thanks, but I'll pass. I have plans myself." A lie, but she didn't want to be a third wheel.

Kira leaned on the counter and watched as Emma packed her gear. "I had a visit earlier from the cops about the body you found on the beach."

Emma looked up. "That's my fault, I'm afraid. I was showing them the picture I shot, and they spotted the one I'd taken of you. They asked for your contact information. I'm sorry."

"Don't be. I don't know if it was the same two detectives you talked to—"

"Tall black woman with short white hair and a dark-haired man?"

Kira sipped water and nodded. Swallowing, she said, "That's them." Her voice took on a sultry note. "Detective Matthias Honeywell. What a hottie."

Emma choked. "Hottie?"

"Oh, hell yeah." Kira tipped her head. "Don't tell me you didn't notice."

Emma conjured up an image of the detective. That fierce glare at the cemetery and again when he'd been dealing with Mick. The hint of a grin when she'd asked if she needed an alibi for Friday night, knowing *he* was the alibi. "I guess he's okay. I'm not exactly on the hunt for a man right now, so I didn't pay attention."

"You're in a committed relationship?"

She laughed. "More like I *was* in a relationship with a man who should've been committed."

"Ah. I hear ya, sister." Kira held out her bottle. Emma tapped her own to it. Not quite a clinking toast. "What'd he do? Cheat on you?"

"Among other things." Emma didn't want to risk summoning the devil by talking about him. "What about you? Married?"

"Now, I just told you Detective Matthias Honeywell was a hottie. Does that sound like I'm married?"

"Married doesn't mean dead."

Kira erupted into laughter. "I like you. You're right about that."

"Your dinner plans tonight … big date?"

Kira waggled her eyebrows suggestively. "If he's lucky. A guy I met at a teacher training a few months back. I told him to look me up if he was ever in the area, and he did." She drained the bottle. "So how long's it been since you and the jerk broke up?"

"Three months." Emma eased her Nikon into its slot in the bag and zipped it closed.

"What happened?"

The question rang in her head. What *hadn't* happened? "I better get going. You have a date, and I have work to do."

"You don't wanna talk about him. I get it. Maybe some evening over a bottle of wine. Or two."

"Maybe."

Emma hoisted the bag onto her shoulder. Kira followed her to the door. "Talk to you tomorrow?"

"I'll call as soon as I have the files ready for you."

"Great." Kira held the door for her. "I'll spring for lunch."

Emma heard the click of the lock once she was outside. Clouds had moved in and carried the promise of rain. She hoped it held off until she hiked the block and a half back to her car. No sooner had she slammed the Subaru's lift gate than the first fat drops splatted on her head, shoulders, car, and sidewalk. She slid behind the wheel seconds ahead of the deluge.

She sat there watching the rivulets stream down her windshield, making trails in the dust.

She liked Kira. The purple-haired yoga instructor had a way of making her and the other students laugh. Right up until she'd asked about Clay. Granted, she had no way of knowing what all he'd put Emma through. Cheating boyfriends were one thing. Men who threatened—no, *promised* —harm were quite another.

Emma sat at her kitchen table, a takeout salad at her elbow, viewing her afternoon's work on the larger computer screen. She'd been right about not needing much in the way of Photoshopping the images. Not only was Kira photogenic, but she'd also chosen lithe yoga students who were equally so. The thought crossed Emma's mind that older, less flexible potential clients of both sexes might be intimidated if all of Kira's promotional material featured these young women.

Marketing wasn't Emma's bailiwick and how Kira used the photographs wasn't any of Emma's business, but she might mention it the next time they spoke.

Emma's phone rang. She checked the screen, which identified the incoming caller as *ErieNOW*. Again.

"Emma," said an enthusiastic voice, "this is Rudy Springstein. How are you today?"

Not interested in small talk, she ignored the question. "What can I do for you, Rudy?"

"I'm calling again about that photograph."

She'd feared as much.

"I've been authorized to up our offer to seven fifty. My boss says he appreciates a woman who knows how to play hardball."

For once, she was glad of the other two offers, even though she'd turned them down. "Sorry, Rudy. Yours is the low bid."

"Really? Okay. What's the high bid?"

"Twenty-five hundred." She imagined his jaw dropping and grinned. "To be honest, he told me to name my price."

"Who offered you that kind of money?" Rudy's voice had turned sharp.

"I'm not giving away that information."

"You said it was a bid. You haven't sold the image yet, have you?"

"I'm still trying to decide what price I want to name." Rudy didn't need to know she had no intention of selling the picture.

"Listen to me, honey. I'll make that same offer. Name your

price. But there's an expiration date. Right now, the case has slipped from the front page. The minute the police make an arrest, it'll be page one, above the fold. That's where your photo will be. After that, no one will care, and no one will pay you one red cent for it."

The idea of that damned picture being of no interest to anyone suited Emma just fine. While messing with Rudy's head had been fun, she was tired of the game. "Then I guess it'll be my loss." She tapped the red button and set the phone down.

As before, Rudy called back immediately.

She considered blocking the number, but she didn't want to completely cut ties with the news outlet. Although she might have already.

Chapter Fifteen

"Joe Platt worked at Great Lakes Trust," Cassie mused as she drove them back to the station.

Matthias glanced over at his partner but didn't comment. It was the look in Jake's and Belle's eyes as they'd peered into the kitchen from the other room that occupied the bulk of Matthias's thoughts. Not their grandfather.

"The man works in finance," Cassie continued. "Has for a long time. It shouldn't come as a surprise to learn he's dealt with more than one financial institution."

And yet it had.

When Matthias still didn't say anything, she shot a look his way. "You're being awfully quiet."

"I'm thinking."

"Care to share?"

"Not yet." He needed to let the whirlwind in his brain settle.

They were too focused on Wesley's homicide and not enough on the home invasion. From the beginning, Cassie fixated on Wesley as something more than a wannabe hero. Had he not gotten loose and followed the van to his death, the investigation would've gone in a much different direction.

Cassie still wanted to delve into Wesley's financial troubles, but Matthias decided to remove that part of the case from the equation.

Back at Major Crimes, he checked his messages. Nothing yet from the arson investigator. Lyle and Kollmann were checking area pawn shops and known fences for the stolen items and had left a text stating they'd come up empty so far.

Matthias heard a growl rise from his own throat. What they needed was a break. A breadcrumb to give them direction.

On the trip back from South Shore Drive, a niggling concern had started an itch in the back of his brain. This crew was slick. Hit a home with valuable artwork. One that hadn't armed its security system. Avoid neighboring cameras. Back the van up to the garage door to load the stolen merchandise. Get in, get out, fast. These guys weren't amateurs. They were too polished, too practiced for the Ingram heist to have been their first job.

He shook off the frustration and pulled up the PACIC—Pennsylvania Criminal Intelligence Center—database on his computer. He entered key aspects of two Erie thefts into the search bar, focusing on high-end residences with security systems and four-man crews using a van as a get-away vehicle. Matthias almost deleted that last part. The white van had been stolen recently and was now little more than a scorched steel frame. He decided to leave it, adding "stolen" to the van's description.

For his first run, he limited his search parameters to northwest Pennsylvania. The two matches that came up didn't quite fit and were too far in the past. A second search for the entire state wasn't helpful either.

"Dammit," he muttered.

Before trying again, he expanded into neighboring states, New York and Ohio. While the computer did its thing, he rose, stretched, and ambled into the break room to fill his cup with the dark, thick dregs left heating in the coffee urn. The bitter taste choked him. He dumped the rest of the cup down the drain, pulled the plug, and proceeded to make a new batch.

While the coffee brewed, he returned to his desk and found six cases had come up in his search results. Expecting more old cases that didn't fit, he started reading. By the time he finished the first three reports, his scalp was tingling. After studying all six, he called out to Cassie. "You need to see this."

He rolled aside, giving her room to view his monitor. "Back in March there were three home invasions in Buffalo, New York, all within a few days of each other. Each home was valued at just under or around a million dollars. Each home had a security system that was disarmed at the time. The families in all three cases were gathered into one room by armed assailants and left tied up. In all cases, there was a four-man crew, three inside the house, one standing guard at the door. The stolen merchandise included artwork of considerable value, none of which has been recovered." He looked over his shoulder at his partner. "Sound familiar?"

Cassie's eyes narrowed to slits, her jaw clenched.

He returned his gaze to the monitor and scrolled down. "Last month, there were three home invasions in Cleveland, Ohio. Expensive homes. Disarmed security systems. Armed assailants tying up family members. Four-man crews. Expensive paintings. Merchandise not yet recovered."

"Why are we only now hearing about this?" Cassie asked, her voice an angry whisper.

He didn't mention that she'd been laser-focused on the homicide instead of the robberies. "I got to thinking about how slick these guys were. They aren't new to the game. I figured they must have been doing this sort of thing for a while."

She didn't say anything but leaned closer to study the monitor.

"Another thing I noticed. They hit three houses within a few days and then drop off the map before the police can get a handle on them. They lay low for a couple of weeks and hit again in another city."

"Cities along Lake Erie."

"Now they're here." Matthias's chest tightened as he put another piece into his puzzle. "They hit the Ingrams a week ago today. They hit the Simmons place last Friday." He looked up and saw Cassie making the same connection.

"If they stay true to form, they're going to hit one more house and then vanish."

"And they're going to hit it soon."

She leveled her dark eyes on him. "And now that they've already escalated to murder, there's no stopping them from taking more extreme measures at their next target."

"Which could happen as soon as tonight."

"Shit." She wiped a hand across her mouth. "Wait. What security companies did all these other victims use?"

Matthias wheeled closer to his keyboard and typed, bringing up the full reports. "Buffalo. The first one was Beldon. The second one was Sentry Home Security. The third..." He clicked to the next page. "Safe At Home."

"Two out of three," Cassie said, her voice tight.

"In Cleveland…" Matthias clicked again. "The first one was Safe At Home, the second was Sentry Home, and the third was—"

Cassie didn't wait for him to say it. "Beldon."

"Give the lady a gold star." He pivoted to face her, crossing his arms.

"I wonder how many homes in and around Erie use Sentry Home Security. Has to be in the hundreds. We can't possibly patrol them all."

He shook his head. "We can't rely on them holding to that pattern. Yes, there's obviously a link with these three companies. But I don't think we should assume they won't hit the same security system twice."

"Shit," she said again. "Okay. We put the word out to the media that we have a home invasion crew likely targeting homes with one of these three systems. Tell people to be sure and lock their doors and keep their systems armed."

Matthias thought about it. "We can't possibly reach everyone. Those we do reach are going to panic, risking more homeowners not only arming their systems but arming themselves." He thought about another armed "hero" and shuddered, forcing his mind into the present. "Not to mention the potential fallout from those three security companies."

"I don't give a damn about legal fallout."

Truthfully, Matthias didn't either, but he preferred to still have a job at the end of the day. Lawsuits against the city and the department weren't conducive to career advancement.

She must've been reading his mind. "I'll run it past the LT first, but if he gives it the all-clear, I'm calling the local news outlets."

"I'm going to dig into the three companies and try to find

the common denominator. Maybe they're all under the same corporate umbrella with the same person overseeing them." It was as big of a long shot as trying to predict where the assailants would strike next, but there had to be something tying them all together.

"We should also contact Buffalo's and Cleveland's police. Maybe one of their victims got a better description of the assailants than ours have."

They needed to find answers, and they needed them fast.

Lieutenant Armstrong put the kibosh on singling out the three security companies. Too much concern over it just being a coincidence. Ever the diplomatic leader, rather than suggest potential lawsuits, he voiced concerns over giving families with other home systems a false sense of security. Instead, he agreed to release a statement that all Erie area residents should use caution, lock doors and windows, keep garage doors closed, and report any suspicious activity. He told Cassie and Matthias the warning should automatically encourage everyone who had an alarm system to keep it on.

While Cassie searched for a link tying the three companies, Matthias placed calls to the two other police departments. A Detective Patrick Flynn from Cleveland responded quickly.

"I'm returning your call about the home invasions." Flynn said the moment Matthias identified himself. From the detective's tone, Matthias sensed the Cleveland cases irked Flynn as much as the Erie one vexed him. "Don't suppose you've located any of our stolen merchandise?"

"Sorry. No."

Flynn swore. "We haven't recovered one damn thing from those heists, and the one family lost several heirlooms. Valuable, yes, but priceless to them. Anyway, what can I do for you, Detective Honeywell?"

"I'm working on a pair of home invasions here that sound an awful lot like yours." Matthias ran down the details of the homes, the victims, and the disarmed security systems.

"They do sound alike. Especially the disarmed security systems and the artwork. One of the victims lost four high-priced paintings. The other two lost a couple of bronzes, including a James Earle Fraser."

Matthias tried to place the name.

"He's the guy who did 'The End of the Trail'."

That's why the name sounded familiar. "Wow." Matthias's grandfather back in Oklahoma had owned and cherished a reproduction of the exhausted horse and Native American. "Any descriptions on the suspects?"

"Not much. It's amazing how having a gun stuck in your face or aimed at your child draws a victim's attention away from the asshole holding the weapon."

"That's all I've been hearing. They wore hoodies and ski masks and carried *big* guns."

Papers shuffled on the other end of the line before Flynn spoke again. "We got a little more than that. Two of our witnesses agreed at least one of the weapons was a chrome revolver."

Matthias jotted a note.

"They also agreed that two of the assailants were black and one of the white males was much taller than the rest and rail-thin. One witness actually referred to him as a 'string bean'."

"Anything else?"

173

"Just that if you catch these guys, give me a call. I hate being skunked. Sons of bitches. No sooner did we realize the same crew was responsible for the first two robberies than they hit the third house and vanished. I always wondered where they went. Now I know."

By midnight, Cassie had gone home to her family, and Matthias was struggling to concentrate despite losing count of how many cups of coffee he'd consumed. Breathing a little easier since no new home invasion reports had come in, he gave up and went home to his apartment.

Sleep came in fits and starts, filled with nightmares of gun-toting homeowners and armed robbers, Matthias trying to determine who was who.

His phone's ringtones brought him wide awake but confused. What time was it? Six o'clock. A number showed up on his caller ID but no name.

"Detective Honeywell," he said, his voice ragged from sleep.

He could hear a soft breath, but the caller didn't speak.

He cleared his throat and tried again, softer. "Hello?"

"Hello. This is Belle Simmons. You spoke with me and my brother the day my dad..." The girl's voice trailed off.

Matthias sat up, swinging his feet to the floor. "Yes, Belle. I remember. What can I do for you?"

"You told me I should call if I thought of anything."

"I did."

"I think maybe ... I might have noticed something during the robbery. It's probably nothing."

"Let me decide that. What did you notice?"

There was muffled background noise and what sounded like Jake yelling. "I can't talk now. Can I meet you later this morning?"

"Absolutely. Do you want me to come to your house?"

"No. Do you know Sara's Restaurant?"

He smiled, aware it would come across in his voice. "Of course I know Sara's. *Everyone* knows Sara's."

The smile worked. Belle sounded more relaxed. "Good. Can you meet me there around ten?"

"See you then."

She thanked him quickly and hung up.

Matthias set the phone down. He remembered thinking Belle knew something that afternoon at their house. Maybe … just maybe … she could give them the break he'd been praying for.

He found Cassie already at her desk looking battle weary. "Did you get any sleep?" he asked.

"Not really." She lifted her gaze to study him. "You?"

"If nightmares count as sleep."

"I know what you mean."

He told her about his early morning call from Belle Simmons and she perked up.

"Did she give you any hint of what she saw?"

"I heard her brother in the background and got the impression she didn't want him to know who she was speaking to."

Cassie's phone rang and she snatched it from her desk. "It's

Buffalo PD," she told him before answering. She put her cell on speaker and identified herself and Matthias.

"This is Sergeant Atkinson returning your call. How can I help you?"

"We have a few questions about the three home invasions you had back in March," she said.

"What about them?"

Cassie glanced at Matthias then back at her phone. "We've had two robberies here with a very similar MO. Is there anything you can tell us beyond what was in the PACIC report?"

"This crew was good. Damn good. Did their homework. Knew which homes contained big-ticket pieces of art. And they knew where all the nearby cameras were and stayed out of their line of sight."

"What about security systems?" Matthias asked.

"Each home had one, but the families had disarmed them at the time. In all three cases, family members were gathered into one room and were tied up by armed assailants."

"How many?" Cassie asked.

"Four. Three inside the house, one standing guard at the door. Sound like your crew?"

Cassie's jaw clenched. "Little bit. Yeah."

Matthias leaned closer to the phone. "You said the homes had disarmed security systems."

"Yeah, but no links between them. The first home used Beldon. The second one was Safe At Home. The third was Sentry."

Matthias met Cassie's hard gaze.

When neither of them spoke, Atkinson broke the silence. "I gather you know something I don't."

"Those companies may not be a link between the victims," Cassie said, "but they do link the crimes."

"You may want to get in touch with Detective Sergeant Patrick Flynn with Cleveland PD," Matthias said. "They had what we assume is the same crew there last month."

"I'll do that."

"One more thing," Matthias said. "Did any of your victims give you a description of the suspects?"

"All were wearing black hoodies and ski masks. Only one witness gave us anything useful. He specifically said all the handguns were black semi-automatics. He also stated all four men were white, tall with broad shoulders, and reminded him of the Marines he'd served with."

Cassie shot a look at Matthias. "Thank you for your time, Sergeant. We'll keep you posted on our investigation."

"Please do. And catch these assholes before they use those guns and kill someone."

Matthias exhaled. "Too late."

"Thanks, Sergeant," Cassie said. "I appreciate the information." She ended the call and swiveled to face Matthias, but before she could say anything, her phone rang again. She snatched it from her desk. "It's Alissa," she told him before answering. "Hi, baby."

Matthias let her talk to her granddaughter and headed for the break room to refill his cup with black crud from the urn. At least it had been replenished since the batch he'd made last night.

Cassie was still on the phone when he returned to his desk. She glanced his way. "We'll talk about it when I get home, okay? Love you, baby." She ended the call. "I forgot how much fun it is raising kids," she said sarcastically.

"She still getting bullied?"

"No, thank God. My talk with her counselor seems to have done the trick."

Cassie's scowl didn't reflect the relief Matthias would've expected. "What is it then?"

"Now the little punk is pushing around one of her friends at school. Alissa's gone from scared to mad. She wants me to arrest the bully, and I might just do it too."

He chuckled. "I'll help if you want."

"I'll hold you in reserve in case I can't put the fear of God into a grade-school boy all on my own."

"Deal."

Her eyes narrowed. "I've been thinking about the descriptions of these different victims."

Matthias had expected her to bring that up. He crossed his arms and waited.

"Two of the Cleveland heists' witnesses stated that at least one of the weapons was a chrome revolver. The man from Buffalo said they used black semi-automatics."

"So they had access to more than one handgun."

"The Cleveland witnesses stated two of the assailants were black and one of the white males was taller than the rest and thin. The Buffalo guy's description didn't match that at all."

Matthias leaned back. "Eyewitness accounts are notoriously inaccurate."

"That's very true, and I'd view these reports with a healthy dose of skepticism were it not for the Buffalo witness being military. Takes one to know one and all that. Combined with two different witnesses from two different families being in agreement about the tall, skinny white dude and two black men, I'm thinking we have different crews."

"You seriously believe the cases aren't related?"

"I didn't say that."

"Then what are you saying?"

She glared at him. "I'm saying we once again have more questions than answers."

Which seemed to be status quo with this case. "Let's just hope Belle can give us something useful."

Chapter Sixteen

E mma finished with Kira's photos and was pleased with the results. She was in the process of loading the files into a new Dropbox folder, when a red SUV pulled in next to her Forester. She rose from her computer and walked to the front of her camper, peering out through the window above the futon. Bob DelGrosso climbed out and looked around.

She stepped onto her deck and immediately wished she'd put on a sweater. "What are you doing here?" she asked, keeping her tone light.

He smiled, perhaps a little too brightly. "Emma. Good to see you. How've you been?"

More small talk. Rather than invite him to join her on the deck, she stepped to the edge of it and crossed her arms against the chilly breeze. "You didn't come here to check on me. What's up?"

He shoved his hands in his trouser pockets and gave her a sheepish grin. "You're right. I didn't. I was hoping we could talk about that photo. I've been waiting for a call from you, setting your price."

"Are the police close to making an arrest?"

The grin faded. "Not that I'm aware. Why?"

"I've been told the case has lost its appeal, but once an arrest is made, it'll regain its frontpage status. That's when the photo becomes valuable."

"That's true. But I hate pushing these kinds of purchases off until the last minute."

"You'd better get used to it if you're getting into the news business. That's what news is. Last minute."

He laughed, nervously. "I suppose you're right. There's a lot I still have to learn in the transition." He brought his hands out of his pockets and rubbed them together. "What do you say? Let's sit down and crunch numbers." He stepped towards her, obviously expecting her to invite him onto her porch.

Instead, she stood her ground. Unlike with Rudy Springstein, she didn't want to risk losing a job connection by messing with Bob's head. "The photo isn't for sale. At any price."

The words staggered him. "You can't be serious."

"I'm afraid I am."

"For God's sake, why?" He gestured at the tiny camper, swinging around to include the old Subaru. "I know you need the money. This one photograph could go a long way toward getting you out of your hole."

She was glad she had her hands tucked under her folded arms. It kept him from seeing her clenched fists. "I'm not in that big of a hole that I'm willing to profit from a tragedy."

His mouth dropped open. When he closed it, he swallowed

and nodded. "You're a good person, Emma. I really wish you'd reconsider though."

"Not gonna happen."

"If you do…"

"You'll be the first person I call."

"I appreciate that." Bob did a slow turn and shuffled back to his car. Before getting in, he looked at her. "Do me a favor, okay? Watch out for yourself." He climbed behind the wheel, backed out, and drove away.

His parting words brought a shiver having nothing to do with the weather. *Watch out for yourself.* Why the hell would he say that? A photograph of a dead body almost completely obscured by lake debris had stirred up a bidding war among *ErieNOW*, WERI-TV, and Bob DelGrosso, but it certainly wasn't worth threatening her.

The paranoid sensation of being watched returned and put her on high alert. Emma's gaze swept her neighboring campsites and RVs. She expected and feared that she'd see Clay peering back at her. *Stop being stupid*, she thought. *Stop letting him control you when he isn't anywhere around.*

When the feeling passed, Emma went inside and closed both the screen and exterior doors. She dug into her computer case and retrieved the external hard drive that held the picture. She clenched the cord, intent on plugging it into her computer and deleting the damned photograph. She'd already deleted it from her camera.

But she stopped. Was it evidence? Would deleting it get her in trouble with the police? She couldn't imagine it would. Wesley Simmons's face wasn't visible on it. What good could it be?

She made a mental note. The next time she encountered Detectives Honeywell or Malone, she'd ask. And if they told her she couldn't delete it, she'd give them the entire hard drive just to get it out of her possession.

Satisfied with her decision, she stuffed the device back into the bag. She stood, lifted the bench seat, and deposited the case into the storage space beneath.

As she gazed out the window, she thought of Bob DelGrosso's visit. She didn't know him well enough to determine whether or not his behavior was normal, but he'd seemed on edge. His smile appeared forced. Then again, he probably wasn't used to offering that kind of money for a picture. He had never paid her anything close to that in all the years she'd worked with him.

She sat down at her computer and jiggled her mouse to wake up the screen holding the Dropbox files but froze.

In all the years she'd worked with him, their dealings had always been online, email, text, or Dropbox exchanges like the one she was setting up for Kira. He'd never come to her to talk face-to-face. He'd paid her through deposits to PayPal.

He didn't have her address beyond the Post Office box she'd set up for tax and business purposes.

How the hell did he know where to find her?

Emma had barely shaken her apprehension over Bob's visit when she heard noises coming through the closed window over her sink—the window that faced Joe's Jayco. She stood and stepped over to check out the source.

Joe's pickup sat in its parking spot and the Jayco's exterior door was open.

In the middle of the week.

She grabbed her sweater and hurried outside and around to his deck, calling his name.

He appeared at the screen door, hesitated, and stepped out. While his cheeks were ruddy, his bloodshot eyes carried a haunted look.

"Are you okay?" she asked, certain that he wasn't.

"Been better."

She considered not telling him, but she had to. "The police have been looking for you. I was worried."

"The police? Why?" The red in his cheeks drained. "Oh my God. Did something happen to Barbie?"

"I don't believe so. They were asking questions about Friday night."

Joe clamped his mouth shut.

"Where've you been?" she asked softly.

She caught a glimpse of some emotion—anger or perhaps mere impatience—before his expression mellowed. "I've been out on my boat. Being on the water soothes my soul. And with everything that's happened, it needed some soothing."

She got that. While she had no experience with boats beyond her father's little fishing canoe, simply standing on the beach with her feet in the water had the same effect. "You should probably call those detectives and let them know you're back."

His eyes hardened again. "They can go to hell." Joe turned and reached for his door. He paused and turned back. "I'm sorry. I know you mean well, but you should stay out of it."

Before she could respond, he went inside, slamming the door harder than necessary.

"Stay out of it?" Emma said to herself. "You're the one who brought me into it."

Chapter Seventeen

Sara's Restaurant was a long-time fixture of Erie. The red and white décor harkened back to a more innocent era when jukeboxes played the music of the fifties. At one time, vintage cars—or at least the shells of them—had added ambiance in the parking lot. But the business kept growing and the cars were removed to make room for additional dining space, which consisted largely of picnic tables under red and white striped awnings.

Situated at the entrance to Presque Isle State Park, the place fed ice cream, hot dogs, hamburgers, and other fast foods to tourists, as well as being a hotspot for locals seeking a family-friendly outing.

Being mid-morning on a chilly, gray Wednesday, Sara's was only moderately busy. Matthias and Cassie easily spotted Belle Simmons seated by herself at one of the outdoor tables.

"Good morning," Matthias said with an easy smile. "Do you remember Detective Malone?"

Belle glanced at her. "Yeah." She brought her gaze back to him. "Thanks for meeting me here."

"Not a problem."

She gave a short, sad laugh. "Not for you maybe. Jake's so freaked out, another visit from the police might push him over the edge. And Mom? She's mad at everyone and everything. I couldn't dare let either of them know I was talking to the cops. I had to lie. Tell them I was going to the park with a couple of friends. I guess it wasn't a total lie. I just had them drop me off here first. I'll meet them in the park later."

"We appreciate you making such an effort," Cassie said.

Matthias stepped over the bench and sat across from the teen. He rested his elbows on the table and folded his hands. "You said you think you noticed something during the break-in." In his peripheral vision, he noticed Cassie, who remained standing, pull out her pen and notebook.

Belle lowered her eyes to the beverage in front of her. "You asked if we'd seen anything like a scar." She glanced up at him —and he assumed at the scar on his lip—before again studying her drink. "Or if any of them spoke with an accent."

"That's right."

"None of them did. At least not that I noticed, so I didn't lie."

"Okay."

"But one of them … the one that stayed by the door … was smaller."

"Smaller?"

Belle nodded. "And was getting impatient because the others were taking too long. She only spoke once and said, 'Hurry up'."

Matthias inhaled. "She?"

"Yeah. I mean, I can't be one-hundred-percent sure because she was trying to make her voice sound gruff. But I'm maybe ninety-five percent sure." Belle met Matthias's gaze, her shoulders hunched.

He shot a look at his partner and could see masked excitement on her face. Returning his focus to Belle, he asked, "Can you tell me anything else about her? You said she was small. Small, how? Height? Weight?"

"Both. And it may sound odd, but she moved like a cat."

"You mean graceful."

"Yeah. Like a dancer maybe."

"This is all good stuff, Belle. You're doing great. What about the others? Were they tall or short? Heavy or thin?"

She chewed on her lower lip, thinking. "It was hard to tell because of the hoodies and masks they wore."

"I understand. How about their skin color? Were they white, black, brown?"

"White. They were all white."

"Are you sure?" Cassie asked.

"Positive."

"Is there anything else?" Matthias asked.

"Maybe." Belle squirmed. "The woman who stayed by the door?"

"Yeah?"

"She had on the same kind of hoodie and mask as the men so I couldn't see much, but at one point, her hair kinda slipped down in her eyes and she tucked it back real fast."

Matthias leaned closer. "Did you notice whether she was blonde? Brunette? A redhead?"

"Neither." Belle met his gaze. "Her hair was purple."

"How many women in the Erie area have purple hair?" Matthias asked once they were back in the car, watching Belle Simmons cross the parking lot to the trail leading into Presque Isle.

"Probably more than you'd think." Cassie fingered her close-cropped white curls. "I've been thinking of dying mine blue or green. Purple might be fun."

He pinched the bridge of his nose. "We already know of one person involved in this case who has purple hair."

Cassie let her hand drop to her lap. "The yoga instructor."

"And she moves like a dancer too."

"Yes, she does." Cassie looked at him. "You wanna go question her again?"

"About what? 'Hey, are you part of a home invasion crew?'"

"We need to look a little deeper into her past."

Matthias gazed through the window at the campground directly behind the restaurant. "There's someone else we need to look deeper into."

Cassie followed his gaze. "The photographer."

"She's acquainted with both the yoga teacher and Joe Platt."

"I didn't think you suspected Platt."

"But you do. And believe it or not, I respect your instincts."

Cassie made a show of pressing a hand to her chest. "I'm touched." She turned serious. "But I thought since we'd changed our focus from the murder to the home invasions—"

"They might be more connected than I first thought. Look. If Wesley's murder was simply the tragic result of him playing hero…" The word raised a lump in Matthias's throat. He swallowed hard. "Then yes, we need to focus the investigation on the home invasions in order to solve the homicide. But what if…" He let the sentence fade as he tried to process the new information they'd received this morning.

"Yes?" Cassie said. "What if?"

He closed his eyes, organizing his thoughts. "The eyewitnesses in Buffalo agree on the descriptions of the assailants there. The eyewitnesses in Cleveland agree on their assailants too, but the descriptions are different from Buffalo's. Now we're getting yet another set of descriptions here in Erie."

"Yet we agree the cases are all connected."

"Have to be. There are too many coincidences otherwise."

"What are you thinking?"

"I'm thinking different cities, different crews." He met Cassie's gaze. "One mastermind."

Her eyes shifted. Came back to his. "Joe Platt? Criminal mastermind?"

Matthias once again gazed towards the campground. "Stranger things have happened."

"I wonder if he's shown up at his campsite."

"Only one way to find out." Matthias started the car.

They made their way through the parking lot and around the pizza joint next door to the campground entrance. As they climbed the gentle slope toward Joe's Jayco, his pickup truck came into view.

"Looks like we're in luck," Matthias said.

"Photographer's home too." Cassie pointed out the white Forester nosed in toward the smaller camper and the bicycle on the deck. "Two birds, one stone."

"So is your favorite music lover." He could already hear the cranked-up radio even with the car windows up.

"*My* favorite? What about you? You're the one who showed off your pitching skills with his batteries."

"From the sounds of it, he didn't learn anything about respecting his neighbors."

"Do you want to give him another lesson?"

"Not right now." Matthias drove past Emma Anderson's camp and parked in the grassy space between her Subaru and Joe's pickup, in plain view of the noise polluter. As soon as they opened their car doors, the volume dropped.

"Apparently, he doesn't want another lesson either," Cassie said across the roof. She stepped in front of the pickup and turned toward the rock and roller's place. "Good day, Mr. Harper."

He'd been sitting in the shadows beneath his deck roof. He stood. "Go to hell." He stormed inside, slamming his door behind him.

Cassie rounded the vehicle to join Matthias on the downhill side. "Yep, you made quite the impression. What do you think? Cute photographer first, then Platt?"

Matthias studied the Jayco. The exterior door was closed but a light shone from inside. "As long as we keep an eye on him so he doesn't rabbit."

By the time they reached Emma's deck, she was stepping outside. Matthias could read her expression. *You again.* "Ms. Anderson," he said, "do you have a few minutes to talk?"

She replied with an open palm aimed at her folding lawn chairs. Cassie claimed one. Matthias settled one hip on the deck railing and mimicked Emma's gesture back at her and the remaining chair. She looked like she was going to protest but after a moment, dragged the chair to face them and sat.

"I see Joe Platt's back. When did he arrive?" Matthias asked.

"Maybe ten minutes ago."

"Have you spoken with him?"

"I said hello."

"Did he give you any indication of where he's been?"

She shifted in her chair. "He doesn't want me involved in this."

"What's 'this'?"

"Police business, I assume. If you want answers about him, he's the one you need to ask."

Matthias gave her a measured smile. "Fair enough. We'll do just that."

"How about Kira Petersen?" Cassie asked.

Emma's gaze snapped to hers. "Kira? What about her?"

"Have you seen her lately?"

"I did some photography for her yesterday. Why?"

"How long have you known Ms. Petersen?"

Emma appeared rattled by the question. Or puzzled. "I met her for the first time Saturday on the beach. The day I—" She ran her tongue over her lips. "The day I sent you her photo."

Matthias leaned forward. "You'd mentioned she wanted you to do some photography for her. That's what you were doing yesterday?"

"Yes."

"So you've only met her the two times? Saturday and yesterday?"

"I took a yoga class with her on Monday. We went out to lunch afterwards."

"What did you talk about?"

Emma's cheeks flushed. "Girl talk. Getting to know each other. That sort of thing. And we made plans for yesterday's shoot." The chair squeaked as she shifted again. "Why all the questions about Kira? You can't possibly think she had something to do with that man's murder just because she happened to be teaching a yoga class on the beach where he washed up?"

The way she said it made Matthias question the likelihood of the Petersen woman being a suspect. Yet Belle had told them about a woman with purple hair who moved with catlike grace. He couldn't dismiss it. "What are your impressions of Kira?"

Emma set her jaw. He feared she wasn't going to reply. When she did, her voice was tight. "I don't know her well enough to have an impression."

He wanted to say, "Bullshit." He had a feeling Emma had a good eye for a photo subject and a good set of instincts for judging people. She clearly didn't care much for him, which only confirmed his suspicion.

Cassie picked up the questioning. "Did she say anything that made you think something might be off?"

"No." Emma glared at Cassie, then brought her narrowed eyes back to Matthias. She climbed to her feet. "You obviously think Kira's involved in your murder case. If she is, which I strongly doubt, I know nothing about it. I'm working on a job right now, so if this is all you wanted to talk about, I think we're done."

Matthias pushed away from the railing. "It's not really the murder case we're working on right now."

Cassie shot him a dark frown. Their job was to gather information, not share it. He knew that.

Emma folded her arms and waited.

"There've been two home invasions in Erie recently," he said

Emma nodded. "One of them was at Joe's daughter's house. That's how his son-in-law ended up dead."

"Right. We have a witness who claims—"

Cassie came to her feet. "A word, Detective." She stomped past Matthias, headed toward the campground road.

Matthias took a step closer to Emma, holding her gaze, hoping she'd be able to read his thoughts. His intentions.

Her expression grew more confused. "A witness saw Kira?" she asked, her voice little more than a whisper.

"That's what I'm trying to figure out," he replied, in a whisper matching hers.

From the road, Cassie shouted, "Detective. Now."

He edged back, keeping Emma locked in his gaze and watching her try to digest what he'd said. And what he hadn't said.

With another nod to her, he turned and strode toward his partner. And toward the ass-chewing he knew she was about to dish out.

"What do you think you're doing?" Cassie asked in a sharp whisper.

"Sometimes you have to give a little to get a little."

"This is not the time for giving, Detective."

He held up his hands in surrender. "You're right."

She hiked an eyebrow. "You only tell me that to get me to back off."

"Is it working?"

"No. But we still have to interview Mr. Platt. This conversation?" She aimed a finger at him, back to her, and to him again. "Will be continued."

He had no doubt.

Cassie led the way to Joe's deck, up the steps, and to the door. She rapped on it. "Mr. Platt? Detectives Malone and Honeywell, Erie Police."

The door swung open to reveal an exhausted-looking Joe Platt. "That didn't take long."

"We'd like to talk to you, if you don't mind."

"Is this one of those 'we can talk here, or we can talk down at the station' moments I've seen on TV?"

Neither Cassie nor Matthias answered.

Platt shrugged and pushed open the screen door. "Come in."

They stepped into a kitchen, dining, and living space with finishes nicer than Matthias's apartment. Stairs to the right led up to what he presumed was a bedroom in the space above the fifth-wheel hitch. Everything was clean and comfortable. Matthias had to admit, he could happily live here.

Platt directed them to have a seat on the sofa in the camper's bump-out extension. He dragged a stool from one corner and perched on it. "I hear you've been looking for me."

"We have," Cassie said. "Where've you been?"

"Out on my boat."

"Fishing?" Matthias asked. He didn't add the real question on his mind. *Were you cleaning up evidence of having dumped a body from it?*

"A little."

"Catch anything?"

Platt glared at him. "You don't look like the Pennsylvania

Fish and Boat Commission."

Matthias gave him a smile. "Just asking."

"If you're gonna ask questions, stop pussyfooting around and ask what you came for."

"Fair enough. How long have you lived in Erie?"

The question threw him off, which was partly what Matthias intended. "All of my adult life. I moved here when I married my wife."

"Where'd you live before that?" Matthias hoped to hear either Cleveland or Buffalo.

"DuBois."

Of course, it couldn't be that easy. "That's a few hours away. Do you still have family there?"

"No."

"How about elsewhere? Do you have family or friends around the lake?"

"Just my daughter and grandkids. But you know that. What's this about?"

"Have you been to Buffalo lately?"

"Buffalo? New York?"

Cassie looked up from her notetaking. "That's the one."

"Not lately."

"How long has it been?" Matthias asked.

"I don't know. Ten years maybe."

"How about Cleveland?"

"My wife has cousins there, but I haven't seen them since her funeral. Why don't you just tell me what this is about?"

Time to change directions. "Just trying to clarify a few things." Matthias crossed an ankle over his knee. "I hear you used to work at Great Lakes Trust."

Once more, Platt appeared off balance. "I did. Years ago."

"Do you know the Ingram family? Grant and Debra?"

Platt's gaze shifted. Matthias could tell he was thinking, apparently trying to remember. "The names aren't familiar," Platt said. But then something appeared to click. "Wait. Is that the family whose home was robbed last week? A few days before Barbie's?"

"That's right." Matthias noticed Cassie's eyes had lifted, watching Platt.

"You think the two robberies are connected."

Cassie drummed her pen on the open notepad. "It's been on the news."

"Like I said. I've been on my boat. I make a point of disconnecting from the world when I'm out on the water. Except for keeping an eye on the weather."

"Where were you last Tuesday?" Matthias asked.

"At work." Platt's reply came a bit too quickly.

Cassie shook her head. "Not according to Eugene Castillo."

Platt's eyes grew wide with surprise. "You went to my office?"

"We did," Cassie said. "You were out."

"On your boat," Matthias added.

"But Mr. Castillo was very cooperative. He gave us a printout of when you checked in and out."

Matthias watched a parade of emotions march across Platt's face and expected to see anger leading the way. Instead, the creases and crevices evoked sadness. Maybe even defeat. "Last Tuesday," Matthias said again, softer this time. "Why'd you take off early?"

Platt took a few moments to consider his answer. Then his chin came up, his face passive, no longer giving anything away. "I was on my boat."

Matthias didn't believe him. He doubted Cassie did either. He also doubted they would get a different answer by pressing. Time to change directions yet again. "I'm curious. With you spending so much time here and on your boat, I bet you have a security system at your house."

"You'd lose that bet, son. I don't have anything there worth stealing."

Matthias couldn't resist taking a glance around the Jayco, wondering how much it had cost.

"I know what you're thinking. Guy's got a lake boat and a nice RV. He must be rolling in the dough. And you'd be partly right. I do okay. But since my wife died, my house isn't something I put a lot of energy or money in. My money goes to two places." He leaned forward and held up one finger. "My toys." He circled the finger to indicate the Jayco, then held up a second finger. "And trust funds for my grandkids." He closed his hand and lowered it to his lap. "You got any more questions for me?"

Matthias looked at his partner, expecting her to close her notebook. She didn't.

"Only one more, Mr. Platt," Cassie said. "And it's more of a request than a question."

Platt opened both hands wide. "Hit me."

"Would you mind if we take a look at your boat?"

His hands returned to his lap to help push himself up. "I do mind. You want on my boat, you show me a warrant. But since you got nothing on me, no judge in his right mind would issue one."

Cassie gave him a smile. "If you have nothing to hide, what harm could it do?"

He smiled back. "Good day, Detectives."

Chapter Eighteen

Emma watched the dark Chevy Impala with the detectives inside back out of Joe's parking spot and out of the campgrounds. The woman detective, Malone, clearly had not wanted Honeywell to divulge anything about the case. He'd overstepped and given her just enough to raise a lot of red flags. And even more questions.

Kira. Bubbly, funny, personable Kira. A witness had identified her, connecting her to the home invasion.

And Joe's son-in-law's murder.

The idea made Emma's head spin. It was a mistake. Had to be.

She stepped back inside her camper and took a long look at her table with the laptop and monitors she'd used to edit the yoga studio photos. Now she couldn't stomach thinking about them.

She grabbed her keys on her way out. After locking the camper door, she dragged her bike from the deck, and coasted down the slope. Rather than making the left where the camp road leveled out and exit through the gate, she leaned the bike into a right turn and pedaled towards the bike path into Presque Isle.

One of her favorite parts of Sara's Campground was its direct connection to the trails and the park. No need to move her car.

The loop circled the peninsula, returning fourteen miles later to the park's entrance, ending across Peninsula Drive from Sara's Restaurant and the campground. Emma often took one of the shorter loops where a trail crossed from the bayside to the lakeside at various points along the way.

Today, she planned to cycle the entire fourteen-mile trail. She needed to sort through her thoughts and clear her mind.

She was glad she'd worn a sweater. The breeze coming off the bay rustled the leaves and undergrowth between the paved path and the water's edge. Once she cleared the wooded stretch, there was nothing to shield her from the wind. The bay's choppy surface reflected the gray sky. Gulls sailed overhead, and a pair of mallards rode the waves lapping at the rocks bordering the path. Emma inhaled deeply and swiped her hair from her face. This was exactly what she needed.

The next few miles were slow going. The heaviest trail-use occurred on that bayside stretch. Locals and tourist walked their dogs or just took a stroll. Rollerbladers and bikers shared the mostly flat path with them, dodging and weaving through the human obstacle course. Today was no different. Eventually, traffic thinned to an occasional bike. Emma's clearer mind was freed to ponder Honeywell's latest visit.

They suspected Kira of … what exactly? No matter what it was, they had to be wrong.

Emma had abandoned her old life in February. She

moved into her current home in early April when the campground opened for the season. In all that time, she'd been a hermit. Her solitude was a personal choice. She needed to lay low.

She'd made exactly two friends. Sort of. Joe Platt, easygoing, protective. Not quite a father figure. More of an older brother.

And now Kira. A girlfriend. Easy to talk to. Funny. Like Nell and yet, not like Nell. Emma had started to open up to Kira.

She hadn't shared any of her secrets with Joe. He never asked. Yet he'd sensed the part of her past from which she was hiding. And he accepted her as she was. The new Emma. Who had gotten away *on her own*. Unlike his daughter.

Could Joe or Kira be involved in criminal activity? Armed robbery? Murder? Was her judgment so impaired that she'd totally underestimated them?

She slowed and swung onto a side trail leading to the Perry Monument. More tourists gathered here, and she coasted around them, gliding all the way to the obelisk rising from a fountain. She braked to a stop, lowered the kickstand, and parked her bike next to an unoccupied concrete bench where she sat and gazed across the bay to the city.

Judgment. She laughed silently at the word. Was her judgment impaired? Hell, yes. How else could she explain those three years with Clay? She leaned forward, resting her elbows on her knees and her face in her hands. She'd thought she had learned something from the experience. Obviously, she had not.

She sat there, letting the breeze from the bay toss her hair as she kept her head lowered and her eyes closed. Around her, voices of tourists filtered through her thoughts. A goose honked.

A sudden chill, not caused by the coolness of the day, prickled her skin. She sensed she was being watched and sat upright, expecting to find Clay standing over her.

"Excuse me, ma'am, are you all right?" A young man who appeared to be in his teens, concern showing on his face, stood next to her.

Feeling foolish, she smiled. "I'm fine."

He returned her smile, his much relieved. "Oh, good. Have a great day."

Emma watched him walk away and join hands with a teenage girl.

Ah, young love.

Emma's gaze drifted beyond the couple to what she guessed was a school group. Through the crowd, she caught a glimpse of a dark-haired man as he turned away.

The old familiar panic gripped her throat. Clay? Or yet another case of paranoia?

Unlike Honeywell and the guy next to her car Monday afternoon, this man wasn't wearing a hoodie. He wore his straight, jet-black hair exactly as Clay did. Part of her willed him to turn around. Part of her feared he would. She pictured Clay's strikingly handsome face. The smirk she'd once thought was fun and sexy. Now, the memory of it reminded her of a wolf. A predator.

He strolled away, headed toward the parking lot. She needed to know. If the man was Clay, he'd already seen her. If he wasn't, she was once again obsessing over nothing.

Leaving her bike behind, Emma started toward him, her gaze locked on the back of his head. She moved into the crowd of school-aged kids, most of whom had their faces lowered towards their phones rather than taking in the park's beauty or watching where they were going. She bumped shoulders with a few as she made her way through the group. Once in the clear, she broke into a jog, closing the gap between her and the retreating man. He never looked back. Never turned to reveal his identity. As she drew within a few feet, she slowed, keeping pace. Now what? Did she really want to give Clay a chance to grab her?

Abruptly, he stopped. She tripped in her effort to pull up short and ended up doing exactly what she hadn't wanted to. She stumbled into him.

He lurched and turned. "Hey, lady, watch what you're doing."

He wasn't Clay. Right age. Similar angry glare, probably because she'd slammed into him. She sputtered apologies. The adrenaline drained, weakening her knees. He probably thought she was drunk.

She staggered backward, wheeled, and broke into a run. Circumventing the school kids, she raced to her bike and swung a leg over it. With one last look towards the man, who continued moving away from her, shaking his head, she pushed off. Pedaling hard and fast, she shot down the sidewalk to the trail.

By the time Emma made it back to the campground, her pounding heartrate was due to the breakneck pace instead of another encounter with a Clay lookalike. Her thighs burned during the last uphill climb to her campsite as they always did.

She swung into her parking spot next to the Subaru and braked to a stop.

Joe's pickup was gone, his camper closed up. Pushing her bike to the edge of the deck, she lifted the front wheel onto it, then gripped the bar supporting the seat and hefted the back wheel up as well. It wasn't until she leaned the bike against the far railing and turned toward the door that she spotted it.

The exterior door was ajar.

She'd closed and locked it before she left. If she hadn't, it would still be bungeed open.

As always, her first thought was Clay. Her initial instinct was to run. Jump in her car and hightail it out of there. She chastised herself for always letting her mind drag her in his direction. Still, she wasn't fabricating the fact that *someone* had broken into her camper.

At least whoever had been—or was still—in her camper hadn't stolen her Subaru despite her car keys hanging on a hook inside the door. But retrieving her keys meant going inside. She could run to one of her neighbors to ask for help. If only Joe was still here.

Mick was. The loud music told her that.

Mick, however, wasn't the protective sort.

Cautiously, Emma picked her way toward the door. She listened for noise from inside, but all was still. Decision time. Did she risk checking her camper on her own? Or run for help?

She reached out and nudged the door farther open.

Nothing happened. No one jumped out at her. No sounds came from inside. Emboldened, Emma peered through the screen door. One thing about living in a seventeen-foot camper —other than the bathroom in the rear, there was nowhere to hide.

"Who's in there?" she called in her most fierce voice.

When no one responded, she grasped the screen door handle and popped it open. She stepped inside, and her shoe crunched on something on the floor. The sight of what was left of her home choked the breath from her.

Her laptops and monitors gone. The refrigerator door hung open, its contents spilled onto the floor, food mingled with broken glass. The kitchen cabinet doors were all open. Plastic plates and glasses were scattered over the counters and the table, where her computers used to be, and onto the benches.

Emma's first instinct was to crunch across the wreckage. First, to check her hiding spot behind the furnace grate. Second, to lift the bench seat and check on the bag containing the hard drive. The one she'd forgotten to give to the detectives when they were here. She quickly reconsidered. Instead, she backed out of the camper, grabbed her car keys from the hook, and jogged to her Subaru. Once inside, she leaned across the console to flip open the glove box where she found the card Honeywell had given her lying on top of her owner's manual.

Chapter Nineteen

All the way back to the station, Cassie chastised Matthias for sharing information with Emma. "You know better than that. You're a better cop than that. We ask questions, not answer them" played on a loop.

He drove without responding. What could he say? She was right.

"Are you even listening to me?" she demanded once they were parked and had climbed out of the vehicle.

"I am."

"Well? What do you have to say for yourself?"

"You're right. I mean it. You're absolutely right. I was wrong."

She straightened, a fleeting look of surprise crossing her face before being replaced with that stony glare again. "Of course I'm right."

At least his admission shut her up as they made their way along the depressingly dark hallways and up the stairs to the detective's floor. They paused in the breakroom to fill their mugs. At least someone had made a fresh pot.

"Joe Platt was lying about Tuesday," Cassie said before taking a sip.

Matthias recalled the man's expressionless face as he'd told them he'd been back on his boat. "I'm not so sure."

"Why?" Cassie trailed Matthias into Major Crimes. "The boat response was too pat. Too easy."

She was right yet again, but Matthias wasn't going to stoke her ego. "I just said I'm not sure. The way he said it ... partly rang true to me. Partly didn't."

"Just because a guy's got a boat doesn't mean he spends every free moment on it."

Matthias had no solid argument. If he owned a boat, he'd be on it every second he could, if only to get his money's worth, but that was him. Joe Platt was another matter.

No sooner had they taken seats in their respective cubbies than Cassie's phone rang and Matthias heard her mutter, "Uh-oh."

"What?" he asked

She hurried past his desk, shaking her head at him as she retreated into the hallway and answered. "Hey, babe. What's up?"

Not a business call. Cassie's husband rarely called her during work hours, so Matthias understood the uh-oh.

He returned his attention to the computer monitor. God, he hated home invasions. Even worse, he knew in his gut there was another one about to happen. Tonight or tomorrow. He was surprised this crew hadn't hit again already. Once they did, if they followed form, the crime spree would be over. They would disband or move elsewhere. The chance to catch them would evaporate.

Was Joe Platt involved? Possibly. The fact he wasn't cooperating regarding his boat didn't help his case. Matthias needed to find out where he kept it moored, although he'd had more than ample time to scrub away any evidence. And then there was purple-haired catlike Kira Petersen.

Matthias's thoughts spiraled back to Emma, who was acquainted with both. Cassie's admonishments echoed in his ears. He shouldn't have shown his cards—or even one of them—to the photographer. He didn't know enough about her to trust her.

Cassie stormed into the office, cursing under her breath. She vanished into her cubicle and slammed a drawer.

"What's up?" Matthias asked.

"Alissa got into a fight at school."

"The bully again?"

"So it would seem. She's in the emergency department at UPMC with a possible broken arm." Cassie slung her purse over her shoulder. "I have to go."

"Absolutely. Call me once you know anything."

She grunted a reply and bustled out.

Matthias pictured the small child who had a passion for pink and tried to imagine her in a fight. The image made no more sense than anything involved with the home invasion investigation. In both cases, he was missing too many puzzle pieces.

He typed "Emma Anderson" into the search engine.

Within a half hour, he'd filled in some of those pieces, at least where Emma was concerned. Her residence was listed as Smith Township, Washington County, some hundred and fifty miles to the south. Further digging revealed her parents were deceased and she had one younger sister, Nell. A quick side trip on his search revealed several news articles about the sister. Multiple arrests for DUI and drug possession, most in Washington County. The most recent, a drunk and disorderly, had been posted back in January on *ErieNOW*.

Emma's sister was in town. Or at least had been four months ago.

He switched to the NCIC database, typed in the case file number, and ran Emma.

She didn't have a criminal record. Not even a parking ticket. What she did have on record were several Protection From Abuse orders against one Clay Bauer. A quick check of his criminal past offered a good hint as to why Emma needed those PFAs. He had outstanding warrants on an assortment of charges ranging from simple assault, aggravated assault, destruction of property, to terroristic threats. Nice guy. Last known address, also Washington County.

Matthias suspected this Bauer guy might be the reason Emma was currently living in a shoebox of a camper in Erie.

His phone rang. "Detective Matthias Honeywell."

"This is Emma Anderson. Can you come to my campsite? Right now?"

The voice on the phone was tinged with pure panic. "What's going on?" he asked.

"Someone broke into my camper and trashed it. I know I should just call 911." Her words tumbled out and over each other. "If you can't come, I'll do that—"

"No, it's okay. Try to calm down. Where are you right now?"

"In my car."

"*Where* in your car?"

"In front of my camper."

"Do you think whoever did this might still be there?"

A damp laugh. "Only if they're hiding in my bathroom."

"Good. I want you to drive down to the entrance gate and wait for me. Can you do that?"

"Yes." Relief mingled with fear.

"I'll be there in ten minutes. Fifteen at the most. Do not go back inside. Do you hear me?"

"Yes. I'll be waiting."

As ordered, Matthias found Emma at the gate, leaning against her car's front fender. She pushed away from it as he braked to a stop.

He aimed a thumb at his empty passenger seat. "Come on."

She rounded his vehicle and climbed in.

"Could you tell if anything was missing?"

"My computers for sure. Those were obvious. I was going to check further but decided I should call the police first."

"Good."

The first thing he noticed when he pulled in was the loud music still blasting from Harper's trailer. The second thing was Emma's camper door hanging open. The previous times he'd been here, she'd had it secured with a bungee. Not fancy but effective.

"Stay here." He climbed out and approached the porch. Stepped onto it, silent except for his pulse echoing in his ears. As a detective, he usually arrived after a scene had been secured and cleared. While he loved his job, part of him missed being in uniform.

He reached down and released his 9mm Glock from the holster on his hip. He paused at a small window and quickly scanned what he could see of the camper's interior, which wasn't much. Taking one big step past the threshold, he claimed a position between the open door and the larger window.

He pounded on the siding-covered wall. "Police! Come out now and keep your hands where I can see them!"

Nothing. No movement. No sound.

At least not from inside. A few campground residents from neighboring sites appeared at windows and in doorways.

He pounded again, repeating the order. Not that he expected a different response. With the toe of one shoe, he nudged the door open wider. He yanked the screen door out of his way and stepped inside.

Emma hadn't been kidding when she told him the culprit had trashed the place. Glass and plastic glittered on the floor. Cupboard doors hung open. The refrigerator had been emptied onto the floor as well. He crunched through the mess to the door at the rear of the camper. No knob, just a handle with a push button. Still gripping his sidearm, he yanked the door open.

The closet-sized bathroom was vacant. The medicine cabinet over the tiny sink was open but the contents appeared undisturbed. And either Emma was a slob, or the closet had been gone through with clothes tossed everywhere.

Matthias holstered his Glock and crunched his way out of the camper. Emma stood at the front of his vehicle with one hand pressed to her lips. "It's all clear," he said.

She started toward him, but he held up a hand to stop her.

"I want to photograph the interior and dust for prints before you go back inside. Then you can check and let me know what's missing."

"I can take the photos if it'll help. One thing I know they didn't take is my camera. I had it locked in my car."

"You're the victim. I'm the detective. I'll handle the photos." He looked around at the other camp residents who were still watching. "But first, I'm going to talk to your neighbors. See if they can give me a description of who did this."

"Then let me help with that," Emma said.

He narrowed his gaze … the look Cassie always told him scared people. When Emma visibly recoiled and he realized Cassie was again right, he softened. "Just have a seat and be patient."

"I hate doing nothing."

"Do you have any idea who might be responsible?"

She shot a glance at the open camper door, and her expression shifted for the briefest of moments. Recovering, she said, "Not really."

She was lying. While she might not *know*, she definitely suspected. "Any idea what Mr. Not Really was looking for?"

Her teal eyes came back to him. "I'll let you know when you allow me in to see what, besides my computer stuff, was taken."

"Fair enough."

Matthias first stops were the residents who had peered out when he'd announced his presence at Emma's door. One older gentleman claimed he hadn't seen anything or anyone out of the usual and stated he couldn't have heard anything over Mick Harper's radio. A woman with a cigarette dangling from her lips thought she heard some noise but didn't know which camp site it came from. A young couple reported seeing Emma's Subaru coming and going but nothing else.

Matthias then made the rounds of the campsites down the hill—the sites which the intruder would have to walk or drive past to reach Emma's. No one claimed to have seen anyone out of the ordinary.

As Matthias stopped at each occupied trailer, his hopes faded of someone having heard the commotion or having seen a vehicle parked next to the white Subaru. Over and over, people reported they couldn't hear anything over Mick Harper's music. And everyone was certain no strange car—other than his Impala—had been parked at Emma's place.

He should've thrown Harper's damn radio into the woods instead of the batteries.

Matthias saved Harper for last and got exactly what he expected. Nothing. Harper snatched his radio from its perch, tucked the thing under his arm, and stomped inside as soon as he spotted Matthias. When he climbed the porch steps and knocked, he was greeted with a loud demand he not come near Harper's RV without a warrant.

Emma was slouched in one of her lawn chairs looking dejected when Matthias returned after snagging his evidence collection kit from his trunk. As soon as she spotted him, she leaped to her feet. "Did you find out anything?"

He scanned the surrounding campers who'd disappeared

once the excitement was over. "You have some of the most unobservant neighbors I've ever encountered."

She attempted a weak smile and failed. "It's part of the reason I like it here. Everyone leaves me alone and minds their own business."

"You might want to consider relocating to someplace with a neighborhood watch."

"You might be right."

"Let me dust for prints. Then you can inventory your possessions and see what all's missing."

"That shouldn't take long. I don't own much."

He broke out his favorite powder and brush and got to work. The door only offered smudges but the smooth surfaces inside the camper provided ample prints, which he lifted and catalogued. As he moved to the table, he heard Emma at the door and glanced back, prepared to order her out.

She raised both hands then stuffed them in her jeans pockets. "I won't touch anything."

He grinned and went back to work. "I don't suppose it matters. You live here. Most of the prints I'm getting are gonna belong to you."

"Oh." She brought her hands back out and gazed at them. "How will you tell which is which?"

"You need to come down to the station and get printed so I can eliminate yours."

"Oh," she repeated.

He eyed her, asking again, "Any idea who did this?"

She thought about the question more this time, but her response was the same. "Not really."

He still didn't believe her. "Any other break-ins around the campground?"

"Not that I know of."

He worked in silence for several minutes, feeling her eyes on him. Once he finished with the table, he turned toward the refrigerator.

"Check under that bench," Emma said.

"Excuse me?"

She pointed at the bench seat. "Take the pillow off and lift the plywood. There's storage underneath. Check to see if it's empty."

He obliged. Under the seat, he found an assortment of camping supplies, a tarp, and a small canvas duffel.

"That."

He looked over his shoulder at Emma, who pointed at the bag. "This?" he asked.

She nodded. "Can I see it?"

He set the duffel on the table, which was still covered in powder. She unzipped the top, flipped it open and reached inside, withdrawing a black device about the size of a cell phone. Her sigh was audible.

"What is that?"

"An external hard drive."

He looked at her, waiting for more.

She jammed the device into her hip pocket and met his gaze. "Finish doing whatever you're doing and then I'll explain. I'll be on my deck."

Chapter Twenty

E mma waited while Honeywell finished contributing to her clean-up chores. The TV shows she and Nell used to watch never showed the mess left behind by fingerprint powder.

She held the hard drive in her hand, turning it over and over. She could only hope the files were still on it. The thief had taken her laptops, leaving her nothing to plug it into. Besides, they probably believed they already had her photos on those computers.

The door swung open. Honeywell stepped out and set his fingerprinting kit on the deck railing. He picked up the other chair, placed it next to hers, and lowered into it.

"Now. Tell me about the external hard drive. I get the feeling you think it might have something to do with what happened here."

She held it out to him. "Take it. I meant to give it to you the last time you were here and forgot."

He accepted the device. "Do you mind telling me why?"

Emma kept her gaze on the small black box. "The photo's on it. The one from Saturday morning."

"The one of Wesley Simmons's body in the debris?"

She nodded.

"We already have a copy."

"I know." She thought of the phone calls and Bob DelGrosso's visit. "Apparently, there's a lot of demand for it."

"Demand?" he echoed. "From whom?"

"The news media." She told him about the bidding war between *ErieNOW* and WERI-TV. "Even Bob DelGrosso told me to name my price."

"Who's Bob DelGrosso?"

"He's the owner and editor of *PA Living Magazine*. He's been one of my biggest clients over the years, purchasing images or giving me photo assignments."

Honeywell's forehead furrowed. "Isn't *PA Living* a magazine that promotes scenic and historical sites around the state?"

She hadn't expected the detective to know that. "It is."

"First of all, I've seen this photo blown up. Other than an arm, there's nothing visually interesting about it."

The way he said it struck her as funny. "Everyone's a critic."

He lowered his head in a failed attempt to hide his grin. "That's not what I meant."

"I know. And you're right."

"As for *PA Living*, isn't it odd that he wants this kind of picture?"

"I asked Bob the same thing. He says he plans to start a new publication focusing on edgier topics."

"If he's only in the planning phase, the home invasions story and Simmons's homicide are going to be old news."

"He did mention the Pizza Bomber. Maybe he wants to cover stories about infamous crimes around Erie or across the state."

Honeywell gazed out at the campground and appeared to ponder the situation. He brought his blue eyes back to her. "How much did they offer?"

"The top bid was twenty-five hundred, but like I said, Bob told me to name my price."

"I'm not familiar with the going rates for something like this…"

"If I had a truly newsworthy image, top quality, timely?" Emma thought of the mound of lake trash and the barely visible limb. "Even then that amount would be like hitting the jackpot."

Honeywell studied her, his expression still intense but thoughtful. "And you turned it down?"

She caught her lip between her teeth. If he was about to call her out for being an idiot, she couldn't really argue. "Yeah. I did."

"Why?"

How could she explain it to him when she wasn't even sure herself? "When I first got into photojournalism, my early jobs involved going to tragedies to document the carnage. The suffering. My bosses were most excited by the images I captured of the grief-stricken widows or families who'd just lost everything. The more heartbreaking, the better. I felt like…" She searched for an appropriate word. "I felt like a vulture, feeding on the misfortune of innocents. I couldn't do it. In spite of making decent money, I quit. Now I take pictures of landscapes, giggling babies, and an occasional wedding."

He seemed to ponder her words. After a glance over his shoulder at her camper, he said, "I get that. And I respect it. But you already have this image and yet you turned down a nice chunk of change when it looks to me like you could really use the money."

"I could, but I keep seeing Joe's face when you told him I was the one who took the picture. That look is precisely why I quit photojournalism. And it's what I keep seeing in here"— she tapped her temple—"when I consider taking the offer."

Honeywell leaned back in the chair, studying her. She couldn't tell what he was thinking. Probably that she deserved to live in abject poverty for being such a moron.

"If you don't like to intrude, why'd you take my picture at the cemetery?"

"I didn't."

His eyes narrowed in skepticism.

"Honest. I didn't." She pointed at the hard drive in his hand. "The photos I made that night are on there. You can check for yourself. I'd show you, but I don't have a computer to plug into anymore."

He still didn't speak.

"I told you I was there photographing headstones for a client who's doing genealogy research."

"When I turned around, you looked like you'd seen a ghost." His lip lifted into a lopsided grin. "Figuratively speaking."

"No, you're right. Until you turned around, I thought you were someone else."

The grin faded. "Clay Bauer?"

Hearing the name choked her. "How did you—"

"You're friendly with two persons of interest in my case. I needed to know if you had a criminal past."

Anger with him for invading her privacy mingled with curiosity over what he might've found. "What do you know about Clay?"

"That he's a bad guy. That you filed a couple of PFAs on him."

"Did you find out where he is?"

"Last known address is Washington County."

So Honeywell didn't know anything more about Clay than she did.

"You think he might be around here?"

"I'm paranoid." She faked a laugh. "I mean, I thought *you* were him. I saw a guy, who I thought was him, by my car the other day. I saw someone an hour ago in the park and was convinced it was him. Yes, I'm afraid he might be around. No, I don't believe he is."

"You have my number," Honeywell said. "Just in case he does show up."

"He won't." If she said it with enough conviction, it would be true. For now, she didn't want to think or talk about Clay anymore. "What's the deal with you drinking beer with a tombstone in the cemetery?"

The sadness playing across his face was the kind of grief she'd been talking about a moment ago.

She shook her head. "Never mind. It's none of my business."

He briefly met her gaze before looking past her. "Nick Tucci was my partner when I was still in uniform. He was the best partner I've ever had." He glanced at Emma. "Don't you dare tell Cassie I said that."

"I won't."

Again, his gaze shifted beyond her, and she could only imagine what he was seeing. "One night, we responded to a home invasion. When we arrived on scene, we could hear screams, yelling from inside the house. Nick kicked in the door. There was a man heading up the stairs with a gun. He turned toward us, and Nick fired. The man died." Honeywell's gaze dropped to his hands holding the hard drive. "It was the homeowner trying to be a hero and protect his family."

"Oh, God," Emma whispered.

"We were cleared. Officially, at least. But Nick never forgave himself. Six months later, he ate his gun." Honeywell's voice caught. "The only reason it was Nick who fired that shot was because he went in first. It should've been me. I'd have taken the same shot." Honeywell shook his head. "Nick was less than a year from retirement. He had a wife and kids. I should've taken the lead." He swallowed. "Anytime I have a rough day, when I would've gone to a bar with Nick to knock back a few, I take two beers to the cemetery. One for him. One for me. And I talk to him. That home invasion—even before Wesley's body washed up—got to me."

No wonder he looked so angry when Emma had interrupted him that night. She was tempted to reach out and touch his arm. But she didn't know him well enough. "I'm sorry."

He still didn't look up but took a deep breath and a slow, raspy exhalation. "And now I'm just waiting around for the third break-in," he said, his voice so low she had to strain to make out his words.

"*Third* break-in?" She thought of the snippets of news she'd caught recently. "There was another home invasion before the one at the Simmons place."

He nodded.

"You expect more." She didn't say it as a question.

"One more. And then the crew will disband or move on."

"How do you know that?"

He looked at her. "Because it's happened the same way in Buffalo and Cleveland."

His intensity chilled her. "People were killed?" she asked.

"No, but no one got loose and followed them either."

"Do you have any leads?"

He gave her a look and a raised eyebrow.

Her heart sank. "Kira and Joe? You have to be kidding."

He shrugged.

"I get Joe. I mean, I don't believe he's involved, but he's family, and he didn't get along with his son-in-law. I get that. But Kira? Come on. You can't be serious."

Honeywell climbed to his feet. The door to his heart that he'd opened to her slammed shut. He held up the hard drive. "I'll hold onto this, but once everything settles down, you can have it back."

"Keep it. I've already backed up the photos I needed for clients on the cloud. That picture from Saturday? I would've deleted it but was afraid you might need it as evidence."

"I appreciate that." He slipped the device into a pocket. "Do you wanna take a look inside and give me a list of what's missing?"

"Sure."

It didn't take long. Laptops, monitors, wireless keyboards.

She understood the laptops. But why the external peripherals if all the thief wanted was the photo?

Unless the intention was to take everything she needed to do her job.

"Do you think you'll be able to get them back?" she asked, already knowing the answer.

"I'll let the local pawn shop owners know to be on the lookout. The majority of them are good about informing us when someone brings in stolen merchandise."

"What about the minority?"

"I pay them unannounced visits from time to time to check their inventory."

"So you might find my stuff?"

He took a few moments before answering. "I realize you think they were after your photos, but usually, these kinds of burglaries are pulled off by addicts trying to make a quick buck to spend on more drugs. If that's the case, I'll be honest. The odds aren't good. Do you have insurance?"

She laughed at the absurdity. "No."

"I'm sorry." Honeywell closed his notebook. "Keep checking with your neighbors. If any of them remember seeing anything, call me. Or if you see anyone lurking around who doesn't belong here—"

"I'll call you. Got it."

"Come on. I'll give you a ride back to where you left your car."

She followed him out and climbed into the passenger side of his black Impala. She'd seen a glimpse of another side of the detective. A sad side rather than the angry one she'd first encountered. Kira's words echoed in her mind. What a hottie. Emma wasn't exactly in agreement—and she wondered if Kira would feel the same when she learned he considered her a suspect—but Emma had to admit he wasn't bad looking.

And he'd offered to help if Clay really did show up.

Once the detective dropped her off at her Subaru, Emma drove back to her camper and went inside. She pulled the door shut behind her. It wouldn't latch. Whoever had broken in must've used a prybar on the exterior door and bent it. Great. Now she needed to pay for a major repair in addition to buying new equipment. Not to mention, she couldn't lock herself in at night.

She grabbed a screwdriver from her junk drawer and squatted in front of the refrigerator. Ordinarily, she'd have gotten down on her knees to access the panel beneath it, but the smears of ketchup and mustard stopped her. She hadn't mentioned her hiding spot to Honeywell. If her thief had accessed it, they wouldn't have taken the time to replace the mesh panel. Right now, she was the only living soul who knew about it. Granted, Honeywell was a cop. And he'd shared a harrowing memory with her. But she didn't trust anyone. Not even him.

She removed the screws and worked the grill free. Bending lower, she reached into the furnace compartment, ignoring the cobwebs, and fingered the vinyl pouch. She checked her windows to make sure no one was looking in before withdrawing the pouch and unzipping it. Inside, the bundles of hundreds and twenties remained untouched.

To some, it might have appeared to be a lot to keep hidden in a camper. To her, it was every cent she had left in the world.

Chapter Twenty-One

On his way back to the station, Matthias clenched the steering wheel while pummeling himself internally. Why the hell had he revealed so much to Emma? Why had he let her vulnerability trigger his own? Sure, she was attractive. Yes, she was easy to talk to. But above all else, she was involved—peripherally—in this case. He should never lower his guard with anyone involved in an ongoing investigation.

Been there. Done that. It had ended badly.

He swung past Namaste Erie Yoga only to find the lights out and the closed sign hanging on the door. The clock on his dashboard told him it was 3:05, and his anxiety started to creep up. Three to four o'clock on weekday afternoons seemed to be the home invaders' "witching hour." Were they approaching the next victim's house at that very moment? God, he hoped not. He wanted to be ahead of them this time because he wouldn't likely get another chance.

Back at his desk, he texted Cassie, asking how her granddaughter was doing. While he waited for a reply, he turned to his computer. Playing a hunch, he pulled up the yoga studio's website and clicked on the menu tab labeled "Class Schedule".

Morning classes. Early afternoon classes. Several evening classes beginning at seven o'clock. But the only one held in the three to five range was at four thirty on Saturday afternoons. He needed to speak with Kira Petersen again and find out exactly where she'd been last Tuesday.

He checked his notes for her contact information and called the number she'd given him. A bubbly recording answered. He left a message to call him back. The home address he had for her was a few miles south of downtown. Swinging by Petersen's house on his way home was a definite possibility.

He checked his watch. Three twenty. Still no call about another home invasion.

Tamping down his nerves, he dug Emma's hard drive from his pocket and plugged it into his computer. As the photos loaded, his phone chirped with an incoming text from Cassie.

Broken humerus. Needs pins. Waiting for surgeon.

Poor kid. He'd had his fair share of broken bones as a rambunctious, adventurous child. At the time, he hadn't considered the strain it had placed on his parents. He'd only been interested in how cool his cast would look to his buddies.

He texted back. **Call if you need anything. Give Alissa a hug for me.**

Less than a minute later, the phone chirped again.

Let me know if anything happens with the case.

He texted a thumbs-up emoji. But short of the next break-in, he wouldn't bother her. She had enough to deal with.

Bringing his attention back to the photos, he clicked on the first file. A shot of the cemetery. He wasn't in it. Several more photos followed. Closeups of monuments and their engravings. One, he noticed, was for a family with the surname Anderson. Emma's relations? He kept clicking through a series of more stones. The last one was of Nick's grave with the two crushed beer cans. Matthias backed up, scanning through the cemetery pictures again. Emma wasn't lying. She hadn't photographed him. Only the grave after he left.

He closed that folder and opened the next, which contained the pictures on Presque Isle. Multiple shots of the beaches on a gray day, the choppy water reflecting the leaden sky. Mostly, a lot of nothing. Gulls. Trash littering the sand. More driftwood than usual. Then the shot of purple-haired Kira striking a flamboyant pose.

He studied the shot. Was this the face of a thief or even a killer? Most would say no. But he'd been a cop long enough to realize the worst offenders often had the most innocent faces.

The final few shots were of the jumble of wood and trash in which Wesley Simmons had become entangled, dragging his body onto the beach much earlier than it would've surfaced if left to decomp. Only one of the pictures—the one Emma had emailed Cassie—showed anything. An arm. Nothing to identify the victim. Or the killer. Unless…

He clicked the back arrows to again view Kira.

Had the assailant who broke into Emma's trailer really been searching for these photos? Is that why he—or she—stole the computers? The police already had the picture of the victim, which was useless in solving or prosecuting the case. And if Kira was trying to conceal her identity or presence at the crime scene, why pose for a picture?

Matthias was about to exit the folder when something else

struck him as odd. Emma said her editor at *PA Living* had wanted the crime scene photo so badly, he told her to name her price.

Why?

He'd mentioned the Pizza Bomber. There had been an iconic photo of that incident. Memorable and horrific at the same time. Emma's shot wasn't even in the same league.

But it hadn't been released to the public, so how would anyone know? That had to be it. These media hounds who were in a bidding war had no clue what they were fighting over.

Emma should've thrown out an outlandish price and, if they accepted, she should take the money and run.

Yet she hadn't.

Matthias couldn't help it. He liked her for that. She clearly could use the money and yet she'd placed principles above profit.

He was familiar with *ErieNOW* and WERI-TV. Other than having thumbed through a copy of *PA Living* at a bookstore, he wasn't familiar with the magazine or its editor, Bob DelGrosso.

Matthias was about to type DelGrosso in his search engine when his phone rang.

"Matthias? This is Lucas." A patrol officer he used to work with.

Matthias's stomach dropped. This was it. The third home invasion.

"I have something I think you want to see."

Maybe it wasn't the third home invasion. "What've you got?"

"A local resident called to report he thought his fishing boat had been tampered with."

Matthias sat up. "What do you mean? Tampered with?"

"He claims it's been taken out. Stuff has been moved. Nothing major but he says he's very particular about how he leaves it."

From Lucas's tone, Matthias gathered he had his doubts.

"The tarp isn't secured as well as he always does it. And he insists he had a full tank of fuel. Now the gauge reads almost full, but not quite. Since nothing appears missing or damaged, I wasn't going to pay it much attention. But when I got to the private dock where he keeps the boat, we found evidence of blood."

"Give me the address. I'm on my way."

Breaks in the clouds allowed the sun through as Matthias arrived at the private dock. Private being the keyword. Located on a gravel dead-end road edged by trees and underbrush, the dock was well out of sight of any nearby residences. No one was likely to just stumble upon the place.

A pair of steel pillars edged the entrance to the road and a heavy chain lay across the road. Signs proclaiming "Keep Out" and "Private Property" were in abundance, nailed to every third tree or so.

Matthias imagined the dock had been someone's pride and joy years—decades—earlier. Weeds now grew up through the gravel parking area. The shelter protecting the boat and pier from the elements reminded him of one of the picnic pavilions at the park. A roof and four corner supports.

Lucas strode out to meet him. "Thanks for coming." He nodded toward a sour-looking gray-haired gent who stood off to one side, conversing with a second uniform. "That's our RP, Archie Richardson. He owns the boat and leases the property. Says when he got here, the chain at the end of the road was down and the lock had been cut. Looks like someone took a bolt cutter to it."

"Any other security? Cameras?"

"Nope. He says up until now people have respected the signs."

"You said there was blood?"

"See for yourself."

Lucas led the way to the dock. Matthias scanned the ground as he followed. Between the gravel and the recent rains, any footprints or evidence of a trespassing vehicle had been obliterated.

A rickety wooden pier ran alongside the boat, an older but well-maintained Tracker Pro 170. Matthias judged it to be a seventeen-footer. A cement walkway edged the water, a cleat embedded in it. Matthias wasn't a mariner by any means, but he'd been around the area docks long enough that even he could tell the line securing the boat wasn't properly tied off.

"This is what I was talking about." Lucas pointed to a rust-colored smear on the cement slab protected by the roof. "For all I know, it's a result of cleaning fish, although Mr. Richardson says it's not from anything he's caught. I know you're investigating the Simmons murder and suspect he was taken out and dumped in the lake, which is why I called you. There's not a lot of blood for someone who's been stabbed, but I haven't been on the boat."

Matthias thought of Wesley's autopsy and Dr. Browning saying there would be more blood from his nose than from the stab wound. "I'm glad you called. Tell Mr. Richardson I need to talk to him. And I'm afraid he's going to have to put off his fishing plans. I need to get the crime scene unit in here."

Matthias introduced himself to Archie Richardson, who stood with his hands stuffed in the pockets of his khaki cargo shorts. "Tell me what happened when you got here," Matthias said, his notebook and pen at the ready.

"I already told that other cop."

"Humor me."

Richardson's dour expression didn't improve. "I intended to do a little fishing. When I pulled in, I found someone had cut the lock." He waved a hand toward the drive and the chain. "I was afraid someone stole my boat, but as you can see, it's still here. It's been taken out though. I would never do such a sloppy job docking it. Did you see that mooring line? Saddest excuse for a mooring hitch I've ever seen. Hell, even my ten-year-old grandson does a better job of it."

"Any idea who might've taken the boat out without your permission?"

"None."

Matthias gazed toward the dock. "Did you board your boat?"

"Today? Nah. Didn't want to disturb any evidence."

"Good." Still looking at the watercraft, Matthias asked, "Do you have your keys?"

Richardson brought a hand from his pocket, holding a key on a ring in his palm.

"Who else has access to those?"

"At home? Me and my wife."

"Do you have a spare?"

"Sure." Richardson pointed at the dock. "I keep a backup key hidden in the rafters."

"Show me."

Together, they walked to the shelter. Matthias made sure they stayed clear of the possible bloodstain. At one of the corner posts, Richardson reached up, standing on tiptoes, fingering a notch where the upright met the header. He came down with a key. "I keep this here in case I forget or lose mine. And so my two boys can take the boat out if they want."

Matthias held Richardson's gaze. "Your sons know where you hide the key?"

"Sure do." The boat owner frowned. "Don't go accusing my boys of doing this. They wouldn't be caught dead tying that poor excuse for a knot."

"I'm sure, but I need to clear them." Matthias flipped to a blank page and extended the notebook and pen to Richardson. "I'll need their names and phone numbers."

As his witness wrote the requested information, Matthias asked, "Do your sons have keys for the padlock on the chain?"

"Yep."

"Do you have any other keys to your boat floating around?"

"Just these two."

"Anyone else know about your hiding spot?"

Richardson returned the pad and pen and scowled in thought. "It's possible, I suppose. Like I said, my boys take the boat out whenever they want. I'm sure they've taken friends out with them."

"And the friends may have seen them retrieving the key."

Richardson stuffed both hands back in his pockets, storm

clouds in his eyes. "I'm gonna kick their asses into next Thursday," he muttered.

Matthias held up the notepad. "Before you do, give me a chance to talk to them."

The forensic techs made a presumptive determination that the blood on the pavement was indeed human. It would take further testing at the lab to establish if it belonged to Wesley. While the crime scene guys went over the boat, Matthias made a call to his partner who greeted his news with a string of profanities.

"We finally get a break on this case, and I can't be there."

"I didn't tell you to make you feel guilty," he said. "I'm simply keeping you posted on developments."

"Have you had a chance to call the boat owner's sons yet?"

"Next on my list."

"If the blood's a match to Simmons and if CSU lifts prints from that boat, we might be able to match them to one of the sons' cronies. We could have our killer."

"Those are a couple of big ifs. For all we know, one of the sons took the boat out alone to clear his head and cut himself on a beer can."

"You're just trying to make me feel better."

"Is it working?"

Her resigned sigh reached through the phone. "Maybe. A little."

"How's Alissa?"

"In surgery. I hate sitting here doing nothing."

"Don't you dare sneak out and come here."

"That's not what I meant. You couldn't drag me away from my baby's side right now. Except that's exactly what these doctors have done. I want to be in there, holding her hand while she's going through this. And before you say it, yes, I know I can't."

One of the techs stepped off the boat and headed straight for Matthias. "I have to go. Keep me posted."

"You do the same," Cassie said as he ended the call.

"Well?" Matthias asked.

Despite looking like a fourteen-year-old, Billy Everett was one of the best forensic investigators Matthias had ever worked with. "Something definitely happened onboard this boat. We found trace amounts of dried blood on the floor by the back seat."

"Trace amounts?"

"My guess is someone attempted to clean it up but missed a few spots. Including a smear on the gunwale."

"The gunwale?"

"The edge of the boat. If you want my educated opinion, this is the vessel from which your body was dumped overboard."

Cassie might've been right about a break in the case. "What about fingerprints?" Matthias asked.

"We're still dusting. I can tell you there aren't many. A few on the steering wheel and instrument panel but nothing at the stern of the boat where we found the blood. We'll have to get prints from the owner for a comparison, but I'm willing to bet our assailant either wore gloves or wiped the boat clean. I'll let you know as soon as we run everything through the lab."

"Expedite it. Time is of the essence."

"Roger that."

Matthias thanked him and ambled back to his car. Instead of climbing in, he made his first phone call while leaning on the front fender, allowing the breeze, warmer now than it had been even an hour ago, to wash over him.

A recording answered, beckoning him to leave a message. He identified himself. "It appears someone may have tampered with your father's boat." A helpful son would be more likely to return a call about the boat if words like "murder" weren't mentioned. "We were hoping you could help us with the investigation. Give us a call back as soon as you're free." He left his number and Cassie's.

The second son answered Matthias's call. While expressing concern for his father, he claimed he hadn't been out on the boat in almost a year and had never allowed any of his friends to see where the key was stashed.

Matthias thanked him, asked him to contact Erie PD if he thought of anything else, and ended the call.

So much for the break Cassie had hoped for.

Chapter Twenty-Two

T he sun was dropping low in the western sky by the time Emma finished cleaning the pickle juice from a broken jar on the floor and the fingerprint powder from every other surface. She lugged the heavy-duty trash bag out to her deck and stopped to soak in the last of the day's warmth. The sunset was going to be gorgeous. At least her burglar hadn't broken into her car and stolen her camera. She considered walking over to the lakeside beach to take some sunset images. Or maybe she should leave the Nikon behind and simply go stand at the water's edge, letting the cool waves lap at her feet and carry her concerns out into the lake.

Then she realized she still had a lot of work to do. Her door wouldn't latch the way it was. Her paranoia regarding Clay combined with the very real knowledge that someone had broken into her home, small though it might be, and stolen over a thousand dollars' worth of equipment she needed for her work. Sleeping in an unlocked trailer freaked her out.

As she bent over for a closer look at the bent door, a voice behind her startled her. "Are you okay? I heard there was trouble here earlier?"

She spun to find Joe at the front corner of her camper. "You could say that. Someone broke in and took all of my computer equipment. But I'm fine. I wasn't here when it happened."

"Good lord. What's the world coming to?" He ran a hand through his gray hair. "I should've been here. I could've stopped this."

Emma had a feeling he wasn't simply talking about her theft but about his daughter's losses as well. "Or you could've gotten hurt. It's just stuff that can be replaced."

"Do you have insurance?"

"No."

"I know it's a matter of locking the barn door after the horse has been stolen, but you should really get some coverage."

The phrase made her smile, however briefly. She'd had a barn and a horse, so the cliché meant more to her than to most others. "Don't rub it in." She made sure to give Joe a grin as she said it so he wouldn't feel bad. The fact was her lack of insurance had less to do with money than with not wanting her name in one more system. One more way Clay might track her down.

Joe stepped onto her deck. "Good heavens. They really wrecked your door."

"You should see what they did inside."

He shot a glance around at the surrounding campsites. "And no one saw anything?"

"That detective, Honeywell, was here and questioned everyone but apparently the thief was sneaky."

"Or they just wouldn't talk to a cop. Let me ask around."

"Thanks." Emma stood, glared at the warped door, and hip-slammed it to no avail.

"You can't stay here with it like that."

"I know." She looked at her Forester. "I guess I can sleep in my car." She'd done it before.

"Don't be ridiculous." Joe pulled a ring loaded with keys from his pocket and started working one of them free. "You stay in my trailer tonight."

She looked at him. With any other man, she'd have suspected sexual undertones. But Joe had never said or done anything even remotely inappropriate.

He met her gaze. Despite the waning daylight, she could see the flush rising in his cheeks. "Oh, I didn't mean with me," he stuttered. "I'm going back to my house."

She laughed. "I didn't think—"

"I'm an old man and you're a young woman. I would never suggest anything unseemly." He held the key out to her.

"I can't accept that. I wouldn't feel right."

"Of course you can accept it. What's that saying? *Mi casa, su casa*." He took her hand and pressed the key into it. "I won't be able to sleep if I'm worried about you staying in a camper with a broken lock. Or in your car, for crying out loud."

Emma looked down at the key and felt heat behind her eyes. "Thank you." Without thinking, she flung her arms around him.

He returned the hug, chuckling. "Now now, girl. *You're* the one acting unseemly."

She stepped back and laughed. "I'm sorry. It's just been a long while since I had someone worrying about me."

Joe dismissed her with a wave. "I'll call the guy who does

all my RV repairs and have him come out to look at your door. Heck, maybe he'll even fix it so you don't have to use that bungee to keep it open."

"Right now, I'm only concerned about it staying closed."

Joe gestured toward the broken door. "Get whatever you need for the night. I'm gonna take a walk around and play private eye before I swing by my daughter's house. I want to make sure she and my grandkids are okay before I go home."

"Oh? Are you two getting along better?"

His smile was sad. "Not really, but I can't stop trying." He wiped a hand across his mouth. "I'll be working for the rest of the week, so you can have the run of the place until Friday afternoon."

She thanked him again and watched as he shuffled away. The sun had melted below the horizon. She'd missed the sunset, but thanks to Joe, she no longer needed to let the lake wash her troubles away.

Staying in Joe's Jayco felt akin to staying in a fancy hotel. Emma couldn't bring herself to sleep in the queen-sized bed in the front of the trailer, but she found a second bedroom in the rear with bunkbeds. Joe had probably hoped his grandkids would stay with him when he bought the rig. Instead, the beds were unmade and the space used for storage.

Emma retreated to her camper for her pillow and sheets as well as her pajamas and toiletries. And the money pouch. She shoved her door as close to latched as she could and braced one of her lawn chairs against it. A human intruder could easily gain access, but it might keep the raccoons out.

The Jayco's door locked. The bathroom and shower were at least twice the size of hers. And the mattress on the bunkbed was easier on her spine than her futon was. Still, Emma lay awake, staring into the darkness.

Who had broken into her camper? Had she been a random victim of someone looking to make a quick score? It was possible. Perhaps her thief had seen her leave on her bike and seized the opportunity.

Or had she been deliberately targeted? Was the culprit after that photo? Bob DelGrosso had found out where she lived. She needed to pin him down on how he'd located her, and she needed to patch that hole in her personal security. But the photo? It showed nothing of value. Nothing worth breaking into her trailer for. And yet twice she'd been told to set her own price for it.

Another thought set her nerves on edge. Was the burglar another camper? One of her neighbors? She sat upright, banging her head on the upper bunk in the process. She swore, briefly distracted from her fear. Once the pain subsided, the suspicion returned. She padded into the living room and kitchen area, checking that the windows were latched. She peered out. The grounds were quiet and still, lit by dusk-to-dawn lights. Even Mick had turned in at a reasonable hour.

After she was convinced no one was lurking around either the Jayco or her camp next door, she closed the blinds, making sure there were no gaps.

She stood in the center of the RV, in the dark, and laughed. The absurdity struck her as funny. She was an idiot. A paranoid, terrified-of-the-shadows idiot. Every dark-haired man she encountered was Clay. Except time and time again, they weren't. Now the boogie man was after her, lurking outside, watching her from the dark crevices all around.

Still snickering, she made her way back to the bunkroom and her hiding spot for the night. As she sat—careful of her head—she laughed again.

And then burst into tears.

Chapter Twenty-Three

Thursday morning, Matthias texted Cassie to check in. When she didn't immediately get back to him, he figured either she was still at the hospital with Alissa's doctors, her phone battery had died, or she was finally at home getting some sleep.

He'd noted Kira Petersen's Yoga on the Beach class listed on the website for Tuesday, Thursday, and Saturday mornings, weather permitting. With clear, sunny skies greeting him, he decided to head to Presque Isle and catch her as class wrapped up.

His phone chirped as he parked near the kite beach. **Running late.**

He typed back, **Take your time. Interviewing Purple Hair. Will catch up with you at the office.**

The kite flyers were already set up. Matthias skirted them and made his way down the beach, probably following the path Emma had taken last Saturday. He spotted the yoga class in the distance and recognized Kira seated cross-legged as a half dozen students stretched out in *savasana*. He stopped, faced the lake, and watched gulls soar and dip over the water only to settle onto one of the breakwalls, manmade islands of rocks, constructed to minimize erosion. Each was numbered and painted with "Keep Off."

The trespassing seagulls couldn't read.

Minutes later, he noticed the students coming up to sit. Kira brought her palms together with the others mirroring her and bowing. *Namaste.*

He'd taken a few yoga classes in the past. Bikram's or Hot yoga. Intense and exhausting. Not the more classic version Kira taught. He preferred martial arts but respected the meditative mindfulness of this cousin practice.

The students gathered their beach towels and mats and gradually dispersed. Matthias approached as the last one spoke with Kira, not wanting to disturb them but not wanting Kira to get away either.

He needn't have worried. The moment her final student walked away, she turned to face Matthias with a sexy-as-hell smile.

"I saw you over there and hoped you were here to see me." She rested one hand on her hip and thrust her shoulders back, the stretchy fabric of her tank top leaving little to the imagination.

God, he hoped she wasn't involved in this case.

"I have a few more questions for you."

"I'm glad. I'll take whatever excuse you give me to see more of you." Her gaze slid down to his crotch and back up.

Damn, he *really* hoped she wasn't involved in this case.

"You've already said you were home alone Friday afternoon and evening—"

"And will be tomorrow too. You're more than welcome to keep an eye on me and provide me with an alibi."

He cleared his throat. "How about Tuesday a week ago? Where were you?"

The come-hither look drained from her eyes. "Now why am I getting the impression you aren't here with an excuse to ask me out?"

"Tuesday." he repeated. "A week ago."

She heaved a dramatic sigh. "Let me think. I taught this same beach class in the morning. Then I had a class at the studio at noon. I was done and out of there by two." Her mouth drew to one side as she thought. "I think that was the day I came back here to lay in the sun." She met his gaze, the flirtatious slant to her grin creeping back. "There wasn't anyone around so I may have taken off my bikini top. Tan lines, you know?"

If she was trying to distract him, the mental image she conjured up did the trick. He caught himself looking at her breasts, picturing the non-existent tan lines, and forced his eyes up to her face. The grin had bloomed into a she-wolf smile.

"It would really help if you had someone who could confirm your whereabouts," he said.

"You're bound and determined to stick to business, aren't you? Well, fine. I don't have an alibi." She held out her wrists. "Handcuff me, handsome. I promise I'll comply."

Sexy and curvaceous or not, Kira was starting to play on his last nerve. "Can you get serious for a minute?"

"I am being serious." She planted her fists on her hips in frustration. "But fine. We'll play it your way. What is it you think I did?"

"Are you familiar with the Ingram family? They live on Pepperwood Circle."

"Ingram? The name is familiar." Her mouth pursed in thought. Then her eyes widened. "Ingram. Isn't that the family that's been on the news? They were robbed at gunpoint."

"That's them."

"I remember all my students. Even the ones that only come once. None of that family has taken classes with me."

"Have you ever been at their house?"

"No." The lightbulb went on behind her eyes. "You think I had something to do with that robbery?" She choked a laugh. "Man, you are either desperate for suspects or you're doing a helluva job of finding any excuse to spend time with me."

He didn't smile.

Hers dissolved. "Okay, Detective. I don't have an alibi for Tuesday evening. But I sure didn't break into a house and rob it."

He believed her. No. He *wanted* to believe her. But she was messing with him, distracting him, making him question his gut.

"You have my card. If you think of anyone who could place you somewhere—here on the beach or anywhere other than the Ingram residence—call me." He pivoted and started to walk away.

"You're hurting my feelings, you know," Kira called after him. "But once you catch whoever really robbed those people, I'll let you make it up to me. Bring the handcuffs."

Dammit. If they needed to question Kira Petersen any further, Cassie could do it.

Matthias was studying the whiteboard when Cassie dragged in, her eyes bloodshot. She clutched an extra-large coffee from the café down the street he usually patronized.

"You paid for coffee?" Matthias said. "Aren't you the one who's always telling me there's nothing wrong with the stuff we have here?"

"No one asked you," Cassie muttered. "I needed an extra shot of espresso. We don't have that here."

"One extra shot?"

"Okay, smart ass. Two."

"How's Alissa?"

Cassie sipped from her high-octane brew. "Better than me. Shawn's with her."

"Will he be bringing her home today?" Matthias asked.

"That's the plan." She moved to Matthias's side to review the whiteboard. "Catch me up. Start with the break-in at the photographer's trailer. Any connection to the Simmons case?"

"Doesn't appear to be."

"What was stolen?"

"Two laptops and monitors plus wireless keyboards."

"Same sort of thing our home invasion crew has been taking."

Matthias gave her a look. "Except our home invasion crew hits expensive homes with burglar alarms that are shut off so they can walk right in. Emma's camper isn't exactly mansion material. And they had to force the lock."

"Emma, huh. You're on a first-name basis now?"

He clenched his jaw trying to come up with a suitable comeback. When he couldn't, he chose to ignore the comment. "One thing they didn't get was an external hard drive she had hidden."

"Why'd she hide it?"

"It has the photos she took Saturday morning on it. The ones at Presque Isle."

"There's nothing of any value in the one photo showing Simmons's arm."

"You know that, I know that, and Emma—" He winced. "Ms. Anderson knows that. But there seems to be a bidding war going on." When Cassie gave him a puzzled look, he explained about the three-way battle with the two media outlets and DelGrosso.

"Who the hell is Bob DelGrosso?" she asked.

"Editor of a magazine Anderson contributes to. But he claims he wants it for a different publication. One that doesn't exist yet."

Cassie rested her fingertips on her top lip. "Odd."

"That's not the half of it. DelGrosso told her to name her own price for the photo."

Cassie's dark eyes swung on him. "Has he even seen the picture?"

"Not as far as I know. And to answer your next question, Anderson doesn't understand it and neither do I."

"We need to get our hands on that hard drive."

"I have it. She gave it to me."

A hint of an impish grin played across Cassie's lips. "How much did you have to pay for it?"

"Nothing. That's probably the oddest part of all. She turned down the money the media sites offered."

"Seriously?"

He didn't respond.

"Huh. If someone told me to name my price for a picture I took that didn't really show anything, I'd quote a number that would cover a Caribbean vacation for me and my family and then take the money and haul ass."

He couldn't argue.

"What if," Cassie mused, "there's something else on that hard drive. Another picture that we've missed. Maybe she caught something on film she shouldn't have."

"That's what I thought, but I've been over it three times and haven't found a thing."

"I'll take a look at it." She took another slug from her coffee. "What else did I miss? The boat. What have we got on it?"

Matthias told her about the owner's insistence that someone had taken it out without his permission. "Still waiting on the lab to get back with us regarding the blood, fibers, and fingerprints, although Billy Everett believes the guy either wore gloves or he wiped down the portions of the boat he had contact with."

"Just our luck." Cassie turned to face Matthias and smirked. "And how'd your interview with Purple Hair go?"

He cringed. No way was he going to tell his partner about Kira's overt flirting. He'd never live it down. "She doesn't have an alibi for either of the home invasions, but when I asked her about the Ingram family, she genuinely appeared clueless."

"Did she flash her tatas at you?"

He didn't answer. Nor did he meet Cassie's eyes.

"Uh-huh. She did. And your ability to use your head went out the window." Cassie closed her eyes and sighed dramatically. "Men."

Her phone rang. Averting her eyes from Matthias, she answered. "Malone here. What's up, Lieutenant?"

Matthias watched her expression grow ominous.

"We're on our way." She ended the call and faced him. "We have another homicide."

"Home invasion?" he asked.

"Not really. But the address is South Shore Drive. The Simmons house."

Chapter Twenty-Four

The scene wasn't much different than last Friday. Patrol cars lined the street. Neighbors stood in front of their houses, watching the live-action police drama playing out on their street once again.

This time, a pickup truck sat in the driveway. Matthias had seen it before. At the campground. Parked in front of Joe Platt's rig. Lyle and Kollmann stood at the open driver's door as Matthias and Cassie approached.

"Here we are again," Cassie said without an ounce of humor in her voice. "What have we got?"

Lyle stepped aside, allowing them a view of the victim. Other than the crimson hole in his forehead and a gelled trail of blood down his face, Platt appeared as though he'd parked in his daughter's driveway, leaned his head back against the rest, and fell asleep.

"Where's Mrs. Simmons?" Cassie asked.

"Inside." Lyle thumbed over his shoulder. "Officers McKay and Szramowski are with her and the kids. Story is they had stayed at a friend's house overnight. Just to get away, she said. When they returned this morning, she found him like this and called 911."

"What about the coroner?"

"He's on his way."

Cassie nodded. She met Matthias's gaze. "You wanna take the kids again?"

Not really, he thought. He had a shitload of questions for Barbara Simmons and wanted to hear firsthand what she had to say. But he knew what Cassie's argument would be. He had a rapport with Jake and Belle. Cassie had established a relationship with the mother. Best to go with what stood a better chance of working. "Sure."

Inside, the Simmons family was once again clustered in the kitchen at the rear of the home. Brief introductions were polite reminders of their identities. Matthias moved to the breakfast nook where the teens sat, slump-shouldered. "Hey guys." He gestured at the French doors. "Let's go outside and get some fresh air."

They didn't agree or disagree, but simply followed him like a pair of automatons. Matthias didn't want to gather them at the same spot where they'd met when their father was missing. Too much had transpired since then, and he didn't want to stir up additional bad memories. He led them to a round table with an open umbrella shading it and extended a hand toward two of the chairs. Both kids collapsed into them. Matthias took the third.

"I'm sorry to have to talk to you again like this," he said. "How've you both been holding up?"

Jake kept his gaze on the table's surface and shrugged. Belle interlaced her hands on the tabletop and squirmed. "Okay, I guess," she said.

"Tell me what happened, starting with yesterday. You went to stay with friends?"

Belle made a sour face. "Mom's friend, not ours. Mom said she needed to get us out of this house before we all went crazy. Funny thing is, Mom's the only one who's been acting crazy. Jake and me? We're just trying to keep busy."

Interesting. Matthias wrote a note. "How's she been acting crazy? What's that mean?"

"She's been mad a lot. At us. At everyone. Before … when Dad was still alive … she'd be mad at him. They'd argue when they thought we couldn't hear."

"What did they argue about?"

"Money mostly," Belle said.

Jake lifted his face and Matthias noticed a spark of anger in his young eyes. "And women."

Belle shushed him.

Jake glared at his sister. "It's true and you know it. Dad had girlfriends. More than one. We all had to pretend it wasn't true, but it was."

"Did you ever meet any of them?" Matthias asked.

Jake lowered his head again. "No. But I heard Mom and Dad yelling about it more than once."

Tears shimmered in Belle's eyes. "I never met her. I mean, I don't know if there was more than one. But I did see Dad having lunch and holding hands with another woman once."

"Where?"

"At a restaurant downtown."

"Did you recognize the woman?"

Belle shook her head.

"Did you mention it to your mom?"

"Oh, God, no. She'd have killed him." Belle's eyes widened and she brought her fingertips to her lips. "I didn't mean that. I mean, I did, but not, like, for real."

Matthias gave her an understanding smile. "I know. What about last night? What time did you leave for your mom's friend's place?"

"Right after supper," Belle said. "About six or so."

"What's your mom's friend's name?"

"Mrs. Nelson. Her first name's Gloria. She's divorced and lives down in Kearsarge."

Jake looked up again. "Belle and I wanted to stay home. Mrs. Nelson doesn't have any kids. There aren't any video games to play. All she has is books. It's boring over there. But Mom wouldn't let us. She claimed it was because of what happened last week. The break-in? But I told her we'd keep the alarm turned on."

Belle faced her brother. "We don't have much in the way of games here either. Those thieves stole them."

"If we'd stayed here, I could've had Kayden bring his stuff over."

Belle glanced at Matthias. "Kayden's our next-door neighbor."

"Besides..." Jake's eyes brimmed. "If we'd stayed home, we might have been able to save Granddad."

Matthias dug a handkerchief from his pocket and handed it to Jake. "Did you know your grandfather was coming over?"

Both kids shook their heads emphatically. "He keeps calling, and Mom keeps telling him he's not welcome here," Belle said.

"Have you seen your grandfather since last Saturday?"

Belle and Jake exchanged a look that told Matthias all he

needed to know. Yes, they'd seen him and no, their mom wasn't aware of it. "When and where?" he asked.

She heaved a big sigh. "We met him in the park. Presque Isle. At that observation deck. The Feather?"

"I know it. When?"

"Tuesday afternoon. Granddad called me. He said he'd been thinking. Said he wanted to patch things up with Mom and hoped we could help."

"Help how?"

"You know, telling her how much we loved and missed him. I mean, we never did see a lot of him before. Only when Dad wasn't around."

"Dad hated him," Jake added.

Matthias met his damp gaze. "Do you know why he hated him?"

Jake mumbled and looked away.

"Dad thought Granddad was always trying to convince Mom he wasn't good enough for her," Belle said, her chin quivering.

"Was he?" Matthias asked and realized his question was too vague. "Did your grandfather try to convince your mom that your dad wasn't good enough?"

Belle looked away. "I dunno. Maybe."

Matthias sensed he was asking the kids to divulge the grownups' secrets, something they weren't comfortable doing. He typed in a quick text to Cassie. **Ask B if she knew W was having an affair**. He wished he could be there to see Barbara's reaction to that one. Pushing the phone aside, he asked, "Did you do as your grandfather wanted? Did you say anything to your mom about missing him?"

"*I* did." Belle emphasized the "I" as if Jake had not.

"How'd she react?"

Belle sighed. "She said she never wanted us to mention Granddad again." She swallowed hard. Her next words were barely audible. "That if he knew what was good for him, he'd better never set foot around here again."

Matthias caught the knowing look of dread that passed between the siblings. He hated to ask but had to. "You said you left for Mrs. Nelson's house around six?"

Both nodded.

"Were you all together the entire evening?"

"Yes," Jake said quickly. Too quickly.

Matthias shifted his gaze to Belle. She didn't reply. At least she didn't speak the words. But her eyes told him what he needed to know.

She and her brother hadn't been with the adults the entire time. And Belle was terrified of what that meant.

Matthias and Cassie left the Simmons family in the kitchen where they'd found them and moved outside to compare notes.

"Barbara denied Wesley was having an affair," Cassie said flatly.

"You don't believe her." Not a question. Matthias recognized his partner's tone.

"She knows. Moreover, I'd be willing to bet she knows who the girlfriend or girlfriends are. Were." Cassie gazed toward Joe's pickup. The coroner's wagon had arrived, and Felix Hamilton was leaning in the open door to examine the body.

Cassie faced Matthias. "What else did you learn from the kids?"

He gave her a recap of the conversation, from Barbara's ongoing anger with her father and the kids sneaking a visit with their granddad, to their overnight stay with Barbara's friend and the implication that the kids couldn't vouch for the grownups' whereabouts the entire evening. "Anything new from Barbara?"

"Her version is slightly different."

"How so?"

"She claims she's distraught over her father's death. Says they'd been talking regularly and were making plans to put the past behind them."

Matthias huffed. "Yeah, that's *slightly* different."

"She also claims while she and the kids stayed at Gloria Nelson's home, they were together the entire time."

"I'd like to hear what Gloria has to say about that."

"I get the feeling she and Barbara are tight, so she'll likely back up anything Barbara tells us."

Matthias surveyed the houses along South Shore Drive. "We need to canvass the neighbors again."

"And look at more security footage. Maybe Joe's killer wasn't as camera savvy as the home invasion crew."

Matthias had his doubts. "What makes you think they aren't one and the same?"

"I'm not thinking anything right now. Let's go talk to Ham. Maybe he can shed some light."

They crossed the lawn to the pickup and the coroner.

"Hey, Ham," Cassie called.

The blond beachboy turned his head. "Detectives." His attention returned to the victim.

"What can you tell us?"

"About the homicide? Not a whole lot you can't already see until I get him into autopsy. Gunshot wound to the face. No weapon found on or around the body, so my initial assumption is this wasn't a suicide."

"Initial assumption?" Matthias said. "It's pretty hard to shoot yourself in the head and then dispose of the gun."

"Downright impossible. But he's been here overnight. Rigor is fully set, so TOD is between twelve and twenty-four hours ago. During that time, someone could have happened by, seen the gun and helped himself."

Cassie's forehead creased. "Pretty ghoulish."

Hamilton shot her a grin. "How long have you been in this line of work?"

"Don't be a wiseass, Ham."

"Just sayin'. We can't rule anything out at this point."

Matthias added Hamilton's signature line. "Until you get him into autopsy."

"You got it."

"What else can you tell us?" Cassie asked. "Initial assumptions accepted."

"It wasn't a robbery."

"And you know this how?" she asked.

"Put on your gloves."

Once she'd complied, Hamilton straightened and tossed a wallet to her. "That was still in his pocket," Hamilton said. "Check out its contents."

Matthias wiggled his fingers into his own gloves and moved to his partner's side.

She opened the billfold. The ID window held Platt's driver's license. An assortment of credit cards filled the slots.

Cassie spread the bill compartment and counted out a hundred dollars in tens and twenties. In addition to the currency, one folded slip of paper remained. She removed and thumbed it open. And whistled. "I'll be damned."

Matthias took the check from her, expecting to see a payout to the victim. Instead, Platt's name and address graced the top of the check. The date was yesterday's. And it was made out to Barbara Simmons for the amount of a quarter million dollars.

Cassie recovered from the shock before Matthias did. "If someone happened upon Platt and took any gun he may or may not have used to kill himself," she said to Hamilton, "they didn't have the stomach to search the body."

"Even thieves have their limits. Their loss in this case."

She snorted and took the check from Matthias. "I wonder how Joe Platt got this kind of money."

Matthias could think of one way, and it curdled his stomach. Blood money. And the blood belonged to Wesley Simmons.

"We need to have another chat with Mrs. Simmons." Cassie wagged the check and wallet at him. "But first we need to bag these."

Hamilton backed out of the truck. "No signs of other injuries at this point." He looked to his assistant who stood nearby. "Let's get him packaged for transport." Facing Matthias and Cassie, he said, "We'll do the autopsy first thing in the morning."

Barbara Simmons sighed dramatically when she opened her door to them. "You again? I've already told you all I know."

"We've spoken with the coroner and just have a couple of additional questions," Cassie said.

Barbara shot an uneasy glance toward the driveway before stepping aside. "Come in."

Matthias kept his hands in his pants pockets as they headed to the kitchen. He looked around for the kids, but they were nowhere to be seen.

At the huge island, Barbara spun to face them. "What do you want to know?"

"Did you know your father was coming to visit last night?" Cassie asked.

"No. I told you. I took my children to my friend's house for the evening."

"That's not what I asked."

Barbara raised an eyebrow. "You think I went to Gloria's to avoid my father?"

Cassie didn't answer.

Barbara's annoyed scowl grew harder. She shook her head. "I had no idea he planned to drop by last night."

"When was the last time you saw him?"

She huffed. "I've already told you all this. I haven't seen him since Saturday when you were here to tell me my husband was dead. I haven't talked to him except to tell him over the phone to leave me and my family alone. You said you had *new* questions. What are they?"

Matthias's still gloved fingers closed around the small bundle in his pocket. Cassie met his gaze and gave an almost imperceptible nod.

As he pulled out the evidence bag, he asked, "Did your father owe you money?"

Barbara stiffened. "No."

"Did he owe your husband any money?"

"Of course not."

Matthias unwrapped the wallet, withdrew the check, and unfolded it. "Can you explain why your father had this on him?" Matthias extended the check toward her.

She reached for it, but he snatched it away.

"Sorry. Evidence." He held it so she could read her father's handwriting.

Barbara squinted. Her lips parted, slightly at first, but opening into a round O at the same moment her eyes widened.

"Did you know about this?" Cassie asked.

"No," Barbara said emphatically, then repeated, "No."

"Any idea where he got this money?" Matthias asked. "Or why he was giving it to you?"

"No," she said again.

"I do," came a small voice from the shadows of the hallway. Jake stepped into the kitchen, his shoulders slumped, his face tear-streaked.

Matthias replaced the check and wallet in the paper evidence bag and handed it to Cassie. He approached the teen. "Jake? What do you know?"

He inhaled a soggy breath. "Granddad sold his boat."

Matthias shot a look at his partner before coming back to Jake. "When?"

"Last Tuesday. He told me he wanted to help with money for the house so we wouldn't have to move."

"How did he know your folks needed help with money?"

Jake's chin quivered. "I told him. I'd overheard Mom and Dad fighting about it. So he took some guy who was interested in buying his boat out on the lake last Tuesday."

The day he'd missed work. The day of the Ingrams' home invasion.

"The guy bought it, so Granddad took it out one last time earlier this week."

When they hadn't been able to find him. "Did you know he was bringing the money to your mom last night?" Matthias asked softly.

"No. Or I'd never have gone." Jake's voice shattered into racking sobs.

Matthias slammed their car's trunk, locking the evidence inside while silently replaying Jake's story.

Cassie stared at the Simmons house, her arms crossed. "That answered a few of our questions. Assuming the boy isn't lying."

"You think he is?"

She took in a slow breath and let it out before replying. "No. I don't."

"Neither do I." Matthias saw only sorrow and devastation in Jake's eyes as he'd spoken.

"Unfortunately, the answer we *don't* have is who killed Joe Platt. And why."

Matthias turned his back to the house and gazed across the street. "Let's go do a walk-and-talk with the neighbors."

Cassie caught his arm. "No. *I* will talk to the neighbors."

He looked at her, puzzled. "I didn't alienate any of them."

"There's someone else you need to interview. Alone." She shook her head. "I can't believe I'm saying this. You need to go talk to Emma Anderson." There was no smirk, no humor glinting in her dark eyes.

Matthias held her gaze, unsure what she was thinking. "You don't really believe she's involved in this, do you?"

Cassie didn't reply right away. "I think she knows something more than she's already told us. Whether she's aware of how much she knows...?" Cassie shrugged. "Go. If you haven't returned by the time I wrap things up here, I'll catch a ride back to the office and meet you there."

Could Emma possibly be involved in any of this? Matthias's gut told him no. Emphatically, no. And while Cassie may have been right about Kira throwing him off his game, with Emma, his feelings were much more grounded. "I'll text you after I talk to her."

Cassie gave one nod, and he climbed behind the wheel.

Chapter Twenty-Five

After a rough start to the night, Emma had fallen into a deep and dreamless sleep to wake confused and lost. Where the heck was she? It took a moment to get oriented. The bunkroom in Joe's camper. The memory of her broken door and stolen computers slammed her wide awake. She pulled the sheets over her head, hoping to go back to sleep and find yesterday had been a nightmare.

She knew better.

She climbed out of the bunk and considered stripping the sheets but decided to hold off. Joe had said he'd be gone until Friday afternoon. If she couldn't get her lock fixed today, she might need to stay here a second night.

After washing up in Joe's bathroom, she dressed and stepped outside, locking up behind her. During the day, she had no qualms about being in her own trailer, although the thought struck her that whoever broke in had done so in broad daylight.

Who would be so brazen?

Clay, of course. But she needed to quit seeing him every time she turned around. And she needed to quit blaming everything bad that happened to her on him.

She moved the chair she'd used to keep her door closed against critters and settled in to make breakfast. For once, she had ample space on the table to eat. She debated driving down to the Mill Creek Mall in Kearsarge to buy new computer equipment. Should she give the police time to catch the culprit and retrieve what was stolen? Or was that wishful thinking?

She suspected the latter.

But it gave her an idea. She unlocked her phone, pulled up her web browser, and typed **pawn shops near Erie** in the search bar. Rather than fork out money she didn't want to spend on new equipment, she might find something sufficient for sale used. Or she might stumble across her own missing laptops.

While she was online, she logged into Facebook, typed in Clay's name, and held her breath. He'd made no updates since she'd checked it two days ago. She exited his page, uncertain if his lack of social media activity was a good thing or bad. Likewise, Nell's profile showed no new posts. Emma stared at her sister's photo, willing her to call. Or email. Or text.

Emma decided while she explored the local pawn shops, she'd also swing past Nell's old haunts. During Emma's most recent sweep, no one in any of the bars and dives reported seeing Nell for several months. Emma had searched their faces for signs of deception and found none.

Not that she trusted her judgment in that department.

As she washed her breakfast dishes, her phone rang with a number she didn't recognize. The chill was back. Clay?

Stop it, she chided herself. The last time, it had been Nell, and she'd missed the call. "Hello?"

"Is this Emma Anderson?" an unfamiliar male voice asked.

"Yes?"

"This is Timothy Callaghan from Lakeside RV Service. Joe Platt called me last evening and gave me your number. He said someone had forced your door and now you can't lock it."

Emma exhaled. "Yes. Joe mentioned he planned to contact someone for me."

"We've done a lot of business together. I'm in the area and can swing by in a bit. I understand your site's next door to Joe's?"

As they finished setting up an appointment, Emma noticed the same black Impala Honeywell and his partner drove crawl up the hill and park next to her Subaru. She thanked the repairman, ended the call, and stepped outside.

Honeywell was alone once again. "Did you catch my thief?" she called as he stepped out of the car.

"I'm sorry. No." He shot a glance at Joe's place before approaching her deck. The look on his face unnerved her.

"What's going on?"

He looked around, at the surrounding camps this time. Several of her neighbors were out and about. Bringing his eyes to hers, he said, "Can we talk inside?"

Her throat tightened as she flashed back to the cops who'd come to her door four years ago. They'd worn that same look when they asked to speak with her and Nell "inside." And then they proceeded to deliver the news that destroyed hers and Nell's worlds.

Emma felt the deck tilt. She reached out to catch hold of something. Anything.

The detective was at her side in an instant and caught her in his arms. "Hey, hey," he said softly. "Are you okay?"

She wet her dry lips, blinked to clear the haze, and nodded. She stepped back from him. "Yeah. Come on."

Breathing deeply to maintain clarity, she led the way inside and dropped onto one end of her futon. Honeywell lowered onto the other end, shifting to face her.

"What's happened?" she asked.

"I'm sorry to have to tell you, Joe Platt's dead."

Her eyes fogged again. The first part of the sentence was identical to four years ago. "Joe?" She heard the squeak in her voice. "How? When? What happened?" Her questions poured out.

"When was the last time you saw him?"

Emma covered her face with both hands, seeking sanctuary in the darkness. But there was no sanctuary. She lowered her hands. *Think.* "Yesterday."

"What time?" Honeywell asked the question, but she'd already been trying to remember.

"It was right at sunset. Whatever time that was."

"He didn't stay here last night?"

"No." She dug in her pocket and came up with his key. "He said he'd be back Friday afternoon. Until then ... until I got my door fixed, he gave me this. Told me to stay at his trailer rather than here or in my car."

"Did he say where he was going?"

Emma pictured Joe walking away. "He was going to talk to some of the other campers. Play private eye, he called it, to see if anyone had noticed who did this." She looked at her empty table.

"Did he?"

"I don't know. I didn't see him again."

"Do you know where he went?"

She searched her memory for his exact words. "He was going to his daughter's place to check on them. Then he was going home. I asked him if things were any better between them. He said not really but he was gonna keep trying."

"You didn't hear from him after that?"

She shook her head. "I should have called or texted him to see how it went."

"Is that something you'd normally do with him?

"No. But he's been so kind. I should've."

Honeywell gave her a comforting smile. "It wouldn't have changed anything."

Which is when it struck her. He hadn't said how Joe died. "What happened to him?"

"It appears he was shot."

She leaned back against the overstuffed pillow she kept on the futon. "Shot? Where?" She hadn't listened to or read any news this morning. Had he been caught in yet another robbery or one of the drive-by shootings happening more and more?

Honeywell hesitated, seeming unwilling to answer. "Has he said anything to you about his relationship with his daughter? Other than he was still trying?"

"It's not a subject we've talked about. Until he found out about the break-in here, he's been reserved around me. I was afraid he was still angry because I didn't tell him about finding his son-in-law's body." Emma paused. The detective had answered her question with another question about Joe's daughter. "Did she have something to do with it? Joe's daughter, I mean?"

"Why would you ask that?"

Frustrated, Emma clenched her fists. "Will you please stop asking me questions instead of answering mine?"

The pained look was back on his face. "Sorry. Hazard of the job. It's going to be on the news, so it's not going to stay quiet for long. Joe's body was found in his pickup in his daughter's driveway."

Emma recalled the angry exchange last Saturday morning at that house. Joe pleading with "Barbie". She ordering him out instead of accepting his offer of support. Could a family squabble have turned that violent? Emma met Honeywell's gaze but didn't ask the question. At least, not out loud.

"I know what you're thinking," he said. "And I really don't know."

Emma stared at the key in her hand. "What can I do to help?"

Honeywell stood. "You've already done it by telling me what you know."

She climbed to her feet, facing the detective, and held out the key. "If you need to search Joe's camper, you'll need this."

The detective looked at it but shook his head. "You're right. I'd like to look inside, but not without a warrant."

"But he gave me the key and is letting me stay there." She extended her hand farther.

"You don't own the trailer. If I found any evidence, a good defense attorney could get it thrown out."

"Oh." Emma closed her fingers around the key. Another thought struck her. "Should I even be staying there?"

He made a face that Emma translated as *not really*.

But before he could say it, a small box truck rumbled up the hill, slowing as it approached. Emma noticed the lettering on the side—Lakeside RV Service. "It may not matter," she told

Honeywell. "This is a friend of Joe's who's supposed to fix my door."

Honeywell caught her gaze and held it. "You've been inside Joe's trailer. Did you see anything questionable?"

"What do you mean?"

"Anything that might explain what happened to him? My partner and I questioned him the other day, but we were only in the main area. Did you notice anything ... off ... in the bedroom?"

"I didn't go into his bedroom. I stayed in the second one in the back. It's set up with bunkbeds. I did think he probably hoped his grandkids would stay there at some point, but the bunks weren't even made up. I got my own sheets, which are still in there, by the way."

Honeywell smiled, the kind of smile Emma decided she liked. Easy. Genuine. Not the patronizing cop smile she'd seen from him numerous times. "I don't think it would hurt if you retrieved your bedding. But if this guy can't fix your lock, you should find someplace else to stay tonight." He pushed open her screen door, stepped outside, and held it for her. As they stood on the deck watching the repairman gathering his tools, Honeywell leaned closer to her ear, speaking softer. "While you are clearing your stuff out over there, if you see anything that looks suspicious or interesting, don't touch it. Call me."

"I could photograph it and send it to you."

"That would be great."

The man from the truck ambled toward them. "Ms. Anderson?"

"That's me."

"I'm Tim Callaghan. We spoke on the phone."

"Thanks for coming."

Honeywell touched her arm. "I'll be going. Don't lose my card."

"I won't. Thanks for coming by and letting me know what happened, Detective."

He gave a nod. "Call me Matthias."

Chapter Twenty-Six

Matthias phoned Cassie as he made the left onto Peninsula Drive, informing her of Joe's intention to visit his daughter last night as well as Emma's report that the relationship hadn't improved in the days prior. Cassie seemed subdued as he spoke. "Anything new there?" he asked.

"Affirmative. The same neighbor who caught the van on their security cam Friday afternoon caught some interesting footage last night too."

"Oh?"

"It shows Joe Platt's pickup pulling in at eight forty-five last night and parking just as it was found this morning. At eight forty-six, a second vehicle pulled up at the end of the driveway and backed in beside him."

Matthias's grip on the steering wheel tightened. "Just like the van."

"Exactly like the van. Two minutes later, there was a flash."

"A muzzle blast?"

"Sure as hell looked like it, although the second vehicle

blocked the view. Less than a minute passed before it pulled out fast. The windows were all tinted, so no good shot of the driver. It was too dark to make much out anyhow. The tech guys will try to clear it up, but from the shadows of the dome light, looks to me like there was only the driver. No passenger."

"I guess we can rule out the suicide theory."

"So it would seem."

Matthias eased to a stop at the red light on West Sixth and noticed one of those big ass SUVs riding his bumper. "Are you still at the scene?"

"No. We're having the pickup towed to the garage for processing. Ham left with the body. Patrol is continuing to canvass the neighborhood, asking if anyone heard the shot or saw anything. I hitched a ride with a uniform. We're on our way to talk with Gloria Nelson."

That altered Matthias's planned route. "I'll meet you there."

"Don't bother. We've got this. Go back to the office and start coordinating the information coming in."

"On it." Matthias checked his mirror again. "By the way, that security cam didn't happen to pick up what make and model the vehicle was, did it?"

"As a matter of fact, it did. A dark-colored late model Lincoln Navigator. It even caught the license number. The Lincoln was reported stolen yesterday afternoon."

"I keep coming back to the similarities with our home invasion crew. They torched their van, so they had to find a new set of wheels. Maybe they decided on a classier ride."

"Maybe."

The light turned green, and Matthias headed straight, then pulled into the left-turn lane. The SUV followed, still too close.

If he'd still been in uniform, he'd have done a traffic stop. "You don't think this is the same guy?"

"I'm trying to keep an open mind."

"For once."

"This feels like an execution to me," Cassie said. "If—and I do mean *if*—Platt was killed by the same gunman who killed Wesley Simmons, we have to ask ourselves some hard questions. Was Platt planning to meet his killer? If so, why there? Did Platt know something he shouldn't and need to be shut up? Or was he just a loose end?"

All good questions.

The left-turn light turned green, and Matthias swung onto West Eighth. The SUV continued to ride his ass. He took a closer look in his rearview mirror and noticed the emblem on the grill. "You said the suspect was in a dark Navigator?"

"Yeah. Why?"

Matthias slowed to a crawl, expecting the SUV to move into the left lane and pass. Instead it stayed with him. "Because I have a dark Navigator riding my six right now."

Cassie fell silent for several moments. When she spoke, she asked, "Coincidence?"

Although he was always highly skeptical of them, he replied, "Probably."

The next light turned yellow as he approached. At the last moment, Matthias wheeled into the right-turn-only lane and veered into a shopping complex. In his mirror, he saw the Navigator stay in its lane and stop at the red.

"I'm gonna try to slip behind him and get his license number."

"Do you want me to send backup?"

"Not yet. But text me the number of that stolen Lincoln."

"Done."

The strip mall he'd pulled into happened to be one that didn't connect to the next plaza. His only option was to turn around and exit at the same light. By the time he got back to the entrance, the light had changed twice, and he had the red. The Navigator had moved on. Matthias spotted it still eastbound on Eighth, but by the time the light turned green, the big SUV was long gone.

"Looks like I lost him," he told Cassie.

"In this case, I'm glad. If it was the same guy, you wouldn't want to take him on alone."

"Roger that. I'll see you at the office." Matthias tossed the cell onto the passenger seat and continued east on Eighth. Rather than battle the stop signs and lights all the way into downtown, he made a left onto the Bayfront Parkway. Traffic was light at this hour and the views of the marina with its yachts and sailboats always brought a smile to his soul. Not that he ever had any hope of owning one.

Before he reached those views though, his cop's Spidey sense raised the hair on the back of his neck. His gaze shot to his mirror.

The Lincoln emblem on the Navigator's grill filled it. So much for coincidences.

Since slowing down hadn't worked, Matthias sped up and managed to create some breathing room between them. But the Navigator swerved into the passing lane. Matthias imagined the guy pulling alongside and firing on him. He prepared to stomp his brakes, hoping the SUV would roar past and he could swing in behind.

Except the Navigator's driver apparently had other plans.

The jolt bucked Matthias's Impala sideways. The back tires

lost traction as Matthias fought to control the steering wheel. Around him, the scenery spun. He caught the briefest glimpse of the Navigator roaring past his windshield. Then he was looking back the way he'd come. His head filled with the screech and smell of rubber on pavement. He steered. Counter steered. The hillside next to the road blurred, and the passenger side kicked into the air. His stomach rolled. But no. It was the entire car. The sickening crunch of steel replaced the screech. He was upside-down. Airborne. Crashing back to earth with a brain-jarring crunch.

And then all went black.

Matthias had no clue how long he was out. When light filtered back into his consciousness, it was through a red haze. His head throbbed, but at least that meant he was alive.

His memory of the crash was spotty. Concussion? Or had it simply happened in a blur?

His hearing returned with the scream of sirens. He blinked but his vision remained hazy and tinged with crimson. He blinked again, trying to see through the red fog, but all he could make out was a spiderweb. The web slowly morphed into a shattered windshield. Whatever lay beyond was indecipherable.

He turned his head toward the door. A mistake. Lightning bolts of pain exploded in his skull. But he was able to discern the car and the world beyond were right-side-up. How many times had he rolled? One thing for certain. He'd never get on an amusement park ride again. He'd survived the wildest one possible. Barely.

"Sir?" A man in firefighter's turnout gear stood outside the missing driver's side window peering in at him. "Can you hear me?"

"Yes."

"Don't try to move. We're going to get you out of there. Can you tell me where it hurts?"

Matthias swore. "Everywhere." As he spoke, he tasted metal. No. Not metal. Blood. He swore again. "I'm bleeding."

"Yes, you are. You have a nasty scalp wound and they bleed a lot."

He knew that much. He'd seen plenty of vehicular collisions in his years.

"The ambulance just pulled in," the firefighter said. "Can you remember your name?"

"Detective Matthias Honeywell. Erie Bureau of Police."

It was the firefighter's turn to swear. Over his shoulder, he yelled, "He's a cop. Will you guys hurry it up!"

Time crawled and raced at the same time. A paramedic applied a bandage to his head and flushed his eyes with saline. "I think the blood in your eyes is all from the gash on your head. I don't see any glass."

They asked him how many fingers they held up but didn't tell him whether his guess was right or not. He thought it was. Against his protests, they strapped a stiff plastic collar around his neck. The damn thing hurt worse than the head injury.

The firefighters covered him with a heavy blanket and cranked up some power tool. He wanted to pull the blanket from his face but when the car started to whine and groan as the port-a-power wrenched open the door, he thought better and left the cover where it was.

When they removed the blanket, the door had been ripped

open and folded back against the front fender. He couldn't turn his head because of the damn collar but saw two medics approaching with a litter.

"I don't need that," he said and reached for his seatbelt. Another bad idea.

"I told you don't move."

He ignored them and the pain and released the restraint. "I'm fine. Just let me out of here."

"As you can see, he's as muleheaded as the day is long."

He recognized that voice. "Cassie?" When had she gotten there?

She leaned in, positioning her face in his line of view. "Stop being an ass. Let these people do their work."

"Yes, Mom," he said.

She grunted as she backed out. "At least your sense of humor hasn't improved."

"Cassie," he called out.

Her face floated back in front of him. "Yes?"

"It was that Navigator. He pulled a PIT maneuver on me."

At his mention of the Pursuit Intervention Technique, Cassie's expression turned stony. "You're sure?"

He swore yet again. "Yes, I'm sure. It may not be the same Navigator involved in Joe Platt's homicide. I never got a plate on him. But it's damned sure the same vehicle that was tailing me on Peninsula and West Eighth."

"Ma'am?" one of the rescue personnel said.

"We'll talk at the hospital." She backed out.

"I don't need a hospital. I need to find out who the hell tried to kill me."

He couldn't see Cassie, but her voice reached him loud and

clear. "Make sure you tape his mouth shut if he keeps arguing."

Every inch of his body hurt. But after hours of X-rays, CT scans, and blood draws, the diagnosis came in. He was one lucky son of a bitch. Sixteen stitches closed the gash in his head, which Cassie proclaimed was hard as granite. Otherwise, he was bruised and contused, but nothing was broken. He won the argument with the discharge nurse, refusing the recommended wheelchair ride to the exit. She muttered something about Cassie being right and handed him a prescription for painkillers, telling him he'd need them even more in the morning. He tore it into bits and tossed it in the trash bin at the nurses' station on his way out.

Cassie shook her head. "I'll drive you home."

"You can drive me back to the office."

"No." Her tone told him there would be no arguing.

He patted the pocket of the same filthy trousers he'd worn when they brought him in. "I'll call an Uber. Where's my phone?"

"Probably still in what's left of your car."

"Then I'll walk." Any other time the four blocks between UPMC Hamot Hospital and the police station would be a breeze. But halfway down the hall, the floor slanted, and he had to grab for the handrail edging the walls.

Cassie caught his arm. "You need to rest."

"I need to catch this asshole before he hurts anyone else. If he is part of the home invasion crew and killed both Wesley Simmons and Joe Platt—and tried to kill me, a cop—he's more dangerous than ever. We need to stop him before they hit the next house."

"You keep saying 'he.' Did you see the driver? Do you know for certain it's a male?"

He thought about it and stopped to face Cassie. "No, I did not."

"I think we have to consider the possibility our killer is a woman. It doesn't take masculine brute strength to drive a mammoth SUV and fire a gun. And the fact they followed you and tried to take you out tells me they suspect we're getting too close."

"Too close?" he echoed. He truly wished he was close to solving these crimes. But at this moment, he was as clueless as he'd been Friday evening.

Chapter Twenty-Seven

Emma watched Tim Callaghan shake his head at the damage done to her door before proclaiming it beyond repair. Joe had warned him such was likely the case. Moreover, Joe had given Tim the make and model of her camper.

"I pulled a door off a junked trailer I have on my lot," he told her. "I'm pretty sure it'll fit. Got it in the back of my truck."

Emma left him to his work and wandered over to Joe's Jayco. Honeywell—Matthias—hadn't told her to stay out, just that *he* couldn't go in without a court order. As long as she didn't leave her fingerprints all over everything, she figured she could snoop. If she found anything that might explain who killed Joe or why, she'd leave it be and call the detective.

She climbed the steps to Joe's bedroom and hesitated outside the door. Last night, she hadn't entered out of deference to his privacy. Today, Joe was dead. Privacy was no longer an issue. Still, she felt uncomfortable entering his personal space.

She detoured into the bathroom, grabbed a clean washcloth from the linen cabinet, and used it to open the door. She wished she had a pair of those gloves the cops used. If she ever planned to riffle through another's belongings again, she'd have to borrow a pair from Matthias.

A search of the room's storage revealed nothing more than shirts, pants, socks, and underwear. She didn't move anything, partly because the idea of touching Joe's things unnerved her. Partly because the words *tampering with evidence* flitted through her head. She'd leave emptying the closet and drawers to the professionals.

Coming up empty, she retreated through the bathroom, closing the door behind her, and entered the living space. The items she found in the kitchen storage were the same stuff she kept in hers. The only paperwork she found anywhere was the owner's manual for the Jayco.

A rap on the screen door brought her reeling toward it, stashing the washcloth behind her back.

Tim stood there. "Door's been replaced. The one I brought was a perfect fit."

"Oh, good." Relief mingled with guilt over having been busted. "How much do I owe you?"

He shook his head. "Joe told me to put it on his tab."

Her mouth went dry. "Joe's…"

"Dead. I heard. But he wanted to do this for you. Said you've been going through a rough spell, and he could afford it more than you could."

Hot tears burned her eyes. "Joe was a good guy."

"The best. I hope like hell they catch whoever killed him."

"Me too."

"Well, I'll be going." Tim started to turn, then swung back.

"Almost forgot." He pulled a pair of keys on a ring from his pocket. "You'll need these."

She opened the screen door, accepted them, and thanked him. After he drove away, she stuffed the keys in her own pocket and headed to the bunkroom. She'd failed at finding any evidence to help the police find Joe's killer. Just like she'd failed at finding her missing sister.

As Emma reached across the bunk to tug the fitted sheet loose from the mattress, Joe's death and everything that had transpired over the last few years rushed up and overwhelmed her. Her knees weakened, dropping her onto the edge of the bed. She couldn't breathe. All she could see was her parents, their smiling faces in anticipation of the vacation they'd planned. Their disappointment when Emma and Nell joined forces and refused to go along. Waving to them as they headed down the driveway, telling them to have fun. Mere days later, awaiting their return, only to have the state police knock at the door. Mom and Dad would never come home. Never be there to argue with or comfort their daughters again. In so many ways, her own life ended that day as well. Or shortly thereafter as Nell spiraled away into the dark abyss.

Emma doubled over, gasping through her tears. She'd lost her parents and could only blame herself. The decision to stay home had been hers. Nell went along with it. But if Emma had said, "Sure, let's go", Nell would've been all in. The blame for Mom and Dad's death was Emma's alone. Nell's disappearance, a direct result of the loss, also sat squarely on Emma's shoulders. Even the emotional trauma Clay had inflicted had taken root because of that day.

Now here Emma sat, trying to create a new life. Make new friends. Joe was the first real connection she'd made, and he was dead too. Her fault? No. And yet she felt responsible, as if every loss she suffered was her responsibility.

The tears gradually subsided. Her breath grew less ragged. She dried her eyes and her face with the washcloth. She stood, her legs still shaky. After gathering her toiletries and the money pouch, she placed them and her pajamas in the middle of the bed and finished stripping the sheets. She balled them around her stuff, tucked everything under her arm, and headed to the door. She fumbled for the key—Joe's, not her new ones—and locked up behind her.

On her way around the front of her camper, dodging the hitch, she dug in her pocket for her own new keys, eager to see Tim's handiwork.

She froze. A dark-haired man sat in one of her lawn chairs, his back to her. For a split second, she thought Matthias had returned. But her heart knew better.

He stood slowly. Not Matthias's heavily muscled gym-rat physique. Instead, he was broad-shouldered but trim, like a runner. He turned, his face ablaze with a too familiar, too charming smile. "Hey, babe."

Emma could barely squeak out the name. "Clay." Instinct told her to run but her feet had rooted to the earth.

Her worst nightmare stepped off her deck and strode toward her, reaching for the wadded sheets. She tried to hold on, knowing her entire life savings was inside. But he forced the bundle from her, tossed it aside, and pulled her into his embrace. "God, I've missed you, Red."

She stiffened, her arms tight against her sides.

If Clay noticed her tension, he ignored it. He released her but reached up to touch her hair. "What have you done? You know how much I loved your long red hair." His hand lowered. "No matter. It'll grow back. And I'm sure you can dye it back to its real color."

"How did you find me?" she whispered.

He laughed the laugh she'd once found sexy. "It was easy. I just followed my heart." He tapped the center of his chest with one slender finger. "We're connected, you and me. You may not realize it yet, but we are."

She stepped back. Considered bolting for her car only a few feet away. But not without her money stash, which Clay clearly didn't realize hid within those sheets. Besides, the keys to her Subaru hung on the hook inside her trailer, and Clay stood between it and her.

"I know you've been going through some shit. Your head's messed up. I get that. I've given you some space. Let you get away from it all up here. Riding your bike, walking on the beach, even practicing yoga again. I'm sure it's been good for you. You look great, Red. Well, except for your hair."

His words crept into her brain, sinking in all the way to her bones. She wasn't crazy, thinking he was always around. Lurking. Watching. He really had been.

"I'm sorry for the way we left things back home. I was pushing too hard, too fast. But you know I love you with every ounce of my being. We're soulmates." He held up both hands. "Like I said, your head's been messed up. I understand. I have work to do. I need to win you back, and I fully intend to do just that." He took a step closer.

Emma backed away, maintaining the few feet that separated them.

"It's going to be fine. I'm coming into some money, so I can take you home. I'll even build us a new house. You can design it however you want. All the obstacles between us are gone now, so there's nothing to keep us apart."

Obstacles? The only obstacle was his insanity.

And her sister.

"Have you hurt Nell?"

"God, no. Nell's fine. At least as far as I know. She's still missing, right?"

Emma couldn't speak. His singsong cadence. His voice, as smooth and intoxicating as fine whiskey. His way of saying things without really saying them. He'd known all along where Emma was. He knew where Nell was too. "Where is she?" Emma demanded.

"I have no idea. I thought maybe you'd heard from her."

That phone call. Not that she'd tell him about it. "I haven't."

"I'll help you find her."

"You're the reason she disappeared."

He shook his head slowly, his expression tolerant. "That's nonsense. And you'll come to realize it soon enough." He moved toward her.

She backed against her car, but he closed the distance and again drew her into his arms.

"I love you, and I know you love me. You've just needed a little time to figure that out." He held her even closer and brought his mouth next to her ear, his voice dropping to a whisper. "Time's up, Red. I will win you back, make no mistake. I'm the *only* man for you."

He eased away, and she thought he was going to release her. Instead, he pressed a hard kiss to her lips.

She wanted to bite him, but before she could do it, he let

her go. Giving her that predatory smile again, he turned and strode to the road and down the hill.

Inside her head, a voice screamed, *run*. But she remained frozen. Clay had walked here. From where? He didn't look back as he kept walking, keeping left at the bend.

The paralyzing spell broke. She scooped up the laundry still concealing her money pouch, charged onto the deck, and grabbed the doorknob only to find Tim had locked up after himself. Tremors shook her hands as she tried to fit the key into the lock on her new door. It slipped from her fingers, pinging onto the deck and into one of the cracks between the planks. Emma dropped to her knees. The keyring had kept the key from slipping all the way through to the ground beneath. She rescued the key, stood, and unlocked the door. Inside, she stuffed the bundle into the storage cabinet above the futon. Scurried back outside. Relocked the door. Grabbed her bike and rolled it off the porch. Jumping astride, she pedaled in the direction Clay had disappeared, skidding to a stop at the turn.

He was well ahead of her, still ambling away. She scrambled backward so he wouldn't spot her if he happened to glance over his shoulder. But she could still see him. He made another left at one of the campsites, vanishing from view.

Emma dared not trail him. Not on this road. She needed stealth on her side instead of on his. Looking around, she steered her bike to the right. The camp road made a sweeping U-turn to the left and paralleled the one she'd just been on. The one Clay had walked. She rode slower, peering through campsites, around the double row of trailers separating the two roads, until she stopped across from the camp that she believed Clay had entered. She maneuvered her bike so she could see without being seen.

She hoped.

A large black SUV was parked at the camp in question. The passenger-side front fender was dented. She spotted movement in the shadows under the trailer's awning. And there he was. Clay opened the door and stepped inside.

Emma remained still, one foot on the ground, the other on her pedal. Now what? She needed more information. Squinting, she made out the campsite's number painted in red on a white placard nailed to a post.

She shoved off, pumping hard and fast, only slowing for the speedbumps, until she reached the campground entrance. Watching for traffic, she pedaled to the crosswalk at Peninsula Drive and stood to push even faster across the four lanes and into the Beach Side half of the campground. She leaned into the sharp bend, coasting to a stop at the office.

Inside, Emma bypassed the camping supplies and touristy trinkets sold in the front and headed straight to the registration desk in the rear. A woman looked up at Emma's approach. "May I help you?"

Emma fought to catch her breath and explain who she was and on what site she camped.

"Yes, Ms. Anderson. What can I do for you?"

"Site 356. Can you tell me who camps there?"

The woman's eyes narrowed. "We don't like to give out our residents' names."

"Please. It's important."

"Your site is near there. Why don't you stop and introduce yourself?"

Emma battled to control her breathing and her racing mind. She didn't dare divulge her reason for asking. She could imagine Clay's rage if she messed up whatever plan he had.

She plastered an apologetic smile on her face. "I intend to, but, you see, I accidently broke one of the garden gnomes they have out. Playing ball with some kids on the road." She rolled her eyes. "I'm not blaming the kids, mind you. It was my bad. Anyway, I'm going to replace the gnome plus give them a gift card as restitution. I just wanted to have a name for the card."

Emma expected the woman to call her out on the lie, but she apparently bought it. "I understand. Things happen." She tapped on her keyboard. "That site is leased to Mrs. Connie Schultz. I see a note here that she's in a rehab facility for PT following hip surgery, so there's no one staying there at the moment." The woman looked over the top of her glasses at Emma. "You know, you *could* just replace the gnome, and no one would be the wiser."

"That explains why she hasn't tracked me down and read me the riot act," Emma said. "But I'll be sure and confess what I did as soon as I see she's back." Emma thanked the woman at the desk and backtracked through the store, leaving her fake smile behind.

Somehow, Clay had located a vacant camper and had taken up residence. And conveniently for him, Emma drove past that campsite every time she came and went.

Emma returned to her site by way of the road with the double row of campsites between it and Clay's temporary residence. She could only hope he hadn't noticed. At her camper, she ditched the bike in the grass and unlocked the new door without dropping the key this time.

Inside, she surveyed her home. Her car's fob still hung

from the hook. The refrigerator door was closed. No one had miraculously returned her stolen computer equipment.

It had to have been Clay. He was the one who broke in, took her laptops, monitors, and keyboards, and trashed everything else. No one was after that blasted photo. Clay was simply trying—and succeeding—in freaking her out.

She had no evidence. She didn't need any.

She pulled the door closed behind her and flipped the deadbolt. She needed to throw what little she owned into a bag. Grab her money pouch from its current hiding spot. Her car had a full tank of gas. If she left now, she could put several hundred miles between her and Clay by nightfall. She had started over once. She could do it again.

But had she? She'd thought she was free, yet he'd found her. How? And how long ago? Had he been hovering nearby since mid-February?

What made her think he wouldn't find her again? No matter where she ran.

No. She needed to stand her ground. To end this, here and now.

Emma dug Matthias's business card from one pocket, her phone from the other. She slid into the bench at her kitchen table and placed the call. It went directly to voicemail.

She almost disconnected without leaving a message but changed her mind. "This is Emma Anderson. The man I told you about ... Clay Bauer? He was just here." She hesitated. Should she ask the detective to call her back? Come to the campground?

Send SWAT to the campsite Clay had taken over?

Instead, she ended the call and placed the cell on the table before burying her face in her hands.

Her brain started reeling off a nightmarish scenario.

Clay had been in town all along. Watching her, yes.

But what else? He told her he was coming into some money. What on earth had he been doing in Erie to earn the kind of money that would build a house?

Chapter Twenty-Eight

The pounding in Matthias's head refused to subside. Even with his eyes closed, concentrating was pure hell. He sat at his desk forcing his way through the pain in search of clarity. And in search of what he'd done to make a killer believe he was closing in.

Cassie returned to Major Crimes after finally visiting Barbara Simmons's friend. She stormed past Matthias's cubicle to her own and slammed her purse into its drawer.

The reverberating *thunk* bounced around inside his contused skull. "Easy there," he said with a groan.

"Sorry." She didn't sound it. Returning to his desk, she asked, "Do you want to know what Gloria Nelson had to contribute?"

He met his partner's scowling gaze without replying.

"Nothing," Cassie said. "That's what. She totally backs up Barbara's story. When I pressed about the two of them leaving the kids alone, she claims they went for a walk around the neighborhood to get some air."

"You believe her?"

Cassie shrugged. "She did give me the names of some people they allegedly encountered on their stroll. I'll add them to the list of people I want to talk to." Muttering, she returned to her desk. Through the partition wall, he heard her shuffling papers.

Matthias's unsettled mind wandered back to the campground and Emma. She always seemed to be at the center of whatever was going on. If not the bullseye, then damn close. She'd found Wesley's body. She'd been close with the now-deceased Joe Platt. She'd become friends with Kira Petersen, who very well might be part of the home invasion crew. Emma's trailer had been burglarized and her computers stolen. But not the hard drive containing a much sought-after photograph. A photograph that showed next to nothing of legal or news value.

Matthias opened his eyes. He'd gotten sidetracked before having a chance to look into Bob DelGrosso. Curious, he typed the name into his computer's search engine.

Robert DelGrosso was the editor in chief of *PA Living Magazine*, which Matthias already knew. There was no mention of a second publication. Digging into the magazine's website yielded nothing. If he was indeed planning to create a new crime-focused publication, he either had the worst marketing team on earth or his plans were in their infancy. In which case, why blow the budget on Emma's photograph, sight unseen?

"Hey, Cassie," Matthias called out, instantly regretting having raised his voice.

She came around to his cubicle, took one look at him, and winced. "You look horrible. Go home."

"I'm fine," he lied. "I need a favor."

"What?" She shifted her attention to his monitor. "*PA Living*?"

"I told you about the bidding war for Emma's photo."

Cassie hiked an eyebrow at him. "So you really *are* on a first-name basis now?"

"Stop," he said in a hushed growl. "Something feels off with this Bob DelGrosso."

"Off? How?"

"Why would he want to buy that picture?"

"Why would anyone?"

"He told Emma he was starting a new publication, but I can't find anything about it."

Cassie shrugged. "He's not far enough along with it yet."

"Exactly. Why put out that kind of money for one photograph at this stage?"

She rested her fingertips on her upper lip, thinking. "I have no idea. Where are you going with this?"

"I don't *know* where I'm going with this," he said, again too loud. He cringed. "That's the favor I need. Help me dig into this guy. I have a feeling there's something hinky going on with him."

"All right. On one condition. You go home."

"I'm not going home."

She glared at him. All Matthias wanted to do was close his eyes, but he held her gaze, unblinking. Just as he was about to cave, she heaved an exasperated sigh. "Fine. I'll make some phone calls."

Less than an hour later, Cassie wheeled her chair out of her cubicle. "I hate to say this, but you may be right."

Matthias stood, wavered, regained his balance, and circled to her side. "What'd you find?"

She rolled back to her desk. "Until a couple years ago, Robert DelGrosso lived in Scranton. He and his wife divorced. Shortly afterwards, he moved his business headquarters to Erie. I called in some favors and was able to learn he was struggling to keep his magazine afloat even before the divorce. Add alimony and child support on top of that and…"

"We have yet another man up to his eyeballs in debt."

Cassie held up a finger. "You're half right. He *was* in debt. Two months ago, he suddenly came into an unexplained influx of capital."

Matthias reached up to rub his throbbing head but thought better of it. "Two months?"

Cassie's dark eyes gleamed. "Shortly after the home invasions in Buffalo. According to my informant, he received a second influx a month later."

"Coinciding with the Cleveland break-ins?"

Cassie brought a finger to rest on the side of her nose. "Ding, ding, ding. Give the man a prize. But that's only part of it. DelGrosso has a brother by the name of Gerald with a G, who owns a business down in Butler."

Matthias didn't understand the light gleaming in his partner's eyes. "Is his business in trouble too?"

"Not at all. His business is called GDG Galleries."

Matthias's head throbbed, and Cassie wasn't helping. "And?"

"GDG Galleries handles high-end works of art."

Matthias sat up, his headache almost forgotten. "Like the stuff that's been stolen in the home invasions?"

Her smile grew even wider. "I made another call to my friend at the FBI who investigates art thefts. She says GDG Galleries has been on their radar for the last few years, although she hasn't been able to come up with any solid evidence. How's that for interesting?"

"I found something too, although probably nothing to do with DelGrosso." Matthias returned to his desk, Cassie on his heels. "Beldon, Sentry Home, and Safe At Home."

"The three security companies."

Matthias reclaimed his seat. "I've been doing online searches on them and finally found what might be the link." He tapped his monitor. "This news story triggered my search alert. An independent security firm identified a system vulnerability, specifically naming those three companies."

Cassie leaned over his shoulder. "Vulnerable? How?"

"According to this, the system could potentially be hacked, allowing outside parties access to customer timeline histories and patterns." He swiveled to look up at his partner. "Like when they armed their systems and when they were likely to leave them turned off."

"Holy crap." Cassie's eyes had widened. "Maybe they've fixed it, which would explain why there hasn't been another break-in."

Matthias scrolled down in the story. "According to this, a patch is in the works and should be installed soon."

Cassie continued to stare at the screen, her lips moving as she read the piece. Straightening, she fixed her dark eyes on Matthias. "You said this has nothing to do with DelGrosso. Are you sure about that?"

"What are you thinking?"

"What if he hacked those companies?"

"Did your source happen to mention computer skills in DelGrosso's background?"

"No," Cassie admitted. "But I would love to have a talk with this guy."

"Let's go."

"Not you. You need to go home and rest."

"Not on your life."

She glared at him. He glared back. No way was she winning this one.

Cassie blew a rumbling sigh. "Fine. But I'm driving."

"No problem. Except we'll need to sign out a new car."

The drive to the address listed on *PA Living*'s website took only minutes. They could've walked but Cassie gave him an exaggerated head-to-toe inspection and vetoed the idea.

From the passenger seat, Matthias pondered what he knew about DelGrosso. He'd been in the red with his business. After the first home invasion in Buffalo, New York, he'd come into some cash. He'd told Emma to name her price on a worthless photograph for a magazine that showed no signs of existing. A hacker might be the link between all the invasions. Did DelGrosso have the computer skills to be a hacker? Having seen *PA Living*'s meager online presence, Matthias had his doubts.

The art dealer brother, on the other hand…

Cassie parked in front of the red brick building on French Street. "You sure this is the address?"

"It's what's listed on the website."

With a doubtful grunt, she turned off the engine and stepped out. Matthias climbed from the passenger seat, stifling a groan. He felt like rigor mortis was setting in. Maybe he hadn't really survived the roll-over crash and was in some new version of that movie where the kid saw dead people.

No. If he was dead, he wouldn't hurt this much.

Hopefully.

The storefront housed an insurance company. But a plain steel door set into the brick next to the window wore a small sign. *PA Living Magazine*, suite 201. Matthias tried the latch and found it unlocked. The door swung outward, revealing a steep staircase to the second floor. His legs were as heavy as lead, but he wasn't about to complain in front of Cassie. He started the climb.

At the top, they were faced with two doors. One was a unisex restroom. The other had another small sign with the magazine's name taped over the frosted glass. Matthias expected the door to be locked, but like the street-level one, the latch clicked open without resistance.

The minimalist office housed a wall of file cabinets, shelves containing binders, possibly holding back issues, and a long, cluttered worktable.

A man looked up from his seat at the lone desk. "Can I help you?"

Cassie strode forward. "Detective Malone. This is my partner, Detective Honeywell. Erie Bureau of Police. We're looking for Robert DelGrosso."

The man stood. "That's me." His gaze bounced from Cassie to Matthias and back. "What seems to be the problem?"

"Who said there's a problem?" Matthias asked.

"There are police detectives standing in my office. I doubt you're here to buy ad space in my magazine."

Matthias gave him a tight smile. "You're right about that. We're here to ask you some questions."

DelGrosso ran a tongue over his lips. "Please. Pull up some chairs." He indicated a pair of beige metal Samsonites.

Cassie glanced at Matthias. He tipped his head at one and gave a quick shrug. "I'll stand, thanks," he said, as much to her as to DelGrosso. The truth was, he feared he'd need help getting back up. He caught a trace of a grin cross his partner's lips. She knew he was hurting.

Cassie dragged one of the chairs closer and fluttered her fingers at DelGrosso. "Please have a seat." She thumbed at Matthias. "He's been sitting too much today."

DelGrosso eyed both of them, clearly debating whether to oblige the lady or remain standing and eye-level with the male. His gaze settled on Matthias, probably wondering about the bandage and assorted cuts and bruises. Then DelGrosso lowered into his chair, although his discomfort was palpable. "What kind of questions?"

Matthias started with a softball. "How long have you been in this office?"

DelGrosso visibly relaxed, just as Matthias had intended. "A couple of years or so."

"And where were you before that?"

"I was in Scranton."

"Why'd you move?"

DelGrosso lowered his gaze. "Marital problems."

"That's rough, man." Matthias feigned sympathy. "Women. First, they break your heart. Then they break your bank."

DelGrosso huffed. "You got that right."

"That why you had to downsize? I imagine you had a bigger office in Scranton."

"I did. Yeah, I've had to trim the fat, so to speak."

"Then why offer upward of twenty-five hundred dollars for a photograph that's basically an arm sticking out of a bunch of lake trash?"

DelGrosso visibly recoiled. After a few false starts, he said, "You spoke with Emma Anderson?" When Matthias didn't answer, DelGrosso's expression darkened. "She called the police about that?"

"No," Matthias said. "But we're investigating a homicide. She found the body. And you want the photo. You can see why we'd be curious."

"I'm not the only one who wanted to buy that image. Have you talked to WERI? Or *ErieNOW*?"

"They're both news organizations. You publish a family magazine that features tourist spots."

"I was thinking about starting a new publication. *PA Living* isn't exactly bringing in the advertising money or a bunch of subscribers."

"You *were* thinking?"

"I've changed my mind."

"So you no longer want that picture?"

He shook his head. "I'm out of that bidding war. Besides, like you said, it's nothing more than an arm and some trash."

"You've seen the image in question?"

He blinked. "No. You just said—"

"Mr. DelGrosso," Cassie broke in. "Can you tell us where you were last night between eight and ten o'clock?"

His eyes danced between Cassie and Matthias, settling on Cassie. "I was here. I'm always here."

She made a point of looking around the space. "Alone."

"Yes, alone." His gaze shifted to Matthias. "What is it you think I've done?"

"You tell us."

Something in DelGrosso's eyes shifted, like the currents of his conscience swirling, the silt of guilt floating to the surface. "Is Emma okay?"

The question startled Matthias. "Why do you ask?"

"I don't know. You two make it sound like you think I did something to her."

"Did you?"

He hesitated a moment too long before stuttering, "No."

Matthias waited. Humans, especially those with a guilty conscience, tended to despise silence.

DelGrosso was no exception. "It wasn't my intention. I didn't mean to." His voice and his demeanor began to crumble. "No one was supposed to get hurt. I had no idea who he was when I hired him."

Matthias looked at Cassie who appeared as puzzled as he. "Who did you hire?" he asked.

DelGrosso, eyes damp, leveled his gaze on Matthias. "A guy by the name of Clay Bauer."

Chapter Twenty-Nine

Emma remained seated at her kitchen table and ran the events of the last few weeks through her mind. She'd thought she saw Clay at every turn. Each time, she was proven wrong. Matthias at the cemetery. The guy standing by her car. The man at Presque Isle. She'd come to believe she was paranoid. Now she knew she wasn't. That feeling of being watched? She hadn't imagined it.

But when exactly had Clay arrived in Erie? And how was he about to come into a large amount of cash?

Her mind settled on last Saturday. Joe's daughter's house. The home invasion.

The murder.

Emma buried her face in her hands. She was taking a huge leap in logic.

Or was she?

When she first met Clay, almost a year after her parents' deaths, he'd been charming, attentive, not to mention handsome. He'd comforted her, held her as she wept over her loss. As time went on, he became possessive. Demanding.

Threatening.

Clay didn't want her spending time with her friends because it took time away from him.

Meanwhile, Nell had been numbing her grief by self-medicating with alcohol. Then with drugs.

Clay started insisting Emma was an enabler for Nell and her demons. Tough love was the only answer, he claimed. He pressured Emma to cut Nell off financially.

Like an idiot, she had. Only, instead of providing a wakeup call, the tough love threw Nell deeper into the abyss. She'd vanished, lost to the world of addiction, resurfacing occasionally, claiming to be getting her act together. And then she was gone again.

Clay continued to manipulate Emma, forcing her to cut ties with everyone important in her life. He pressured her to stop going to yoga classes. He insisted she give up her fledgling photography business, claiming he would take care of her.

Late last year, she'd finally had enough and told him to leave. He'd gone into a rage and beat her senseless. She took the blows to her face and torso until she fell to the ground. He kicked her. She heard her ribs crack. The pain was overwhelming. She knew in that moment he was going to kill her.

He didn't. He stopped just shy of murder. Kneeling next to her, he cradled her in his arms, stroking her hair, her face. Smearing the blood from her nose. He didn't apologize. He told her she shouldn't say things like that. They were soulmates. She belonged to him. If she ever left him, he would die.

But he would kill her first.

If he couldn't have her, nobody could.

That night, she hatched her plan to get away.

She'd thought she'd succeeded.

Thinking back on that night—the broken bones, the blood and the bruises, none of which he'd permit her to see a doctor about—she thought of Wesley Simmons, dead on the beach, and knew, in her heart, Clay had done it. Clay was part of the home invasion crew. For whatever reason, Clay had killed Wesley.

The next thought doubled her over. Clay killed Joe. Why?

The answer was obvious. Joe had befriended her.

Emma rose from her seat and paced the short span between her bathroom and futon. Five steps one direction, five steps back. She stopped at the table and looked down at Matthias's business card. He still hadn't returned her call. She picked up her cell and tried again. She needed to tell him what she suspected—what she *knew*—and let the police handle it.

The call once again went to the detective's voicemail.

"It's Emma. Call me as soon as you get this." She disconnected and debated what to do. Wait. She should wait.

Except she knew Clay. He was slick. The police wouldn't find any evidence on him. He was too smart for that. And as soon as he realized they were after him, he'd vanish into thin air.

Which wasn't a bad thing. However, it wouldn't last. He'd found her once. If she ran, he'd find her again. If she stayed, he'd be back. Only she wouldn't know when. At least right now, she knew he was here. Better to know where her enemy was than to look over her shoulder every minute of every day.

The only way she'd ever be free was to make sure the

police had evidence of Clay's crimes. And she was the only one who could provide that evidence.

She snatched Matthias's business card and stuffed it into one hip pocket, her phone in the other. Briefly she thought about digging her money pouch from the bundle of bedsheets. Clay had held her life savings in his hands without knowing it. The pouch was probably safer right where it was.

Grabbing her car's key fob from the hook, she charged out and locked her new door. She hurried to her car and checked the floor of the backseat. Her camera bag was still there, Nikon inside, memory card intact.

"Yo, Emily, where are you going in such a hurry?"

She spun to find Mick standing behind her Subaru. She looked down at her camera and then at her neighbor. "I have a photo assignment."

He grunted and started to move on.

"Hey, Mick," she called after him.

The fact that she'd addressed him in a civil manner appeared to startle him. He stopped and faced her.

"Don't suppose you have a pair of binoculars I could borrow."

Confused, he pondered the question before replying. "Yeah. I do."

Emma had a plan. Not a very good one, but she hoped it would evolve into something solid as she thought it through. For starters, she intended to turn the tables on her stalker. She was sick of being the prey in Clay's cat-and-mouse game.

She drove to the intersection below her camper. If she

turned right and made that U-turn onto the parallel road as she had with her bike, she might slip past Clay unnoticed. But before she could become the huntress, she needed to be the bait.

She turned left.

It took every ounce of determination to keep her eyes on the road straight ahead as she crawled past site 356. Was he watching? Did he see her? Would he follow her? If he noticed her looking his way, he'd know she'd made him. She needed him to believe he was still in control.

By the time she reached the entrance, she caught a glimpse of a black SUV behind her, keeping its distance.

"Gotcha," she whispered. But now that she had him on her hook, what was she going to do with him?

She needed to lure him away and then lose him.

He followed her onto Peninsula Drive. With one car between them, he kept enough distance so she wouldn't notice. If she didn't already know he was there.

The light at West Sixth Street was green. She stayed straight. A check of her rearview revealed he and the car between them did too. The light at West Eighth turned yellow as she approached. The car ahead of her squeaked through. She hit the gas and made it through as well. The car behind her stopped, stranding Clay. So far so good.

The next traffic signal was at West Twelfth. She pulled into the left turn lane just as the light turned yellow. "Go, go, go," she said to the driver in front of her. Unfortunately, he chose to heed the traffic laws and stopped. She swore. If she'd been able to make the left, she could've quickly turned onto any one of the side streets before Clay caught up. By the time the light turned green, the black SUV was behind her again. There were several cars between them, but he knew where she was. Still, she stuck with her plan. The abundance of traffic lights on Twelfth Street usually annoyed her. Today, she hoped they'd be her saviors.

She cruised along in the right lane, keeping at or below the speed limit. She didn't want him to believe she was aware of his presence. He was still back there, three cars between them. The first light stayed green. The second light stayed green. The third light turned yellow.

"Let's try this again." She sped up and slipped through as it turned red. The car behind her stopped.

No more obeying the speed limit. Emma gunned it down the street keeping one eye on her rearview. No SUV. She made the next right onto Fourteenth, heading west. At Lowell, she hung another right bringing her back to Twelfth. She stopped and looked behind her. Nothing. She checked left and right. No black SUV. Still not content to simply take the heavily traveled Twelfth back to Peninsula, she went straight.

Shortly after she'd moved to Erie, she'd made a habit of driving around this area, familiarizing herself with the businesses and the streets. She used the knowledge she'd gained, cutting through parking lots, making seemingly random lefts and rights, until she reached the intersection of Sixth and Peninsula without ever seeing Clay's SUV.

She'd lost him. Now, she needed to lay in wait for him.

Emma wished she could swap out her white Subaru for another vehicle, but that wasn't an option. Instead, she tucked her car between two huge pickup trucks parked behind Sara's

Restaurant and hoped Clay wouldn't make a swing through the parking lot. She darted into the gift shop next door and bought an oversized hoodie and sunglasses. Not the best disguise, but it allowed her to blend in with a group of college-age kids who'd claimed three of the picnic tables at the diner. From her vantage point, she watched and waited.

About a half hour passed before she spotted the dented black SUV. Thankfully, it drove straight into the campground's entrance without checking out the restaurant's parking lot.

Emma rose from her seat and slid through a gap in the fence separating the dining spots from the campground. Huddled against a dumpster, she watched Clay drive toward his site. She moved away from her concealment and shadowed him, darting from campsite to campsite, always out of his view.

Not surprising, he drove past site 356 and turned right, heading toward her camp. She said a silent prayer that he didn't go into a rage and set the place on fire. At the idea, she wished she'd grabbed her money and kept it with her.

Less than a minute later, the SUV returned and pulled into his spot. Emma sighed, relieved. He'd merely checked to see if she'd returned. She imagined how pissed he was at having lost track of her. Hopefully, he considered it a temporary situation and would go about his business in anticipation of her eventual return.

After she covertly watched him get out of the SUV and go into Mrs. Schultz's camper, she hurried back to the picnic tables at the restaurant to continue her surveillance of the entrance.

The college kids left. Emma moved under the red and white awning and checked her phone for the time. One thirty.

An hour and a large fries and milkshake later, she spotted the SUV exit the campground.

Emma scrambled to her feet and jogged toward her Subaru, dumping her trash in a can on the way. By the time she got in and made it across the parking lot and onto Peninsula Drive, the SUV had almost a quarter mile lead on her. But traffic coming out of the park was heavy, and the twenty-five-mile-an-hour speed limit allowed her to keep him within sight. Besides, she wanted space between them. The last thing she needed was to have him spot her.

The black SUV stayed in the right lane and, at the top of the hill, made a right at the light onto West Sixth. No other cars in front of Emma made the turn. If she followed, she knew he'd notice her behind him.

She went straight, her heart racing. Ahead, the next light was red. She veered into a gas station sitting on the corner and cut through the lot onto West Lake Road, aware that West Sixth merged with West Lake a block ahead.

She saw him. The dented SUV passed the intersection in front of her, continuing on West Lake. She waited at the intersection, giving two cars a chance to pass before falling in behind. They'd barely gone two blocks when she noticed the SUV pull into a parking lot on the right. Emma hit her turn signal, caught a lucky break with traffic, and managed to turn left into a motel parking lot almost directly across from Clay.

Too close. Emma could only hope he was so focused on whatever he was up to that he didn't notice her.

She snagged Mick's binoculars from the seat next to her. Clay, attired all in black, stepped out of the SUV and strode towards a pair of vehicles at the edge of the lot. A trio, also wearing black, exited the cars and waited for him.

Emma took a closer look at Clay's friends. Two men and a woman. The woman had long light brown hair, and as she glanced in Emma's general direction, Emma noticed the purple highlights.

The woman was not Kira, although Emma had a feeling she'd seen her before. She blew out a breath, grateful her new friend wasn't part of this group.

Emma swapped the binoculars for her Nikon with the long lens, wishing she'd coughed up the money for an even longer one. She zoomed in on the four, snapping photos of Clay and each of his associates.

Putting the camera down, she dug out her phone and Matthias's business card. Time to call in the professionals and to clear Kira's name. Before she had a chance to punch in even the first number, the quartette started moving toward the SUV. Emma swore. The call would have to wait. She didn't want to lose them now.

Clay, she noticed, claimed the front passenger seat while the woman got behind the wheel.

Emma backed out of her parking spot and drifted toward the street, giving them an opportunity to get well ahead of her. Before she was clear to make the left turn, the SUV made a right off West Lake and into a residential area.

It seemed like forever before traffic cleared. With Clay and company out of her sight, she stomped the gas, then veered onto the same street the SUV had. She noted the name, Baer Drive, so she could report the location to Matthias. She caught a glimpse of the SUV's rear as it disappeared into a side street ahead.

Throwing caution to the wind, Emma sped to the intersection. By the time she followed their trail, the street ahead was clear. Fearing she'd lost them, she gunned it again to the next stop sign. Looking both ways, she saw no evidence of the black SUV.

She slammed her steering wheel with both fists. Why hadn't Matthias returned her call? Maybe she should just call 911.

And tell them what?

She looked left, then right, again, thinking. Left would only take them back to West Lake. Right? She'd never explored these streets but considered what she knew of the lay of the land. Right should take them toward the lake's shore.

And probably some home-invasion-worthy homes.

Emma decided to head that way. If she spotted the SUV, she'd stop and make the call. If she couldn't find it, she'd also make the call. At least she'd be able to give the police a starting point.

She steered right and crawled along the residential street. The homes here were nice but nothing like Joe's daughter's place.

The road came to an intersection. Thick trees grew along the left leaving no option to turn that way. The paved road hooked right. Straight ahead, a gravel lane sloped down through thick foliage toward Lake Erie. A no-outlet sign warned her off.

A voice inside her head agreed. Do not enter. Instinct told her Clay had gone down there. She lowered her window and listened for the sound of a motor running. Only the breeze through the leaves responded.

She let off the brake and coasted forward, tires crunching on the gravel. Leaning toward the windshield, she kept her eyes on what lay ahead.

And there it was. The sunlight reflected off a hint of black paint gleaming through the trees. Time to end her private investigating and call in the professionals. Emma braked and reached for her phone.

She was so focused she missed the movement to her left until it was too late. A black-clad arm reached through her open window and pressed a gun against her neck.

"Put the phone down," Clay ordered.

For a split second, she considered hitting the gas.

He must've read her mind. "Don't," he ordered, his voice low and threatening. "I'll blow your head off."

She believed him and let her cell drop from her fingers.

Chapter Thirty

M atthias's breath grew still. "You hired Clay Bauer? For what?"

DelGrosso clasped his hands on his desk but that didn't stop them from trembling. "A job opening."

Matthias shot a glance at Cassie, who met his gaze, wide-eyed. She gave a subtle nod, ceding the interview entirely to him.

"What kind of job?"

DelGrosso lowered his head as though speaking to his desk. "A short-term local position."

"On your home invasion team?"

DelGrosso's face came up, terror in his eyes. "How did you—?"

"What did you do?" Matthias asked. "Hire a different crew in each city? Buffalo? Cleveland? Now Erie?"

All color drained from the editor's face. His mouth worked, trying to form words and failing. He gave up, pressing his lips shut in a tight, thin line.

The last thing Matthias wanted was to have DelGrosso utter the word *lawyer*. "Look. I get it. I really do," Matthias said, still pouring on the empathy. "The last few years have sucked. You're doing what you need to do to stay afloat."

Cassie's phone buzzed softly. Matthias watched as she checked the screen. She looked puzzled before her eyes registered recognition. "I have to take this," she said. Then softer for Matthias's ears only, she added, "It's the boat owner's son."

He gave a nod of understanding, glad he'd left her number along with his on the voicemail. She rose and strode away.

He brought his gaze back to DelGrosso and, keeping his voice soft, said, "You seem sincerely concerned about Emma Anderson's safety."

"I am."

"Clay Bauer."

DelGrosso's eyes glistened. Choking, he said, "I should've never hired him."

"For your home invasion crew," Matthias said.

DelGrosso gave a nod of confirmation.

"Tell me about them."

He took a long inhalation and let it out, shoulders sagging. "I was on the verge of losing my business. A business I've worked my entire adult life to grow. I was desperate. Then an old college friend of my brother's and mine came to town."

The mention of the brother cleared what remained of Matthias's trauma-induced brain fog.

"This guy runs a security firm," DelGrosso continued. "We went out for drinks one night. All three of us overindulged. He always did talk too much when he was drunk, even back in school."

"Your friend?" Matthias asked. Without Cassie, he needed to make sure he was keeping the story straight.

"Yes. He mentioned he was investigating a potential system vulnerability affecting certain home security companies. Gerald—my brother—and I must've looked interested because he went into a lot of detail about how a hacker, with the right equipment, could acquire the records of these companies' clients. Stuff like what time they armed and disarmed their home systems."

"And you took advantage of the information."

"I didn't plan on it. But in the next few days, a bunch of bills hit me. My alimony and child support were overdue. I thought, what harm would it do? Rich folks have good insurance they'll collect and not really be out anything. No one was supposed to get hurt." DelGrosso's voice broke. "I swear to God, no one was supposed to get hurt."

Matthias wasn't ready to go there yet. He looked around at the sparse office space. "You mentioned a hacker could pull this off. Excuse me for saying, but you don't sound like a hacker with specialty equipment."

"I'm not. But there's a woman who's a regular contributor for the magazine. I knew she had IT skills and abilities. I also knew she was..." He rubbed his forehead. "I knew she was in love with me. I'm not proud of it, but I seduced her."

"With the intention of getting her to breach these security systems for you?"

He nodded.

"What's her name?"

DelGrosso's quivering jaw jutted. "I'm not giving her up."

Matthias wasn't concerned with that detail right now. They'd find out later, one way or another. "That's fine," he told

DelGrosso. "You got your girlfriend to hack the security companies. Then what?"

"I knew I didn't have a lot of time to pull this off. The news of the vulnerability would be made public soon and the companies would develop a patch. I had to move quickly. I placed an ad on the dark web and hired a four-man crew in Buffalo. The plan was to hit three homes. Three big scores and be done. We'd get our payoff from the sale of the stolen merchandise, and they'd disband before the police got organized enough to figure out what was going on. It worked." He chuffed a laugh. "I called it my rule of thirds."

"Then you moved on to Cleveland."

He lowered his face. "I did the same thing as before. Hired a crew. Three big scores and disband."

"And then came Erie."

"Honestly, I hadn't planned on a third city, much less my own. But it was working so well. I had my girlfriend go in and check to see if they'd installed a patch yet. They hadn't, so I thought, one last time. Three really had become a lucky number."

"You hired another local crew."

DelGrosso's brow furrowed. "Yes and no. I went on the dark web, same as before, but I received a strange message in response. This one fellow was insistent on being part of the crew. You know how when you're hiring for a normal job, you accept applications and select those you think might be a good fit? In Buffalo and Cleveland, it wasn't any different than that. But this guy? He was like the applicant who keeps calling and checking to see if you've filled the slot yet. Very determined."

"Clay Bauer?"

"Yeah. He made me a little uncomfortable, but he did seem perfect for the job. I hired him. But then he broke protocol."

"Protocol?"

"With the others, I never met them face-to-face. It was part of my safety net. Everything is anonymous on the dark web. But somehow Bauer knew who I was. The son of a bitch showed up here. In my office."

"Why? What did he want?"

DelGrosso swallowed. Hard. "He wanted Emma Anderson."

Matthias planted a hand on the desk and leaned over it. "How do you mean, he *wanted* her?"

Matthias's posture had its desired effect. DelGrosso sank back. "Just that," he said. "Bauer wanted me to tell him how to find her."

"And did you?"

"No. I really like Emma. She's a sweet young woman. I knew she'd been through a rough patch. Her family dying. Her sister missing. And I knew there was something else going on that had her hiding out, but I didn't know what. Or who."

"What happened when you didn't give him what he wanted?"

"He went crazy. The man is deeply disturbed."

Cassie returned and slid noiselessly into her chair.

DelGrosso continued. "At first, he threatened to turn me into the police for my part in the break-ins. But I wasn't going to trade my life for Emma's. Besides, at that point, a good attorney could've gotten me off."

"You said 'at first.' What changed?"

"The first robbery went off without a hitch. But everything went sideways after the second one."

"At the Simmonses' place."

DelGrosso inhaled a ragged breath. "Bauer called me that night, telling me to meet him out in the middle of nowhere and to bring him a change of clothes. I honestly didn't know what he'd done. But when I got to the location he gave me, I found him and the white van he'd stolen to use in the thefts. He had blood on his shirt and pants. That's when he told me he'd killed the homeowner. *Had* to kill him, is how he said it. Nonchalant. Like he had to pick up a loaf of bread on the way home. He told me not to worry." DelGrosso huffed a hysterical laugh. "He claimed he'd taken care of the body. He'd dumped it out in the lake, and it would be weeks, maybe months, before it was found. By then, we'd have all moved on. And by 'we,' he meant him. Then he stripped down. Changed into the clothing I brought. Put the bloody stuff inside the van. Dumped a can of gasoline all over the clothes and the van. Then he tossed in a match. The thing went up like a rocket."

The only sound in the room was the faint scratch of Cassie's pen on her notebook. The rip of a page being torn. Then she held the piece of paper out to him. He took it and glanced at the scrawl. *Boat owner's son took his cousin out on the water several times. Cousin is Clay Bauer.*

That answered one question.

DelGrosso blew out a breath. "That's when he told me I was in it all the way now. It didn't matter I hadn't been the one with the knife. I was as guilty of committing the murder as if I had."

Bauer was right about that.

"And he told me the only way he'd keep quiet was if I told him where Emma was."

"Did you?"

"I couldn't tell him because I didn't know. I pay her electronically into an online account. He was furious."

"What did he do?"

"Nothing. At least nothing right away." DelGrosso shifted in his chair. "Sunday, a friend of mine at the TV station told me about the photo. Bauer had been wrong about the body not washing up. Not only that, Emma was the one who found him and took a picture. All I knew was there was an image of the victim and other news outlets were bidding on it. I didn't know if it showed any damning evidence. I shouldn't have, but I called Bauer and told him about the photo and that *ErieNOW* and WERI were trying to purchase it. He told me we had to get it away from her. I was to meet with her and offer to buy it."

"What did you do?"

"I wasn't planning to do anything. But I saw her on the street the next day when I was on my way to pick up lunch. I stopped her and asked about the picture. She wasn't willing to sell it. I told her to name her price and she said she'd think about it."

Matthias already knew what happened next but asked anyway. "Did she?"

"I didn't hear back from her. I *did* hear back from Bauer. The odd thing is, he'd found out that she was living at Sara's Campground. Which site and everything."

This news chilled Matthias. Emma's stalker knew where to find her.

"He insisted I get the photo because it might provide incriminating evidence against us," DelGrosso continued. "He emphasized *us*. I went there and met with her. That's when she told me she wasn't going to sell the image to anyone, and she

327

mentioned there wasn't anything identifiable in the picture anyway."

"Didn't you know the police already had a copy of it?"

The look on DelGrosso's face told Matthias he didn't.

"What happened next?"

"I contacted Bauer and told him there was nothing incriminating on the image and told him to leave Emma alone or I'd turn him in. He was holding the murder over me. I figured two could play that game."

"When was the last time you spoke with Bauer?"

DelGrosso lowered his chin to his chest. "Last night."

"And?"

The editor kept his head down.

"Mr. DelGrosso," Matthias said, an intentional threat in his tone. "What did Bauer say to you?"

DelGrosso sighed. Lifted his face and scrubbed it with both hands before meeting Matthias's gaze. "He told me he had a few minor details to wrap up, but everything was on for this afternoon."

"What is on for this afternoon?" Matthias feared he already knew.

"The third robbery. I'm telling you the truth. This one is the last. Three cities. A total of nine jobs. And done."

"Where?" Matthias asked.

DelGrosso squirmed.

"You've cooperated with us so far. We'll let the DA know. He might … *might* … be willing to work with you. But if you allow another homicide to happen, all bets are off."

DelGrosso hedged. Thought about it. "All right. But I mean it. This was always to be the last job." He gave them an address on Lake Front Drive and checked his watch. "It may already be happening."

"You're right about one thing," Cassie said, closing her notebook. "This is the last job you will ever pull." She stood. "Robert DelGrosso, you are under arrest."

While Cassie radioed dispatch to report a possible home invasion in progress at the Lake Front Drive address, Matthias called for a marked unit to transport their suspect to the station for booking.

As they waited for DelGrosso's ride. Matthias held open his palm toward Cassie. "I need your phone."

She handed it over. "What for?"

"I need to call Emma." Except he'd saved her number in *his* phone. Grumbling, he dug out his notebook and thumbed back, searching for it.

Cassie found the number in her notes first and aimed the page at him.

He keyed it in and waited. He needed to warn her. Tell her to get away from the campground. But the call went straight to voicemail.

"Dammit," he muttered.

"No answer?" Cassie asked.

He looked at his partner, then at their suspect. DelGrosso had been searched—no weapons—and handcuffed and now was slumped in the chair Cassie had vacated. A broken man whose life had crumbled from under him. "You can handle things here, right?"

She eyed Matthias. "Yes. Why?"

"I need to get to the campground. And I need to hold onto your phone."

"You really think Emma Anderson is in danger from this Bauer guy?"

"I do. I also believe she's one of the minor details he planned to wrap up before leaving town."

"If this Lake Front Drive job is the last one, leaving town is Bauer's next move."

"Exactly. And I don't intend to let him leave with Emma."

As Matthias approached Emma's camp, he noted the absence of her car. He parked in its usual space and noticed the closed trailer door. Another call to her number again resulted in voicemail. This time he left a message. "Emma, it's Matthias. Call me at this number as soon as you can."

He *should* be relieved. If Bauer had grabbed her, her Subaru would still be here. But Matthias knew that wasn't necessarily the case.

He climbed out and was immediately buffeted with the high-volume rock music blasting from Mick Harper's site. Matthias didn't have time to deal with him right now. Instead, he stepped onto Emma's deck and tried the door. Locked. He knocked. Nothing. He peered into the large window over her table. The lights inside were out and no one was home. Nor was Emma sprawled unconscious on the floor.

Still, the knots in his neck and shoulder, which had nothing to do with the earlier rollover, refused to ease.

He returned to his car. With his hand on the door handle, he looked towards the music, then strode in that direction.

The radio fell silent the moment Harper spotted him.

"Don't you have anything better to do than harass law-abiding citizens just trying to relax?"

Matthias ignored the question. "Have you seen Emma Anderson today?"

"You mean Emily. Yeah, sure."

"When?"

"I dunno. After lunch."

"Any idea where she went?" Matthias didn't expect he would.

"She said she had a photo assignment."

His surprise over Harper knowing anything about Emma's comings and goings was overpowered by relief. She was working. That explained why she wasn't answering her phone. She'd silenced it to not be disturbed. "Did she happen to mention where?"

"Nah. But I figure she was taking pictures of birds."

"What makes you say that?"

"She asked if she could borrow my binoculars. That's what most folks around here do with binoculars, right? Birdwatch over on Presque Isle."

Maybe. Except the tension in his neck and shoulders spread to his jaw. Emma had never mentioned being a birdwatcher. Not that he knew her well enough to be sure. But if she was, wouldn't she have her own a pair of binoculars? No, the only reason she'd have to borrow a pair was if she was spying on something.

Or someone.

Chapter Thirty-One

C lay yanked open Emma's car door and jammed the gun against the side of her head. This was it. With a slight twitch of his finger, her life would be over. Instead of shooting her where she sat, he growled, "Move over."

Climbing across the center console of her Forester wasn't an easy task. She reached over to move her camera to the floor, but Clay grabbed it from her.

"Move," he repeated.

She managed to scramble over the gearshift and tumbled into the passenger seat. Clay was right behind her, sliding behind the wheel. He deposited her Nikon onto his lap. Keeping the gun leveled at her head, he used his left hand to drop the car in gear and coasted down the hill.

A lone gray cedar-shake-sided house sat at the end of the lane with Lake Erie only a few yards beyond. The black SUV was backed up to the attached garage. A man—one of those Emma had seen minutes ago in the parking lot—now wearing a ski mask in addition to his black hoodie—was shoving a framed painting into the vehicle.

Confirmation that she'd been right about Clay's involvement in the home invasions was a hollow victory.

He jammed the shifter into park and shut off the ignition. "Stay put," he said, punctuating the order by jabbing the gun barrel into her shoulder. He stepped out, taking her camera with him, and circled the front of the Subaru, keeping the gun aimed at her through the windshield. He placed the camera on the car's hood, ripped open the passenger door, and gestured with the weapon. "Get out."

She complied.

"Hey!" the man who'd had the painting yelled over at them. "We could use a hand here, you know."

"I'll be right there," Clay shouted.

The man shook his head and disappeared into the garage.

Clay turned his dark eyes back to Emma, a terrifying sneer curling his lip. He brought the gun behind her head, intertwining the fingers of that hand in her hair. The cold steel of the revolver dug into her skull as he drew her face toward him and pressed a hard kiss to her lips.

Terror mingled with anger. This time, she did bite him, tasting blood.

He released her with a yelp. "You bitch," he hissed, drawing his hand back. He swung.

She recoiled, but not fast enough. The butt of the gun slammed into her cheekbone and spun her around. Razor-sharp spikes shot through her face, into her brain. Red-hot light burst behind her eyes. She had a vague sensation of the ground rising around her. But she crashed against the Subaru's front fender. She dragged her fingers along the smooth surface, managing to land on her knees. Clinging to the car, she fought a rush of nausea. Something warm and wet trickled down her cheek.

She gasped a deep breath, fighting to regain her senses and rise above the pain. Blinking, she focused on the black-jeaned legs in front of her, then lifted her gaze, expecting to see the gun's muzzle and a final flash of flame.

Clay still clutched the gun, but it wasn't pointed at her. His other hand was pressed to his mouth, crimson tinting his fingers.

If her final act in this life was to bring him pain, she'd take it.

"I would've given you everything," he said, his voice low and deep and vicious. "Now, I'm going to take away everything you have." He picked up the Nikon, thumbed open the SD card compartment and retrieved the small square from it. "You think you were being so clever, lurking across the road and taking pictures of me and my crew. You're a fool. I spotted you following me before I even left the campground."

Emma swore to herself. He was right about her being a fool. She should've known she couldn't outsmart the master stalker at his own game.

Clay set the memory card on the Subaru's hood. Aiming the gun at Emma's face, he stepped back, swung, and smashed the Nikon against a tree trunk.

Emma winced as if he'd slammed her own face against it. That camera represented her independence, such as it was. Its destruction, the final nail in her coffin.

"In case you haven't figured it out yet, I'm the one who took your computers." His victorious smile revealed bloody teeth as he pointed at her Forester. "I hauled them away in this very car, and you never realized it. My plan was just to hold them for you until you realized I'm the only one who can take care of you. I'm the only one who could've saved you."

"How'd you find me?" she asked.

He lifted his face to the sky and laughed. "It was easy. We were together for three years. I *know* you. I know this is where you and your family vacationed when you were a kid. You think I can't recognize your work? I saw your photos in *PA Living*. And I noticed most of the photos you were selling to the magazine were taken around this area. You didn't know I have family here, did you?"

She did not.

"Oh, and by the way, that new Facebook profile? Using the name Rebecca Manderley? Give me some credit. I heard you and your sister talking about that book—your *favorite* book. If you really didn't want me to find you, you should've come up with something better than that."

Emma wanted to swear. She never suspected he paid attention to those conversations. But she should have.

"Anyhow, once I knew what city you'd moved to, I found an ad on the dark web, seeking a crew to do three home invasions in Erie. It wasn't hard for me to find out who placed the ad. None other than your boss at the magazine."

Her boss? Bob? Emma's mind stumbled over Clay's words, trying to make sense of them.

He moved closer to her. "How convenient for me. A chance to find out exactly where you were and earn some good money at the same time."

Still trying to piece together the puzzle of Bob and the home invasions, Emma kept her gaze fixed on the broken shards of glass and plastic at the base of the tree. The dented metal body and lens of her camera lying on the ground.

"But when I went to Bob DelGrosso's office and asked him to tell me where you lived, he wouldn't say. Claimed he didn't know."

"He didn't." As soon as she said it, she recalled his visit to her trailer.

"Didn't matter. I knew I'd track you down. After I killed that stupid asshole who followed us from the second job, I realized an added benefit. I had old Bob under my thumb at that point. Legally, he was as culpable as I was for the murder."

She hadn't realized Clay knew that much about the law.

"When he heard about the picture you took of the victim, he freaked out and came to me. I told him to meet with you and offer to buy the photo. To pay whatever it took."

"There was nothing in that picture to suggest who the killer was. It was just a glimpse of the victim's arm."

"But Bob didn't realize that. Neither did I, but I didn't care. What I cared about was following him until he made contact with you."

Emma thought of Monday afternoon. Bob stopping her on the street. The man next to her car. The one she was so certain was Clay. He hadn't been. But Clay had been there. Watching. No wonder she felt his eyes on her.

"After that, I followed you to your little camper." He sneered. "How cute."

"And you moved into the empty trailer on the road below me."

"I did. And until today, you never knew."

Not entirely true. She'd sensed his presence but convinced herself she was overreacting.

"Bob came to see me there. Why?"

"He was still freaking out about that photo. So I told him where to find you. I probably shouldn't have. I was afraid he might warn you about me. But he was a good boy and kept quiet."

"And if he had warned me?"

Clay shrugged. "I'd have killed him too."

Too? Somehow, she had a feeling he wasn't talking about Wesley Simmons.

Clay must've read her mind. "I'm the only man who can save you from yourself. You and your neighbor were getting too chummy. He was trying to take care of you. That's my job and mine alone."

Her breath froze in her throat. "You killed Joe."

"Was that his name?" Clay sounded disinterested in her answer. He picked up the memory card from the car's hood. "What exactly were you planning to do with this?"

Emma didn't see the need to reply. Clay had been a step ahead of her all along. The question was rhetorical.

"You thought you'd give it to your cop boyfriend?"

Boyfriend? Matthias? Hardly. But again, she saw no need to answer.

"I saw you two getting cozy on your front porch." Clay tsk-tsked. "How sweet. In case you haven't heard, he's dead too."

Emma choked. She lifted her gaze to meet Clay's soulless dark eyes, hoping to see some hint that he was lying. The gleeful sneer told her he wasn't. "You killed Matthias?"

"Me? No." Clay's grin reminded her of a wolf. "He was

killed in a horrible traffic accident right after he left your place. I guess you hadn't heard. I'm so sorry."

Gut-punched, Emma doubled over. Joe had been kind to her, and for that, he was dead. Matthias? Despite a rough introduction, Emma had begun to trust him. Had begun to have feelings for him. She hadn't even realized it until now. Everyone she felt connected to was dead.

And now she understood why he hadn't answered his phone, hadn't returned her calls.

She almost asked if he'd harmed Kira but decided to keep her out of it. Maybe he wasn't aware of the budding friendship. If that was the case, for Kira's sake, Emma hoped to keep it that way.

"Bauer!" The impatient shout came from the house.

Clay shifted his gaze away from Emma toward the member of his crew.

In that moment, she knew she was dead. He spoke of being the only one to save her but that wasn't his intention. Clay Bauer was going to add her to his body count. She had no way out.

But she'd be damned if she was going to leave this world kneeling at his feet.

She launched up and forward at him. Her shoulder struck him just above his knees. The unexpected attack caught him off guard. He staggered, roaring, balance lost, falling. Emma laser-focused on the gun. She grabbed his wrist and hand as they both tumbled. Knowing her life depended on it, she dug in, grappling with his grip on the weapon. Bellowing like the beast he was, he snared a handful of her hair. Her scalp burned as it was ripped from her head. Still she managed to cling to the gun.

Clay's death grip on her hair weakened her determination. She succumbed, releasing one hand from her hold to clutch his wrist. The revolver's muzzle pivoted toward her face. His ragged breath rumbled in her ears. Helplessness flooded her as she watched the gaping maw coming closer, closer.

This breath would be her last, but at least she was going down fighting.

And then, pressure against her stomach, her throat, lifted her, airborne.

"What the fuck are you doing, Bauer?" a male voice demanded.

Emma's feet hit the ground, but the momentum of having been hoisted off Clay and flung like a ragdoll carried her over. She again fell against her Subaru's steel fender and crumpled. Her scalp screamed, overpowering the bruising impact. Lifting her gaze, she watched a black-clad man drag Clay to his feet, the gun still in one hand, a fistful of her hair in the other.

"Get back to work," he growled at Emma's rescuer.

"Not until you give me that gun. And put on your mask. What's gotten into you? You know damned well no one is supposed to get hurt. And no one for sure is supposed to get killed."

"It's a little late for that," Emma said, breathing through the pain.

The man shot a look her way, brown eyes all she could make out through the ski mask. His gaze returned to Clay. "What's she mean by that?"

"Nothing," Clay said.

His team didn't know. "Wesley Simmons," she said.

The man glanced at her again. "The guy from last week?" Back to Clay. "He's dead?"

Clay glared at her, silent. In that silence, she thought maybe —just maybe—she heard distant sirens.

"You told us you were just going to stash him someplace until after this last job."

"He stashed him all right. In Lake Erie," Emma said. "Simmons washed up on the beach Saturday morning."

The man took a step away from Clay. "You killed him? Why? He couldn't identify us. Even you. We were all wearing our masks. You blindfolded him."

Clay sneered. "You idiot. The one and only way to guarantee he wouldn't be able to ID us was to shut him up permanently."

The man shook his head vehemently. "I didn't sign up for murder. That's on you."

Clay laughed a low soulless laugh. "I hate to tell you but you're a part of the crew. All of us are in it equally. *All* of it."

Sirens. Emma definitely heard sirens. And they were growing louder.

"No way. You dropped each of us off. When you left with him, he was still alive." The man looked at Emma. "I won't be a part of you killing your old girlfriend either."

"Too bad."

Clay's arm came up so fast, Emma didn't have a chance to scream before he squeezed the trigger.

Chapter Thirty-Two

A s a detective, Matthias rarely arrived at an active shooter scene before the uniforms and SWAT teams had things under control. Lake Front Drive's residential street was plugged with police units from the city as well as state troopers. He couldn't get near the address in question. Abandoning his car, he ignored the pain screaming from every pore of his body and pounded along the pavement to the barricade at the No Outlet sign. A flash of his badge, and the uniforms waved him through. He made his way around a dozen or so police units, down the hill. SWAT's armored vehicle had been positioned to block the narrow road. Just beyond it, Matthias spotted the white Subaru Forester. A contingent of five members of the tactical team, the first three carrying ballistic shields, approached the vehicle. Matthias could make out a pair of motionless legs on the ground next to Emma's car—the rest of the body hidden from his view. Before he could get any closer, Cassie stepped in front of him.

"You didn't find her, did you," his partner said, her voice flat, the words not carrying a question mark.

"What's going on?" he asked, hearing the dread in his voice.

"So far we have one dead. And Bauer is threatening to take out the entire family unless we let him walk."

Matthias tripped over the words. *One dead*. "Emma?"

"I don't know."

"What do you mean, you don't know?"

"He fired on the first unit to arrive. No one was hit." She nodded toward the SWAT officers, who'd reached the victim. "This is the first they've been able to get close enough to retrieve the DB."

DB. A quaint acronym for Dead Body. If the DB in question turned out to be Emma Anderson, Clay Bauer would never make it to court. "Where is he now?"

"Inside the house with his crew and the family." Cassie smirked. "And you'll never guess what kind of vehicle is backed up to the garage."

A piece of the puzzle clicked into place. "A black Navigator."

"With a dented front fender, passenger side."

He swore. "Why'd he try to kill me?" Another piece clicked. "He saw me with Emma. He found out from DelGrosso where she lived and was watching her place."

"He seems like one of those *if I can't have her, no one can* kind of stalkers. Probably thought you were his competition." Cassie's brow furrowed. "Explains Joe Platt's murder too. Platt was kind enough to let her stay in his trailer. I can just imagine how Bauer interpreted that."

Another piece clicked. "Bauer's the one who broke into her place. He stole what had some value and trashed the rest."

"Sweet guy." Cassie's tone was thick with sarcasm.

Another of his partner's phrases stuck in Matthias's brain. *If I can't have her, no one can.* Matthias believed two things to be true. If his assessment of Emma was right, she would never give in to Bauer. And after three murders—that they knew of— and the attempt on Matthias's life, Bauer had nothing to lose. Hence the DB next to Emma's car. *Please God, don't let it be her.*

The officers with the shields protected the other two, who knelt over the body. Matthias couldn't see but imagined they were checking for signs of life. "What's the plan?" he asked his partner.

Cassie eyed him. "We're detectives. We come in *after* the scene has been secured."

"And yet, here you are."

"Yes. Here. Behind the insertion team, waiting."

Matthias acted innocent. "And I'm here waiting with you. I simply asked what the plan is."

"We aren't part of the plan," she said, biting off each word. "Not to mention this is a home invasion gone bad. The very last kind of case you should want to be a part of."

Her words stung. But the thought of Emma dead or severely injured, lying out there, created a hard shell of determination through which Cassie's common sense couldn't penetrate.

The SWAT officers stood as a unit and backed away, leaving the body on the ground. Matthias knew what that meant. Any question of whether the victim might still be alive had been answered. Had she been breathing, they'd have brought her back with them. As it was, the body would wait for someone from the coroner's office.

"I have to find out if that's Emma."

Cassie reached out to stop him, but he plowed past, storming toward the group of heavily armed and armored officers gathered behind the SWAT truck. And the five-man team who'd returned to safety.

Their sergeant was giving orders when Matthias arrived, badge in hand, to be greeted with a round of puzzled looks. "Who's the victim?"

"You aren't part of this team, Detective," the sergeant said.

Matthias shot a glance toward the body. "That woman is a friend of mine."

"Woman? The DB is male."

He exhaled, relief draining some of his resolve. "You're sure?"

"I think I know how to tell the difference." One of the officers who'd been with the extraction team removed his shaded goggles and helmet. "Looks like the subject took out one of his own crew."

The sergeant handed Matthias a pair of binoculars. "Take a look for yourself."

Matthias stepped to the edge of the armored vehicle and pressed the binoculars to his eyes, adjusting the focus. The DB was attired in black and wore a ski mask. Definitely not Emma.

It was, however, her car, her license plate. She might still be alive, but she wasn't out of danger. Not by a long shot.

He returned the binoculars. "Do you know where the driver of that car is? Her name's Emma Anderson."

"I know. We ran the plates."

"Do you know she has a PFA against Clay Bauer?"

"I do. And I've also been informed that Bauer is the shooter. Trust me, Detective, I'm well aware of what we're dealing with. A home invasion team led by a man who has already killed, combined with a domestic abuse situation."

"Do you know where Emma is?"

"When the first unit arrived on scene, Bauer fired on the officers, using her as a shield. Claimed if we didn't all get the hell out of here, he'd blow her head off. After some back and forth about exactly how that would end for him, he dragged her inside. She's one of the five hostages."

"Five?"

"Homeowner, wife, two kids, and Ms. Anderson."

Matthias turned his gaze on the DB next to Emma's car. "Bauer has taken out one of his own crew. Do we know how the other two feel about that?"

The sergeant grunted. "Point taken. We don't know if we have three actors and five hostages or one and seven."

Either way, the atmosphere inside that house had to be incendiary.

Chapter Thirty-Three

Obscenities reverberated throughout the modern-meets-coastal living room, amplified and echoing into the vaulted ceilings, raining back down onto Emma and her fellow captives. A fierce but terrified man with his hands bound behind him and duct tape slapped across his mouth sat at one end of a white sectional. A similarly restrained woman with tears streaming perched at the other. Between them, a pair of pre-teen girls, also sporting duct tape, cowered.

Following Clay's barked orders, the smaller of the two surviving home invaders had quickly wrapped Emma's hands with the stuff, but in front of her instead of behind. Emma glimpsed a strand of purple hair escaping from the eye hole of the crook's ski mask. Purple hair, but not Kira's purple hair.

After Not-Kira had shoved Emma down into a plush chair near the other hostages, she'd joined the other still-masked thief in screaming at Clay.

Emma sat motionless, watching as both of them raged, partly because Clay had shot one of their own, but also because he remained unmasked. Even they understood what it all meant. Clay was a stone-cold killer who had no intention of letting the hostages live. Nor were his remaining team members guaranteed to walk away unscathed. For his part, Clay silently paced, his gun hand at his side, ignoring the frantic admonitions from the pair.

The house's wall-mounted landline started ringing, adding to the chaos. Clay ignored it. After several rings, an answering machine picked up with a cheerful greeting and invitation to leave a message.

"This is Sergeant Ted Spurlock. I need to speak with Mr. Bauer. We can work this out. No one else has to die today. But the only way that happens is if you pick up the phone and begin a conversation."

The man and woman in black shut up and looked at Clay expectantly. Clay acted as though he hadn't heard the phone or the message.

"Talk to the man," the woman ordered.

Clay continued to pace.

The man in black crossed to the phone and reached for it. This sparked a reaction. Clay pivoted and extended his arm, aiming the gun at him. "Don't." His tone left no room for doubt. He would shoot his partner without a second thought.

The phrase *no honor among thieves* floated through Emma's mind. Not that she'd ever use honor and Clay Bauer in the same breath anyway.

The answering machine beeped, signaling the end of the message, leaving a red light blinking on the gadget.

Clay lowered his gun. The man in black pointed an accusatory finger at him. "You're a crazy son of a bitch."

Clay returned to pacing.

"You know what's gonna happen here, don't you?" the man in black continued. "The cops are gonna come down here and take us all out. You. Me." He hoisted a thumb at Not-Kira. "JJ."

The initials JJ did little to reveal the woman's real name, but the fact he'd given away her moniker at all told Emma the situation was more explosive than ever.

JJ. The initials sparked a memory. Monday, when Emma and Kira had gone out to lunch. The waitress with the copycat purple hair.

Emma hoped the young woman hadn't noticed the flash of recognition that must've crossed her face.

The man in black continued to rant. "They'll either set up a sniper or they'll shoot a smoke grenade in here and pick us all off as we come out."

The mention of a sniper drew Clay's eyes to the bank of glass windows facing the lake. From her seat, Emma couldn't see any cops but knew they must be out there. According to her minimal knowledge of snipers, she also knew being seen would defeat the purpose. While watching Clay gun down the other crew member outside had more than met her personal quota of violent deaths for one lifetime, she'd rather the next bullet take out Clay right in front of her than having to witness him killing more innocents.

The landline rang again. This time, Clay looked at it but made no move to answer. Emma held her breath and sensed everyone else in the room was doing the same. The greeting played. The machine beeped.

"Mr. Bauer, this is Sergeant Spurlock again. Pick up the phone. Let's talk this out like men. I can make sure you walk out of there unharmed."

"Goddammit, Clay," the man in black snapped. He took one more step toward the phone and reached for the handset.

Clay's arm coming up was a blur. The gunshot, deafening. Muffled screams came from the two little girls and the mom. Emma closed her eyes as the man in black went down. Her ears rang from the blast still echoing through the vaulted ceilings.

The sergeant yelled over the machine, "What the hell's going on in there?"

Emma reluctantly opened her eyes.

Clay snatched the receiver. "One more down. You try anything, and the next victim will be one of these sweet little girls. Got it?" He mashed the handset down, grasped the phone, ripped it from the wall, and smashed it against the marble floor next to a sobbing, trembling JJ who'd dropped to her knees at her gunned-down friend's side.

The two pre-teens had turned their faces, one to the mother, the other to the dad. The mom, unable to embrace her child, bent her head over the girl. The dad glared at Clay with a silent paternal promise to rip his heart out if he followed through with his threat.

Emma watched the family, imagining herself and Nell and their parents. The same kind of family unit, shredded. Clay may have had nothing to do with her parents' death—that was all on her—nor was he to blame for Nell's addiction. But he was totally at fault for her disappearance.

No. Not totally. Emma had to accept her part in driving her sister away. She'd been stupid enough to listen to Clay. He'd placed the wedge between them, but Emma had hammered it home.

She blinked away hot tears and shifted her gaze from the

family to Clay. He was watching her, his lips curled into a smirk.

He turned the smirk to the father. "Don't worry. That was strictly for the benefit of the police." Clay brought his gaze back to Emma. "The next bullet is all yours, Red."

The terror in those children's eyes mirrored the life Emma had been living and flipped a switch in her. Fury overpowered the fear she'd been carrying for months. Years. The next bullet might be hers or it might be JJ's or it might be the mother's. Clay was playing a game with all of them. Power hungry and savoring every tear shed by others, he would change his game plan—if he even had one—at whim. There was only one thing Emma knew for certain. Before this day was over, she'd be dead.

Or he would.

She stood, her bound fists clenched. The movement startled Clay, which pleased her. "Then let's get it over with," she said.

Peripherally, she was aware of the family's eyes on her, but she focused on her tormentor.

The smirk was back. He raised the gun.

As before, her gaze was drawn to the deadly black maw of the weapon. She forced it to Clay's equally black and deadly eyes.

"You think I won't?" he asked.

"I know you will. Now or later." Unless the police sniper got him first. "I'm done with your cat-and-mouse crap. Just do it already."

His gaze flitted over her shoulder to the windows. Like Emma, he must be thinking of the police. He glimpsed downward at his shirt. Looking for a red laser dot? There was none, but she was pretty certain that was a Hollywood trope.

Clay reacted quicker than she could've imagined. He didn't shoot her. He stepped toward her. Grabbed and spun her away from him. He wrapped an arm around her neck, holding her close. Instinctively, she grabbed his restrictive arm with her bound hands. The hard steel of the muzzle pressed into her jaw for a second time. "It's your lucky day," he growled at her ear, but she wasn't sure if he was speaking to her or to the family.

She suspected the latter. Either way, he'd removed any clear shot a sniper might have.

He bumped her forward. "Let's go."

She planted her feet, digging in. "I'm not going anywhere with you."

He pressed the muzzle deeper into her jaw. "I need you as my shield to get out of here."

He *needed* her. That was a first. A powerful first. Ignoring the pain of steel jammed into her jawbone, she dug her heels in deeper. "You aren't going to shoot me. A dead shield isn't very effective with the police."

She felt his hot breath on the side of her face. Heard the guttural rumble of his laugh. "You're right about that, Red, so I'll give you three choices. I can carry you out." The pressure on her jaw released as he lowered the gun to her side. "I can shoot you in the knee. A wounded shield would still work well." He brought the muzzle back to her jaw. "Or I can kill you and use one of those little girls."

The words reached the family, evoking a new round of muffled whimpers.

Clay brought his lips and his hot breath even closer to Emma's ear, lowering his voice to a whisper. "That one reminds me of Nell. Maybe I'll kill her and use the other one."

Rage and terror rose in Emma's throat on a wave of bile. "You bastard." She swallowed as he chuckled. "Leave them alone. I'll do whatever you want."

"That's my girl." He lipped her ear.

She jerked her face away. Only the knowledge that the family would bear the repercussions kept her from head-butting him.

Clay bumped her forward with his chest. She allowed him to steer her toward the entrance, praying the sniper wasn't a figment of her imagination. Praying at some point she'd be able to give him a clear shot.

"Open it," Clay ordered when they reached the door.

She released his arm to obey. The moment they crossed the threshold, he tightened his grip, bringing her to a stop and bringing her hands back to his arm, fighting to create enough space to breathe.

At the time he'd dragged her inside, only a few police units had arrived although sirens promised more. Now it appeared every Erie cop on the force had been joined by every state trooper within a hundred-mile radius. Behind Emma's Subaru, a military-style armored truck blocked the driveway and any chance of escape.

She felt a spiteful smile spread across her face. "I'd say you're screwed," she told Clay.

He jammed the gun's muzzle deeper against her aching jawbone. "Not as long as I have you, sweetheart." He marched her out in clear view of the police while casting furtive glances toward the lake behind him. "Listen up," he shouted, his tone menacing. "You're all going to get into your cars and your little tank there and clear out or this woman's dead."

Emma wanted to scream *no*! She would be dead anyway.

"Clay Bauer," a vaguely familiar voice shouted back, aided by a PA system on one of the vehicles. "This is Sergeant Spurlock. We spoke on the phone."

"I don't care who you are. Pack up and get out unless you want another body on your hands."

"Now, Mr. Bauer, you know we can't do that. This has gone way too far for us to let you walk out of here with a hostage."

"You're right. I don't plan to walk out. I plan to drive out. In that white Subaru. Just as soon as you leave."

"How about this? You put the gun down. Release the woman. And I'll guarantee your safety."

Emma turned her head ever so slightly toward Clay and spoke softly. "In other words, if you don't, they're going to blow your head off."

"You're the one whose head's getting blown off," he said with a snarl.

"I've already made my peace with that. Have you?"

"You've made your peace, have you? You might want to reconsider that."

"Why? You've already told me I'm next."

"Doesn't have to be that way. Besides there's something you don't know."

She didn't dare turn her head any farther. Not with his gun on the verge of dislocating her jaw. But she shifted her eyes as far to the side as she could, trying to figure out what this new game was. Just more BS?

All she could make out was his lupine smile as he said, "I know where Nell is."

Before his words could completely sink in, a rumble of voices from the direction of the cops drew her attention. And Clay's.

A man with a white bandage on his forehead stepped out from behind one of the police SUVs, hands open and out to his sides.

"What the hell?" the sergeant barked in the direction of the man, his voice still carrying over the PA. "Get back here."

Emma blinked and squinted.

Matthias.

Her breath caught in a jumble of disjointed thoughts. He was alive. He was disobeying orders.

He was unarmed.

"Bauer," he called, his voice like ground glass. "Remember me?"

Clay cursed under his breath. "Your new boyfriend thinks he's a tough guy."

"Not that it matters," she replied. "But he's not my boyfriend."

"You and your cop buddies need to get out of here. Now. I won't say it again." Clay released the pressure of the muzzle against Emma's jaw only to raise and aim it at her temple. "If I don't see you guys clearing out of here within the next two minutes, she's dead."

"I don't think so." Matthias took a couple of slow, smooth steps toward them. "You kill her, there's nothing between you and them." He pointed a thumb at the heavily armed perimeter, none of whom were moving.

Clay retreated one step, then another, closer to the house, pulling Emma with him. "I still have those two beautiful little girls in there. I'll just exchange one dead hostage for a live one."

Matthias, arms still open, advanced another step. "I have a better idea. A trade. Me for the woman. Think about it. You harm her, they're going to blast you to bits rather than let you near those children again."

Clay backed up another step. "I'm taking her back inside. You've got about fifteen seconds less than you did. Get them out of here."

Matthias kept advancing. "You don't want to hurt her. And those kids? They'll be screaming their heads off if you force them to go with you. Me? I'm a better hostage. I carry more weight with these guys. They're more likely to negotiate. And I'd be able to help you get a better deal. You want a helicopter to get you outta here? How about an airplane? The airport's only a mile or so away."

Emma watched him edging toward them. Clay's back was against the door. Another moment, he'd be yanking her inside. He wouldn't fall for Matthias's patter. They all knew the police would never get him a plane or a helicopter. Even Clay's demand to drive out in her car was farfetched, although she sensed he believed he had a chance at that one.

The door behind them rattled. It had latched on their way out. With her hands bound in front and clutching the arm Clay held across her neck, she couldn't open it for him. He wouldn't dare spin her toward it, exposing his back to the police departments' weapon power. He either had to release her or use his gun hand.

Backed against the door, every one of his muscles tensed. He must've realized this simplest of flaws in his plan. This was it. And Emma knew in that second what Clay was going to do.

He swung the gun away from her, bringing it to bear on Matthias. She reacted. Still clinging to his arm, she dropped toward the ground, throwing his balance off. He wasn't expecting that. Nor was she expecting the door behind them to suddenly swing inward.

Clay staggered backward. His gun discharged with a deafening explosion. She glimpsed Matthias diving. A second blast. A warm spray against the side of her face as she hit the ground. Already bruised knees sent razor blades through every nerve ending in her body. Falling, Clay pushed her down the rest of the way. Gravel bit into her cheek. Clay's weight crushed her to the ground for the second time that day.

She expected him to roll off. He didn't. The ground beneath her vibrated with footfalls. Voices shouted, "*Drop the weapon. Drop it now.*"

Clay remained still except for the pulse of his labored breath. Emma's shirt grew warm and wet, and she realized it was his blood saturating the fabric. Around her, boots charged past. Others stopped at her side.

"Get the paramedics down here!" someone bellowed.

She squirmed out from under Clay, listening as he fought for air. Hands reached down, sliding Clay off her.

"Emma?" The soft, whispered voice filtered through the others. "Are you hurt?"

Was she? She pushed up to sit. Matthias knelt at her side, concern creasing his brow. "I don't think so," she said, although her body disputed the claim.

She swung away from him, looking for Clay but drawn to the scene at the doorway. A young woman with a streak of purple in her bangs—JJ now minus her ski mask—was being ordered to her knees while keeping her hands raised.

One of the officers seized the gun JJ still held loosely. The gun she'd used to shoot Clay.

Two paramedics worked on him as blood poured from the

exit wound in the front of his chest and trickled from his mouth. More pooled beneath him. His eyes were open, searching ... until they settled on Emma. He attempted a smirk, but it looked more like a grimace. His bloodied lips moved as he tried to speak and failed. His eyes drifted shut.

"Clay," she said forcefully.

His eyes fluttered open, fixing again on her.

"You said you know where Nell is."

His eyes closed but this time he succeeded in smiling. "I do," he rasped, barely audible.

"Where?" Emma demanded. "Where is she?"

One of the paramedics nudged between them. "I'm sorry, ma'am. We need to move him. Now." The medic signaled to a second pair of rescue personnel approaching with a stretcher.

Gentle but strong hands—Matthias's—grasped her shoulders from behind, drawing her away from Clay and up to her feet. Her legs refused to hold her. She thought she was about to hit the gravel yet again until the detective caught her and scooped her off the ground.

Emma sat on the stretcher inside an ambulance, feet on the floor. Despite insisting she didn't need treatment—she needed to talk to Clay—Matthias and a third pair of medics had outnumbered her. Matthias had told her she looked like she'd gone ten rounds with Evander Holyfield.

As the medics checked her vitals, Matthias climbed in and took a seat opposite her on the crew bench. "How's she doing?" he asked the EMT who'd just removed the blood pressure cuff from Emma's arm.

"I'm fine," she said before the medic could respond.

The medic gave her a critical scowl. "You need to be examined at the emergency department. You took a nasty bump to your head."

"I'll think about it."

Matthias caught her gaze. "You should listen to the expert."

"I'm *fine*," Emma repeated emphatically. She studied his face. The healed scar above his lip. The slight crook in his nose, suggesting he'd been on the receiving end of a punch or two himself at some point. But he also bore some fresher injuries. The white bandage taped to his forehead above his eye. Various small cuts. A discoloration on his cheek promising to bloom into a bruise.

"Did Clay do that?" she asked.

Matthias's eye twitched, but he didn't reply.

"He told me you were dead."

"I'm hard to kill."

"Thank goodness."

The look he gave her brought a flush of heat to her face. "Thank *you*," he said. "He might've shot me back there if you hadn't done what you did."

That moment replayed through Emma's mind. The dive she took to throw Clay off balance. Two explosive blasts. The spray of what she now knew was Clay's blood against her cheek. She'd overheard a comment from one of the other cops. The gunshot that struck Clay was through-and-through. It should have hit Emma as well. Only the reactive drop saved her, the trajectory of the bullet somehow missing her

Emma looked away, shifting her focus to the goings on outside the ambulance. The SWAT truck had left. Most of the other police remained, although the urgency of their movements was gone. "Where's Clay?"

"He's not going to hurt you ever again."

"That's not what I asked." When Matthias didn't answer, she brought her gaze back to him, trying to read his blue eyes and failing. "I need to talk to him."

"No, you don't."

"Yes, I do. He knows where my sister is."

Matthias's chin came up ever so slightly before dropping to his chest. "I'm sorry. We got word from the ambulance crew. He didn't make it."

A soft cry bubbled up from Emma's throat. She closed her eyes. Memories played across her mind. The Clay she'd first met. Charming. Sexy. Protective. How he made her heart flutter every time he showed up at her door. How delicious it felt when he held her in his arms. But how his nature turned from protective to possessive, demanding to know where she was and who she was with. Clay had revealed himself to be more of a monster than Emma ever realized, but was he so cruel as to dangle Nell's whereabouts in front of Emma, when he in fact didn't know?

Yes. He was. But had he? Or did he know and take that knowledge to the grave?

"Hey." Matthias touched her knee. "You okay?"

"No." She swallowed her tears and met his confused gaze. How could she explain what she couldn't completely understand herself? She felt no grief for Clay. Her grief was for Nell, out there somewhere, alone.

"We'll find her," Matthias said. "*I* will find her."

Emma managed a weak smile. "Not unless she wants to be found. And she doesn't."

Chapter Thirty-Four

Aweek had passed since that horrible day on Lake Front Drive. Emma's bruises and scrapes were almost healed. The trauma to her heart and soul hadn't even begun to mend.

She sat on her deck, gazing down the hill. The bass beat of an old rock song accompanied rather than drowned the honking of a flock of geese soaring overhead. Joe's daughter had removed the Jayco, leaving an empty lot and nothing to buffer Mick's music. However, following a recent visit from campground management, Mick kept the volume considerably lower.

Emma's camper felt like an empty shell with her computers gone. She still possessed the spare older Nikon body and her shorter lenses. Clay hadn't smashed those. But with Bob DelGrosso under arrest, *PA Living* was officially out of business. The commission on those few framed images she sold around town wasn't enough to replace her equipment. Nor was the paycheck from the cemetery photos.

She did, at least, still have her phone and had contacted the insurance company regarding the fire at her family farmhouse. The ongoing investigation confirmed arson as the cause, but a suspect had yet to be named. She knew in her heart the responsibility fell on Clay. Whether it could be proved remained to be seen. Eventually, she'd see the insurance payout, which she'd much rather use to rebuild than to buy new computers.

The one bright spot of recent days was a Facebook notification she'd received. Nell had accepted Rebecca Manderley as a friend. Emma had used her now unnecessary alias to message her sister. So far, Nell hadn't responded.

But Emma was more hopeful than she'd been in a long while.

A red Jeep made the turn onto her road, rumbled up the slope, and pulled in next to her Subaru. With the sun hitting the glass, she couldn't make out who was behind the wheel … until Matthias stepped out.

Mick's radio immediately fell silent.

In jeans and a faded Harley T-shirt revealing arms that had pumped a lot of iron, Matthias looked more like a burly motorcycle gang member than a police detective.

How had she ever mistaken him for Clay?

"Howdy, ma'am," Matthias said, laying on the Oklahoma accent that only appeared when he wanted it to.

"Howdy." She noticed the bandage was gone, a new scar in its place. No signs of the bruise or other cuts remained. "You're looking better than the last time I saw you."

He grinned. "Thanks. How about you? You okay?"

Okay? She shrugged. "I'm … better. What brings you by today?"

He approached as far as the edge of the deck without

stepping onto it. "Thought you'd like an update on the stolen merchandise."

"My computers?"

Instead of answering, he asked, "Did you know Robert DelGrosso has a brother who runs an art gallery down in Butler?"

"No."

"The FBI has been keeping an eye on him for over a year. Turns out he was your former boss's partner and fence for the paintings stolen in the home invasions. They're still digging, but it looks like Gerald DelGrosso might have a forger on his payroll as well. The home invasion scheme was only the tip of the iceberg, but it may end up undoing an international art theft ring."

"Wow." Emma couldn't think of anything else to say and repeated, "Wow."

Matthias tipped his head toward his Jeep, gesturing her to follow. "I brought you something I thought you could use."

"Oh?" She rose and trailed after him to the rear of the vehicle. He opened the lift gate to reveal the laptops and monitors Clay had stolen. "You found them," she exclaimed.

"We were able to recover some of the other stolen merchandise from a couple of pawn shops. But your stuff was just down the hill, in the camper Bauer was borrowing."

She huffed a laugh. "So near and yet so far. Doesn't it have to be held as evidence?"

Matthias wrinkled his nose. "Technically, your break-in wasn't a part of the home invasion case. And you never filed an official report. Now, if you want to file charges—"

"Against whom? Clay's dead."

"My thoughts exactly. So I liberated your computer equipment."

Emma was tempted to give the man a hug but resisted. Yesterday, over lunch, her new friend Kira had swooned about him and the date they'd gone on last Saturday. And the second date coming up this weekend. Emma didn't want to muddy those waters. Friends were too hard to come by. "Thank you."

He reached in to gather the laptops, which he handed to Emma. "I'll carry the bigger stuff."

Minutes later, the camper felt a lot more like home. She'd have to reconnect everything, but at least she wouldn't need to replace it. "I don't know how to repay you."

"I'm a cop. I can't take bribes." He grinned. "But do you have a beer?"

"Yes, sir."

While she opened the refrigerator, Matthias leaned against the camper's doorjamb. "I do have another bit of official business."

"Oh?"

"Do you know a woman by the name of Judy Post?"

Emma dug a bottle opener from one of the drawers. "Yeah. She's one of the regular writers at *PA Living*. Or was. Bob often asked me to take photographs to go with her articles." Emma uncapped the beers and handed one to Matthias. "Why do you ask?"

"DelGrosso had told us he seduced a woman he knew to get her to help with the IT side of his home invasion scheme. He wouldn't give up her name, but we found out anyway. I just wasn't entirely sure of how she fit in with the magazine." He reached over and clinked his bottle with Emma's. "Thanks for filling in one of the blanks."

"You're welcome." She took a sip. "Have you arrested Judy?"

"We have."

Emma huffed. "I guess I won't be doing any more photography for her either."

They settled on the deck with their beers, listening to nearby children laughing.

Matthias shot a glance in Mick's direction. "How's the noise level been?"

"Better. The camp manager came by a few days ago and had a talk with him. He's kept his radio at a reasonable volume ever since."

A devious smile crossed Matthias's lips.

She realized there was more to that visit than she'd thought. "You had something to do with it, didn't you?"

He took a swig from his bottle. "I may have stopped in at the office to inquire about some noise complaints."

"Thank you."

He shook his head. "No need. According to the woman I spoke with, your neighbors filed a grievance against Harper after Joe Platt's death. Management was preparing to give Harper an ultimatum. Knock it off with the loud music or move out."

Emma looked around at her campground neighborhood. Laughing children played in the road. A younger couple stacked wood inside a metal fire ring. A man walked a pair of well-behaved Shelties. These were good people.

Another person, not so good, and yet possibly having some redeeming value, entered Emma's thoughts. "What will happen to JJ?"

"Joanna Jameson? The woman who nearly shot you?"

"But didn't. She may have saved that family."

Matthias shook his head. "Her fate is in the hands of the legal system. I'm not so sure she was saving that family as much as exacting revenge. The man Bauer gunned down inside the house was her fiancé."

Emma mulled over this bit of news. Even though JJ's bullet nearly took Emma out along with Clay, she still felt empathy for the young woman.

Matthias took another sip. After he swallowed, he asked, "You planning to stick around or are you moving back to Washington County?"

Emma leaned back in her chair. "That's a question I've been asking myself. With Clay gone, I don't need to hide out." She snorted. "As if I was really hiding anyway. He found me easily enough, after all. But Clay wasn't the reason I chose Erie."

Matthias gave a slow nod. "Your sister."

"For all I know, she's a hundred miles away by now. But this is still the last city I've been able to place her in."

He shifted to one side and withdrew a notebook from his hip pocket. He flipped it open and handed it to her. "Write down everything you can about her. Full name. Date of birth. Driver's license number, if you have it."

Emma started scribbling. "I do."

"Do you have a recent photo of her?"

"I have one I took shortly before she disappeared. I think she's posted some newer selfies on her social media sites." Emma lifted her gaze from the notebook to Matthias's eyes. "You really think you can find her?"

He didn't respond right away, taking another long draw from the beer bottle. "I'm going to do my best."

"Thank you."

She noted every detail she thought might help, including Nell's employment at the Blue Goat and Fortune's Bar and her living above the latter. As Emma did so, she felt Matthias watching her. "I have one more thing for you," he finally said.

She looked up again. "Oh?"

"I wasn't going to say anything if you were planning to move back south, but I have a friend who works for *ErieLIVE*."

"Don't tell me they still want to buy that photo."

He grinned. "No. But they have a staff photographer position open. Like I said, I have a friend there, and I spoke to him about you. You'll still have to go through the interview process, but they've seen your work. Basically, if you want it, the job's yours."

"If I want it?" Emma said, more than a little in shock. Kira be damned. Emma stood, bent over Matthias, and threw her arms around him.

He returned the embrace with a deep laugh. "Is that a yes?"

She released him and plopped back into her chair. "You saved my life. You returned all my computer stuff. And you're going to help me look for my sister. I think it would be rude to say no. Hell, yes."

Acknowledgments

This book has been simmering in my brain for several years and didn't come to fruition without a lot of help and support. I'm deeply grateful to my agent, Dawn Dowdle, for her faith in this project.

I'm also grateful to Terry Dawley, always my go-to for Erie police procedure; to Detective Sean Bogart of the Erie Bureau of Police for answering my questions and showing me around the department; and to Detective Adam Richardson of the Writer's Detective Bureau for giving me a glimpse inside the detective's mind through his podcast, Writer's Detective School, and Zoom "office hours." Any inaccuracies or mistakes in procedure are mine alone. These guys tried their best to keep me in line.

Thanks to my good friend and photographer, Holly Tonini, who inspired Emma's profession and who also answered my questions about freelancing. While I've done some photography in the distant past, I appreciate her help in updating my knowledge.

There aren't enough words to express my gratitude to Liz Milliron, Jeff Boarts, and Peter W.J. Hayes, my partners in crime. I hate to think of what my stories would be like without your fierce critiquing skills. And Donnell Ann Bell and Anne Tiller, thank you for being beta readers extraordinaire.

A special thank you to Todd and Marianne Main, my dear

friends and fellow Pennwriters from Erie who have been vital to my desire to set a mystery novel there. Speaking of Pennwriters, I would never have gotten published in the first place without this organization and the friends and mentors I've discovered through them. The same can be said for my Pittsburgh Chapter of Sisters In Crime. They have provided support and knowledge over the years. If you write crime fiction, you need to belong to this group.

Thank you, Dru Ann Love, for being there on Facebook every morning with inspiration and for being such an awesome friend to me and to all mystery authors.

And thank you to the Blue Ladies (you know who you are) for keeping me sane. I love you all.

I feel truly blessed to have been discovered by Jennie Rothwell, my fabulous editor who took my manuscript and raised it to an entirely new level. And to the entire team at One More Chapter, thank you.

Finally, I couldn't do what I do without the love and support of my husband. Ray, you are my best friend forever.

YOUR NUMBER ONE STOP

ONE MORE CHAPTER

FOR PAGETURNING BOOKS

One More Chapter is an
award-winning global
division of HarperCollins.

Sign up to our newsletter to get our
latest eBook deals and stay up to date
with our weekly Book Club!
<u>Subscribe here.</u>

Meet the team at
<u>www.onemorechapter.com</u>

Follow us!
🐦 <u>@OneMoreChapter_</u>
f <u>@OneMoreChapter</u>
📷 <u>@onemorechapterhc</u>

Do you write unputdownable fiction?
We love to hear from new voices.
Find out how to submit your novel at
<u>www.onemorechapter.com/submissions</u>